D1245847

A Political Affair

By
Mary Whitney

The Writer's Coffee Shop
Publishing House

First published by The Writer's Coffee Shop, 2012

The Writer's Coffee Shop
(Australia)   PO Box 447 Cherrybrook NSW 2126
(USA)   PO Box 2116 Waxahachie TX 75168

Paperback ISBN- 978-1-61213-127-6
E-book ISBN- 978-1-61213-128-3

A CIP catalogue record for this book is available from the US Congress Library.

Cover image by: © Jungleoutthere I Dreamstime.com,
© Depositphotos/Steven Heap
Cover design by: Megan Dooley

www.thewriterscoffeeshop.com/mwhitney

About the Author

Even before she graduated from law school, Mary Whitney knew she wasn't cut out to be a real lawyer. Drawn to politics, she's spent her career as an organizer, lobbyist, and nonprofit executive. Nothing piques her interest more than a good political scandal or romance, and when she stumbled upon writing, she put the two together. A born Midwesterner, naturalized Texan, and transient resident of Washington, D.C., Mary now lives in Northern California with her two daughters and real lawyer husband.

Acknowledgments

To paraphrase Yogi Berra, I just want to thank everyone who made this page necessary. That says it all, but it seems incomplete. I owe thanks to too many wonderful women whose humor and smarts inspired and corrected me. In particular, I want to thank Anne Forlines, Annalyse Knight, ECM Connolly, Elizabeth de Vos, Irene Chartofilis, K. Sorrell, Naitasia Hensey, Jada D'Lee, Roberta Curry, and S.L. Scott.

I'm also forever grateful to Fictionista Workshop for whipping me into shape and breathing life into this story and to everyone at The Writer's Coffee Shop for making it a reality. Finally, I thank my dear husband for encouraging my wacky little writing hobby—my love for you goes to eleven.

Dedication

To My Beloved Mother, Lieselotte
May Light Perpetual Shine upon Her

Chapter 1

"Fifty-two. Forty-eight. Fifty-two. Forty-eight. Fifty-two. Forty-eight."

Senator Stephen McEvoy chanted the numbers to the rhythm of his morning run through Rock Creek Park. His mantra worried him, so he tried to find comfort in the birds' inspirational chirps, but the speeding cars drowned out their optimism. Stephen had to agree with his campaign manager. The numbers weren't good.

When Patty told him their latest poll results, she'd warned, "Fifty-two/forty-eight is too close for comfort for a sitting senator up for reelection."

"I know." The two words were loaded with remorse.

Patty wasn't just his campaign manager—she was also his sister, and she sighed at their predicament. "This wouldn't happen to Dad."

"I know."

There wasn't anything else to say. He knew she wasn't blaming him any more than she blamed herself. Politics was a McEvoy family duty, and they were all in it together, though the mantle weighed heaviest on Stephen. It was always assumed he'd take over his father's senate seat, but no one expected it so soon, least of all him.

Throughout the morning, the poll numbers kept him preoccupied. Even during the daily meeting with his circle of senior advisors, he tuned out. As his chief of staff, Greg Miller, reviewed the day's legislation on the Senate floor, Stephen dwelled on how the world judged him. He swiveled his father's creaky old chair to look out the window.

The view was impressive. The Supreme Court building stood floors below him, but it still towered over the tourists taking their proud photos. He often wondered about the people who made up the term "the general public." Polls reflected their opinions about him, yet they knew so little. If they really knew him, would they feel differently?

"Did you hear, boss?" Greg asked in earnest.

"Yes," Stephen answered as though he'd been listening intently. He turned in his seat toward Greg. "It sounds like there are a lot of amendments to that bill."

"Yeah, you'll love this. Monroe is going after LIHEAP again. Can you believe it?" Greg smirked and looked around the room as if to encourage everyone to bring Stephen out of his funk. "Pierce is offering an amendment against it. We're signing on, right?"

"Absolutely." Stephen nodded, crossing his arms. "Great idea. Let's cut off the heat to poor people right before winter. Tell Pierce's staff I'll do anything he wants for the amendment."

"Good. I'll let them know."

"Is that all?"

"No," Megan said and cleared her throat. "We have a new Jennifer issue to deal with."

Hearing one of his female companions' names, Stephen turned to Megan and raised his eyebrows. As his middle sister and de facto press secretary, it was her job to promote and protect him, and she had no problem intruding into her brother's private life.

She ignored his reaction. "I've heard from a contact in L.A. that she's up for a new role. There's nudity involved and some sex."

Before he could respond, Patty jumped in. "Listen, I'll be the first to admit your relationship with her has given you some nice press for the campaign. But—"

"But the senator's sometime girlfriend can't show her breasts to the world?" He chuckled.

"Not during an election cycle," answered Patty. "You've got to tell her to delay the movie until after the election next year. Then she can branch out from her Disney flicks. If she doesn't agree, I suggest breaking up with her now."

"Okay, done." It wasn't a difficult request. Jennifer Hamilton may have been America's sweetheart, but outside of bed, he found talking to her painful. She was no great loss. "I'll handle it soon."

"Thanks, boss," Greg said in relief. "It's just that . . . you know . . . no one expects you to be like Langford, but you need to stick with women who are respectable."

Stephen pursed his lips when Greg mentioned his Republican opponent, Colorado State Treasurer Dan Langford. He was a family man and an archconservative who often said, "Unlike the McEvoy family, I don't have a skeleton in my closet." "Or a cogent thought in your head," Patty always muttered in response. While Stephen was young and brilliant, with a storied family name, Langford was older, dim, but with a hard-fought rise to wealth and power. The election would be a study in contrasts.

Stephen didn't like thinking about it, and his mind wandered back to its bad mood. "Got it. Next subject."

Greg checked his watch and announced, "Time for the interns. And, actually, I should tell you about one of them."

Stephen's phone rang, and after he checked the caller, he held up a finger to stop Greg. "Sorry. I need to take this call."

"Okay, but . . ."

"If it's about an intern, how big of a deal can it be?" With a shrug, Stephen answered his own question by taking the call and continuing to talk as he walked with them to the small conference room.

The month of September brought a fresh batch of interns for the school year, and Megan had cleared his calendar to do a meet and greet with the newbies. She hoped it would make up for the rest of the year when he ignored them.

Just as they entered the packed room, Stephen ended his call. He greeted the staff and interns with his trademark polished smile and personable demeanor. "Good morning, everyone. I hope you're doing well. This is usually such a muggy time in D.C., but it's a wonderful day outside. You should be playing hooky."

The seated group dutifully smiled and said hello.

"I trust the staff have already made their introductions." Stephen took his seat at the head of the table. "So I'd like to hear from our new interns. Let's see. What do I want to learn about you?" He tapped the table for a moment. "Hmmm. Why don't we start with your name? Then I'd like to hear your school, your major. Now, what else? How about your favorite place in Colorado and what town you're from? Does everyone have that?"

All the interns furiously took notes, and one by one they answered his questions. Stephen nodded and smiled as each performed for him, though he was so bored he counted every tile on the ceiling. When he was on his 239th tile, he realized he was almost free of the tedious meeting. He raised his eyebrows in anticipation.

"And I believe we only have one more today."

The table was so crammed with people that he couldn't see who was about to speak. He spotted only a pair of feminine hands resting on a notebook as a clear, female voice answered him.

"Hi. My name is Anne Norwood. I'm a senior at Boulder, but I'm at Georgetown for the year working on my senior thesis. I'm an American history major and—"

"And what's this thesis about?" Stephen asked, leaning forward. "I'll warn you I was an American history major, too." He tilted his head and saw some dark blond hair, but he still couldn't get a good view of her.

The other interns followed his stare because he hadn't asked any of them a direct question.

Her voice rose again from the back. "It's an analysis of Thomas Jefferson's romantic relationship with a slave, and whether it had any impact on his record on slavery."

"I'm sorry," he said with no expression on his face. "I can't see you.

Please stand up."

When she rose, he nodded in acknowledgment. He immediately thought her pretty with a nice figure, though he didn't let on he was checking her out. Instead, he jumped to his question. "So did the relationship alter his position on slavery?"

"Not much," she said in a flat tone.

"And what do you think of this founding father?"

"Not much." She delivered the line plainly again, but her mouth twitched, well aware she'd made a joke.

Everyone in the room laughed, including Stephen.

"Good. I think he's overrated, too."

More laughter ensued as the room enjoyed hearing a Democratic politician buck two hundred years of adoration of the party's idol. While everyone chuckled, Stephen and Anne's eyes locked for a moment. They both smiled, and their eyes held the same mixture of surprise and respect for each other's response.

I like her, he thought, and wanting to hear her say more, he broke their stare. "And what are your answers to my last questions?"

"I'm from Summit County, and I love the meadows of the Gore Range."

"Where?" He also loved those meadows—every one of them.

"Oh . . . I like the Eagle's Nest Wilderness."

Stephen wanted to blurt out, "Me, too," but he saw all the eyes in the room drifting back and forth between him and Anne. He realized he must've paid her too much attention. It was high time to end the meeting and any more interactions with her.

With a final smile for the whole room, he said, "Thank you, everyone, for —" Something clicked, and he turned and pointed a finger at Anne. "Wait. You're from Summit County? And your last name is Norwood? Are you related to—"

"Yes," she said in a firm tone. "Elton Norwood is my dad. He's the district attorney for the county."

"And your grandfather was once attorney general, correct?" he asked, keeping his voice even.

"He was." She smiled. "Yes, my family *are* Republicans, but *I'm* not."

Without skipping a beat, he returned her smile and lied, "We won't hold that against you."

As everyone broke into laughter, he closed the meeting graciously, while Patty, Greg, and Megan gave one another anxious looks. They followed him to his office, where he took his seat and waited for Greg to close the door.

With his office sealed, he grumbled, "So, *she's* the intern you wanted to tell me about."

"Yeah, I tried." Greg took a seat and clasped his hands.

"Why is Elton Norwood's daughter an intern in *my* office?" Stephen's eyes roamed the room searching for an answer.

"If we hadn't hired her, it would've looked bad for us," Megan said matter-of-factly.

As he considered her assessment, Stephen leaned back against the chair and touched his shock of black hair in absentminded thought. It was true, the Norwoods were a respected Republican family in Colorado, and Elton was a popular district attorney in Summit County. At the very least, it would be impolite to reject his daughter for an internship.

He muttered, "Okay. You're right."

"You know," Greg said as he leaned back in his chair and held up his hands in a plea. "The Norwoods are moderates, and Elton and my dad are in Rotary together back home, and they're friends. Elton is—"

"A Republican nonetheless, and I'm sure he's friends with Langford, too," Stephen said with palpable distaste.

"He probably is friends with Langford, but he really is a stand-up guy. He knows I work for you, but he didn't even say anything to my dad when Anne applied for an internship. When I told my dad about it, he asked Elton why he didn't mention it to him. Elton said he didn't want it to appear like he was looking for favors for his daughter. I gotta tell you, that's just like him."

"He is known to be a fair person," Megan said.

"And Anne is just a smart, nice kid, who happens to be from a Republican family. It will be fine," Greg said with finality.

"*Kid* is not the term I would use for her." Patty chuckled. "She's definitely a woman."

Thinking back to how Anne looked and carried herself, Stephen agreed with Patty, but he didn't want to announce it.

Greg grimaced and shook his head at Patty. "Whatever. She graduated from high school with my youngest brother. She's a kid to me."

"Well, regardless," Patty said as she turned to Stephen. "I bet Elton Norwood *is* friends with Langford. I didn't want Anne in this office either, but we couldn't say no to her. She's most likely not a rat, though I'll still watch her. You shouldn't worry about it."

"I can feel her out," Greg offered. "Just to be sure."

Stephen's cell phone vibrated again, and as soon as he saw *Helen* appear on the screen, he motioned toward the door. "I'd appreciate that, Greg. If you don't mind, I need to take this call and talk to my sisters."

"No problem."

The chief of staff was only involved in part of the senator's life; the family controlled everything else. It was an unorthodox arrangement—having not just one, but two family members as part of a senator's most senior staff, but as a McEvoy, Stephen was no ordinary senator.

As Greg closed the door, Stephen answered the phone. "Hello, Helen."

Rolling her eyes, Patty put her feet up on the coffee table and began twirling her red, Irish curls. Megan scrolled through her phone's e-mail and tapped her foot. It was a loud warning for Stephen to hurry.

After less than a minute of conversation, he ended the call and turned to his sisters. "I bet this is the last time."

"Good. I still can't believe you screw around with a Republican, especially *her* of all people," Patty said as she crossed her arms and smirked. "Well, I can believe it. It just disgusts me."

"Helen Sanders really is the Wicked Witch of the West." Megan cringed.

"Now come on. She's much prettier than that." Stephen chuckled. "Though I agree she has an evil side."

"*An* evil side?" Patty sneered. "What side of her isn't evil?"

"Amen," said Megan. "I just heard she refused to do a fundraiser for Michaelson unless he cosponsored her stupid militia amendment *and* gave her top-billing on the invitation—even above the governor of his state."

"And her staff hates her. She has the worst reputation as a boss of anyone in the Senate." Patty snickered. "That's quite an achievement considering how many pompous assholes there are around here. The sooner you stop seeing her, the better. I don't trust her."

"Are things ending because of Matt Smythe?" Megan asked. "I just checked the wires. An AP story says she campaigned with him this weekend. They've been together a lot lately."

"I think they're getting engaged," Stephen replied. "Frankly, I'm relieved to be done with this. It's been difficult to break off."

"So it's not easy having an affair with another senator?" Megan smirked. "Especially from the other party?"

"No, not easy. But it's not an affair. We were just . . . dating."

"Bah!" Patty laughed. "Since when are dates only in a bed?"

§§§§

At nine o'clock sharp that night, Senator Helen Sanders pressed the intercom button outside the giant wrought iron gates of the McEvoy residence. In her home state of Idaho, such a house would be landmark, and she would want her arrival to be in a limousine and televised. In Washington, D.C., the building merely blended in with the rest of the mansions and embassies on Massachusetts Avenue, and she preferred a discreet entrance.

Seconds later the gates opened for her, and after she parked her car out of sight from the street, the house door swung open. She strode inside, enjoying the ease of entry and knowing her favorite amusement awaited her.

As Stephen closed the door, he welcomed his expected guest. "Good evening. It's nice to see you."

"It's good to see you, too, but I don't have much time tonight." She walked into the foyer, turned, and smiled when she saw his jeans. He wasn't much younger, but in jeans he made her feel like Mrs. Robinson, and Helen liked every scrap of power she could get. She saddened once she realized this would be their last encounter—at least until she was safely married. With a few steps, she closed the space between them and touched his T-shirt. Her voice was sweet, but husky. "You're smart enough to know why I'm here."

"You're leaving me for your own kind." He chuckled.

"Something like that. Matt wants to settle down."

"Is it what you want?" he asked with a raised eyebrow.

"Yes. Very much. Tick-tock, you know." Helen controlled everything in her life, and she wasn't going to let her biological clock get away from her without a marriage. Matt Smythe was the remedy. He was the perfect husband—conservative, unobjectionable, and easily pliable.

"Then I'm happy for you," he said, crossing his arms.

"I want something else right now, though," she said as she unbuttoned her coat.

"What's that?"

She tossed her jacket on a chair and walked into the adjacent dining room. In the unlit room, she slipped out of her dress, revealing a black bustier, silk stockings, and lacy panties.

Stephen shook his head and laughed. "Helen, what would the good people of Idaho think about this?"

"The good people of Idaho will never find out about us." She sat atop his mother's antique table and spread her legs, giving him a better view. "Besides, it's just one more time to remember you. And for you to remember me."

"But what about Matt?" he asked with reproach.

"Oh, he'll never know about you. No one will ever know about you because neither one of us will ever tell." She beckoned him with a finger. "That's why we've been perfect for one another."

§§§§

A little after eight the next morning, Stephen sat in the back of his Lincoln Town Car reading *The New York Times*, while his driver, Jim, maneuvered through the streets around the Capitol building. When they stopped at one of D.C.'s interminably long stoplights, he glanced to his right. Standing on the sidewalk near his car was Anne Norwood. The dark windows allowed him to stare unnoticed, and the timing of the light gave him a full minute to study the young woman.

It was a steamy, early-September day, and she dressed like your average Capitol Hill staffer walking from the Metro to work. She wore a suit, but the jacket hung on her arm, and a sleeveless top kept her cool. Stephen again admired her figure; her arms were toned, and a belt accentuated her small waist. Her hair was up off her neck, with stray tendrils damp with sweat. The heat also made her tanned skin pink. She turned her head for a moment, as if she sensed she was being watched. He observed her profile and decided she wasn't generically pretty as he'd thought. There was something both unique and familiar about her. With freckled cheeks and the body of an athlete, she looked like a girl who loved the outdoors, and it was a look he'd always found attractive. Her legs were bare beneath her skirt and, like many women walking to work, she wasn't yet in heels. Instead, she wore a pair of lime green Converse low-tops, which made him smile. He thought she seemed like she'd be fun to be around—to maybe go on a hike with.

As the crosswalk sign signaled the light would soon change, she looked directly into the window of his sedan. Similar cars swarmed the streets of D.C., each one a sign of someone important inside. Though she didn't know it, their eyes met. The light soon turned and his car rolled past her.

The image of her bright and curious eyes stayed with him, making Stephen wince in frustration. When he thought back to the little show Helen put on last night, he felt ashamed. He shook his head in disgust, but quickly shook it faster in disbelief. *What in the hell am I thinking?*

There were always pretty young things as staff and interns in his office, and he treated them all the same way; he avoided them. Those women were off-limits; political self-preservation required it. If Patty ever caught him even glancing at a staff member for too long, she'd mutter, "God damn it, Stephen. Don't shit where you eat."

He grimaced. It would be one thing if he simply was admiring an intern for her looks. *For Christ's sake! I want to go on a* hike *with her?* He hated hiking with other people. Being in the outdoors alone was one of his greatest pleasures. The only person he had liked hiking with was his father. Why would he ever want to hike with her?

Looking out the window, he wondered what kind of girl she really was. Even if Elton Norwood was a moderate Republican, he was still a Republican. He'd endorse Dan Langford. Anne might stupidly mention something she heard in the office about Stephen's campaign to her father, who might tell it to Langford. Then he'd have direct knowledge of how Stephen planned to defeat him.

The girl was trouble in every way. He shook his head and turned back to his paper. The less he thought about her, the better.

Chapter 2

That morning, Anne sat in her cubicle and sorted through constituent mail. Out of nowhere, she heard a friendly voice.

"Anne Norwood, I can't believe you didn't introduce yourself to me."

She looked up to see Greg Miller smiling as he leaned against the partition. She placed the envelopes aside and rose to shake his hand. "I'm sorry. I didn't think you'd know who I was."

"Of course I do." He nodded down the hall. "C'mon. Let's get a cup of coffee. You're the only other person in the office from back home."

"I'd love to. Thanks." As Greg led her out of the office, she asked him how he ended up working on the Hill. While he detailed his career up the congressional ladder, she nodded and took note, but her mind wandered. She was baffled as to how she had gone from sorting envelopes to coffee with the chief of staff.

When they arrived at the elevators, he pressed the button and placed his arms across his broad chest. "So, why did you apply for an internship with Senator McEvoy? Why not another member of Congress?"

"Well, I like his politics," she answered as she looked at his arms. The combination of his question and his stance told her his offer of coffee wasn't a social one. She took a deep, calming breath before speaking again. "And I'd rather work in the Senate than the House. I'm also interested in environmental issues, and Senator McEvoy sits on the Energy and Natural Resources Committee."

"Sounds good." He ushered her into the elevator. "But what does your dad think of you working here?"

"When I told my dad I was applying for this internship, he shrugged it off. He thinks I'm young and naïve. You know, like why else would I want to work for a Democrat?"

"But he didn't stop you?"

"Oh, he and my mom gave me a few warnings, telling me I needed to think about what I was doing, but that's it. They always say my brother and I are allowed to make our own mistakes." She smiled and shook her head. "How's that for confidence in your kids?"

"That sounds like something your dad would say." He chuckled as they exited the elevator into the Hart Building basement.

"I guess you know enough of his sayings from the papers."

"Yeah. Elton has a way with words."

Things were quiet between them as they walked into the cafeteria and got their coffees. When they sat down, he quizzed her on the latest gossip in Summit County. It didn't take long before he asked the question, giving away the real reason behind the impromptu coffee date.

"And what do you think about Dan Langford?" he asked, leaning back in his seat.

"Langford?" she asked, though she knew exactly where he was going. "I don't know. He and my dad are friendly. I've met him a few times."

"So tell me what you think about him." He sipped his coffee. "Your father's a Republican, Dan's a family friend, but you're working for Senator McEvoy. What's the deal?"

"Well, obviously I don't agree with him on anything," she answered and raised a hand in self-evidence. "Langford's way more to the right than my dad, and I think my dad's already pretty conservative—at least for me. I'm the black sheep in my family."

"If you didn't say you disagreed with them, I'd kick you out of our office immediately." He laughed.

"You know, I really appreciate that I got this job, despite my father."

"Aw, hell. It's Colorado. Everybody is related to a Republican somehow."

§§§§

The next morning, one of the receptionists called in sick, so Anne covered the office phones for the day. It was easy enough work, and she liked talking to constituents, even if they were angry. When the waiting area quieted around midmorning, the other receptionist went on a break. Anne took the opportunity to study for a class, and the few minutes of silence lulled her into complete focus on her reading. When the office door opened, she jumped and slammed the book shut.

At first, it only registered that a good-looking man had entered the room. Soon his face clicked, and she found her wits. "Good morning, Senator McEvoy."

"Morning," he muttered as he strode past and into the main office.

His brief glance felt more like a glare to her. She sighed and told herself not to take it personally. She was an inconsequential intern; it had nothing to do with her. She should get used to it. But she wondered if she had done something wrong. Looking around, she tried to see if there was a task she'd missed. If the phones were silent and the office empty, there was little to do. Would he rather have seen her surfing the web or playing solitaire than reading a book? She shook her head and went back to reading.

§§§§

Normally, Stephen wouldn't think twice about the receptionists in his office. He'd give them a perfunctory "hello" in the morning and "good-bye" at the day's end. Otherwise, he ignored them as he came and went throughout the workday.

With Anne at the front desk, it was different. Each time he walked by, he noticed her because she stood out compared to the usual receptionist in her place. The pimply guy, straight out of Georgetown, had been replaced by an attractive woman. Of course Stephen would eye her.

Stephen believed Greg's report that Anne wasn't engaging in political espionage in his office, yet he still wondered about *her*. From the snippets he caught of her conversations with constituents, she had perfect manners, even when taming callers angry over one of his votes. She also read a lot, both books and newspapers. Occasionally, he caught her tapping away on her phone. He assumed the texts were to a boyfriend.

While Stephen pondered Anne, she never acknowledged him again. After their terse exchange that morning, she decided it was best to keep her head down and concentrate on the task at hand when he was around.

Toward the end of the day, she was again alone in the reception area. The door swept open, and she raised her head only long enough to see it was him. Back to her reading, she sensed he'd walked past her, but there was more movement. She spotted dark pants in front of the desk. Folding the paper, she asked dutifully, "May I help you?"

"You know . . ." he said, pointing to the page. ". . . they say no one under the age of thirty reads print newspapers anymore."

"Well, I guess I'm an exception." She wore a proud smile. "I've always loved them."

"Why is that?"

"When I was growing up, Silverthorne was really tiny. Nothing like it is now."

"That's true. It's changed a lot. It's gotten to be pretty commercial." He grimaced in agreement.

"Exactly. So newspapers were like these windows to a whole other world beyond the mountains. I read *The Denver Post* every day. It was different reading the actual paper, rather than the words on a computer screen. Seeing things in print and feeling a paper in my hands made the rest of the world seem more real. Anyway, that's why I read the paper." She considered who she was talking to and shrugged. "It probably all sounds silly to you. You're from the city."

"No, it doesn't sound silly." He stood at ease and smiled. "I had somewhat the opposite experience."

"How so?"

"I was stuck here during the school year while my dad was in the Senate, but I spent my summers at our ranch outside Kremmling. I loved it there. I never wanted to leave."

"It's pretty out there," she said as she envisioned the next county over from hers.

"It is. And much more fun than St. Albans *all-boys* School here in D.C."

"I imagine," she said with a light chuckle.

"I hated leaving the ranch. For years, I'd hide the day we were supposed to leave. It drove my parents nuts."

"Where would you hide?" She grinned at what she thought was an adorable story, especially coming from him. Until that moment, she hadn't thought him very human.

"I don't know . . . closets, cabinets . . . sometimes the hay in my horse's stall."

"Aw," she said, resting her chin on her hands. "I don't miss home at all. I thought I would, but I don't. I do miss my horse, though. It doesn't make sense. I leave him every year for school and don't think about him. Now, I move here, and I'm texting my mom just to see how he's doing."

"What kind of horse is he?"

"A black Morgan named Orion, but I call him Orie."

"Sounds like a handsome guy."

"He is. Do you have a horse?"

"No. Not anymore." He sighed. "My family has a working ranch, so we have some there, but none of them is mine. I don't have the time."

Anne sensed he didn't like his predicament. The look in his blue eyes was also blue, and she felt badly for him. She offered some encouragement. "But you're lucky to see them when you can."

A few seconds lapsed as he held her gaze. A touch of anxiety hit her when she thought he might be debating what to say, but then he nodded and smiled. "You're right. I am lucky. I should remember that." As he turned to leave, he said, "Have a good night."

"Thanks. You, too."

She opened her newspaper again, though she didn't read. She imagined the handsome Senator McEvoy as a sad little boy hiding in the hay. It was a sweet image, and it seemed to hold true today. Why couldn't he remember his luck in life? He was a McEvoy and the son of the revered Patrick McEvoy. His father had recently died, which was tragic, but Stephen was appointed to complete his term in the Senate. No one would say he was unlucky. Her brow furrowed. *I wonder what that's about.*

§§§§

The following day, Stephen spied Anne through the window as he approached his office. Pretending to check his phone, he stopped in the hallway for a minute to watch her as she read. He liked the way she answered his newspaper question the day before. He envisioned a sheltered girl studying the paper every day for news of life outside her tiny Colorado town.

With a loose braid over her shoulder, he thought she looked pretty. She touched the plait as she read, and he wondered what she was concentrating on.

"Good morning, Anne," he greeted as he walked inside.

Her eyes flew up from the page, and she closed the book. "Good morning, Senator. How are you?"

"Good, and you?"

"I'm fine, thanks."

He glanced at the book's cover, John Rawls's *A Theory of Justice*. "Doing some light reading?"

"Oh. Yeah." She smiled. "It's for a class."

Remembering the book from his own school days, he asked, "And what do you think of it?"

"Well, it's a little dry, but I think his thesis is right. Justice should also be about economic fairness."

"You really think that?"

"I *told* you the other day, my *dad* is the Republican. Not me," she said with a wry grin.

"I know that's what you said—"

"You're just going to have to trust me."

"I suppose I will." He'd said it jokingly, but the meaning was serious. She worked in his office; he had to trust her, and at that moment, he *wanted* to trust her because he wanted to talk to her more. She was funny and cute and made him smile. As they shared a grin, he felt off-balance, and he nodded at the door. "I've got a meeting. Have a good day."

When the receptionist came back to work the next day, Stephen was disappointed to see the pimply guy at the front desk, but he told himself it was a good thing. Anne was too appealing to be around all the time.

§§§§

A few days later, Stephen and Megan walked down the office hall, rehashing their latest meeting. In the middle of the same hallway, Anne and another intern stood studying the giant map of Colorado covering the wall. Stephen wondered what they were pointing at, but he planned on walking right by them.

Megan was always polite, though, and stopped to greet them. "Hello, Anne. Hello, Keith. What are you doing?"

"Um . . . Sen . . . Senator McEvoy, Megan, hello," Keith stuttered. "Anne was just . . . pointing out nice places to spend some time outdoors. She really knows her stuff."

"Really, I don't," Anne retorted. "Good afternoon, Senator. Megan."

"Well, Keith says you do," Stephen said and smiled. He was eager to see her reaction to being put on the spot.

"Not as much as some." Anne shrugged. "My dad likes to get away when he can, so I'm familiar with a few remote places."

Keith chuckled and shook his head. "Yeah, she keeps pointing out these wilderness areas where they won't let you mountain bike even though *nobody* is around. I told her she should find me places closer to civilization where I can ride."

"What?" she said in a joking reprimand. "Wilderness is no place for mountain bikes. It's supposed to be serene and quiet, not full of gonzo bikers blasting over trails."

Stephen smiled at Anne's response, and he was jealous Keith could spend his morning talking to her about Colorado's beautiful countryside. "You know, Keith, I love to mountain bike, too, but I have to agree with Anne."

"Keith, where do you ride around Denver?" Megan asked and pointed to the map. "I love finding new places to ride near the city."

As Keith showed Megan spots near his home, Anne smiled at Stephen. He didn't speak for a moment, simply taking her in. He thought she was the definition of a mountain beauty. With her hair streaked from the sun, tan, freckled skin, and bright eyes, she was lovely. Wanting to hear more from her, he threw out the first question to pop into his mind. "So you don't mountain bike?"

"No. My brother rides a bike, but I'd rather hike."

"I would, too."

"Well, really I'd rather ride a horse. He does the work. I'm a slow hiker." She chuckled. "Nobody likes going with me."

He bit his tongue to keep from saying he'd very much like to go on a hike with her. His eyes darted down to her small waist, thinking how easy it would be to pick her up and move her over a fallen tree or any other obstacle in their way. He came to his senses and grasped for another question to continue the conversation. "Does anyone else in your family ride?"

"My mom. She grew up on a ranch. We ride together, except when she's got a baseball game."

"Huh?" His brow furrowed in confusion.

"Yeah, it's odd. My mom, mild-mannered Mary Beth Norwood, is obsessed with baseball. She's like the Rockies' biggest fan."

"So do you like baseball?"

"It's kind of boring to me, but on a nice day, it's great to go to a ballpark and sit in the sun with a beer."

As she spoke, Stephen lost himself. He was no longer Senator Stephen McEvoy, or Stephen McEvoy, District Attorney, or even Stephen McEvoy, son of Senator Patrick McEvoy. He was just a guy at Coors Field with Anne, watching a Rockies game and drinking a couple of beers.

Down the hall, Patty's voice interrupted his daydream. "Megan. You're late."

"I believe we were waiting for you," Megan replied in an annoyed voice.

Stephen snapped out of his daze as his sister gestured for him to walk forward. She smiled at Anne and Keith. "I have to get the senator to his campaign manager. You two have a good day."

Stephen looked at his watch, remembering who and where he was. "Yes, we need to go. Good-bye . . . for now." He walked away without looking back.

After they left the hall, Keith paced excitedly back and forth. "That was too fucking cool!" he exclaimed, turning to Anne. "Wow. He likes to mountain bike. That's awesome. I'm going to tell Gabe."

He left a bewildered Anne standing alone in the middle of the hallway. She decided to walk to the bathroom to think through the last few minutes. She replayed all the conversations she'd had with the senator. It increasingly felt like he wanted to get to know her, but how could that possibly be the case?

She remembered standing in line at Safeway recently and reading a gossip rag with a photo of Senator McEvoy and the actress Jennifer Hamilton at a charity event. When she thought of Jennifer Hamilton's homecoming-queen looks and disproportionately large chest, she self-consciously touched her braid and glanced at her breasts. There was no way the senator could be interested in her. It just wasn't possible.

Yet he always spoke with her, though he didn't have to. She was only an intern. By the end of their latest exchange, he'd been inching toward her. She didn't think she had imagined it. If any other guy acted the way he had, she'd assume he was flirting.

She shook her head. A romance with an intern was political suicide, and Senator McEvoy wasn't stupid. She searched for a reason for his actions. Maybe it was so she wouldn't bad-mouth him to her father?

She took a breath and tried to accept any rational explanation, but the girlie part of her brain wanted to stay confused. Because she found him interesting, she wanted to think he had an interest in her, and because she thought he was so handsome, she wanted to think he found her attractive, too. But she prided herself on being a smart girl. Her mind drifted back to the *People* magazine photo, and she knew she should accept the rational explanation.

§§§§

When Stephen and Megan finally entered his office, Patty slammed the door. "What the fuck was that?"

"What's your problem?" Megan asked as she sank into the sofa. "No big deal. We were just being nice."

"That may be your reason." Patty glared at Stephen. "But *you* were on the make."

"Hardly." He sat down at his desk and scowled to hide his guilt.

"I'll be the judge of that. I'm not a fool. I know you." She turned to her sister. "And Megan, you're supposed to be helping me protect this senate seat. Why didn't you stop him?"

"I didn't notice anything." Megan shrugged and turned to Stephen. "Do you actually *like* Anne?"

"Can we move on?" He shook his head and avoided answering the question directly. "Nothing happened."

Patty raised her eyebrows. "And nothing *will* happen."

"Nothing will happen," he said flatly.

"Good." Patty nodded. "I expect you to go back to treating her like you do every other intern around here. Ignore her."

Megan glanced at her brother the way they always did when they needed to talk without Patty around. He saw her request for a private conversation, and he rebuffed her with a twitch of his nose. This was personal.

With a yawn and scratch of his temple, he shut down the subject altogether. "Okay. Let's move on."

Chapter 3

For the next few weeks, Stephen avoided Anne as he'd promised Patty. With his busy schedule and large office, it was usually an easy thing to do. If he wasn't rushed and he happened upon her, he'd acknowledge her with a nod and move on, but sometimes it was difficult.

Once he heard one of his legislative assistants call the ski resorts in West Virginia pathetic compared to those in Colorado.

"It doesn't matter," Anne replied. "I don't go to resorts much anymore. I usually ski in the backcountry."

As she chatted with the staffer, Stephen was tempted to join in the conversation. Biting his tongue, he kept about his business, but not without another side-eyed glance. He summed her up with one thought: *She's really cool.*

Despite his interest, he stayed away, until one day he noticed her alone in the copy room near his personal office. With some regret, he continued on his path down the hall, but the temptation proved too much. He backed up and peered into the small room. There she was—leaning on the counter as she studied a letter that bore his signature at the bottom. Her finger traced the page as she concentrated on each word.

After a quick look to make sure no one was nearby, he quietly stepped into the room. "What did I say this time?" he asked.

She jumped. "Oh! I didn't hear you walk in. I'm sorry."

"No, I'm sorry. I didn't mean to startle you." He smiled to reassure her. "I asked about the letter. What did I say this time?"

"You mean, what did *I* say this time?" She returned his smile and waved the paper as if to bat him away. "I'm joking. I drafted a new form letter outlining your position on the deficit. This is the final version. I was just seeing what your legislative director kept of what I wrote."

"And?"

"It's pretty similar."

"May I see?"

"Sure." She handed him the letter.

Skimming through a paragraph, he concluded it was well written and persuasive.

As he nodded, she spoke, "The LD left in the part about how an extension of unemployment benefits actually grows the economy. I'm proud of that."

"Spoken like a true policy geek." It was a dismissive statement, but he meant it as a compliment.

"I guess I am." She shrugged awkwardly. "It's always debate night at the Norwood dinner table. My brother never showed any interest in politics—he's in med school now—so my dad talked to me because I kept up with things."

"Sounds like my family." He smiled.

"Except I debate my parents. Everyone in your family agrees."

"We do—for the most part."

"Must be nice." She rolled her eyes.

Stephen paused for a moment, quickly assessing the woman before him who was so different from the women he dated. He liked her irreverence, which she seemed to hold for everything, including her family and even him. Other than his own family, very few people treated him that way.

His eyes drifted from her face down to her shoulders and rested briefly on her small but perky chest. He imagined for a moment what her breasts might look like. Pleased with the image in his mind, he let his eyes wander upward. He noticed the cute freckles from years in the strong mountain sun dotting her nose and cheeks.

Finally, their eyes met again. He admired her flowerlike hazel irises, and the look in her eyes told him she'd noticed him checking her out. She lifted a brow as if to ask him what he was going to do next.

Normally, in such a moment, if he wanted to cut to the chase, he might ask the woman out. If he was really interested, he'd pay her a small compliment beforehand. With Anne, he wanted to tell her she was beautiful —simply to see if he could make her bashful.

Whatever he chose to do, he presumed she'd be receptive. Though she was young, her expression wasn't innocent; it told him loud and clear any advance would be welcomed.

He took a breath of anticipation. Their connection was temptingly easy, but it was also unnerving, like he stood on a precipice with untold consequences. Maintaining his stare for a few more seconds, he debated those consequences—and stopped himself.

Passing back the letter, he broke her spell. "Good job," he said softly. With an abrupt turn of his heel, he left the room, chiding himself for what he'd done.

After Anne watched him pass through the door, she caught her breath while her mind swirled in confusion. *Oh my God. What was that?* It was a silly question because she knew what had happened. In that moment, Stephen McEvoy wanted her, and her rapid heartbeat was evidence of the connection she'd made with him.

Her eyes widened as she realized what it could mean, and she quickly reprimanded herself. *Are you crazy? He's a senator, for Christ's sake, and you're an intern. You'll destroy your career before you even have one.* The thought made her speed out of the room.

§§§§

After the copy-room incident, timing became everything for Anne. Scared to death of the feelings rumbling inside her, she made sure she was never in Senator McEvoy's presence. She worried what he might say, and she feared even more how she would react. In order to avoid him, she was either late or early to wherever she was going and occasionally left conversations in midsentence. If she knew the senator was due in the office, she planned to be absent. If she saw him coming nearby, she'd skulk away so as not to be seen. Sometimes she'd become trapped, though, and she'd had to wait for him to leave an area.

Hiding behind a door or file cabinet, she would observe him from afar. Whenever she lurked, she ridiculed herself for being a stalker, yet she became so engrossed in him that she quickly forgot the creepiness of her behavior. With other elected officials and agency heads, he was congenial but guarded, and with staff, he was firm. His wall only came down when he was alone with Greg and his family.

Patrick and Lillian McEvoy had raised accomplished children who carried the family legacy of public service with a special *noblesse oblige*, but they were still a normal family. Patty and Megan teased and bickered with their brother like they were twelve. He snarled at his sisters' torments and then dished it out right back, causing Anne to cover her mouth to squelch her laughter.

When he was alone, she noticed he seemed glum, his lips pursed in thought. *Why is he unhappy?* she would wonder.

She recalled their conversations and realized he may have given her a glimpse of the real Stephen McEvoy—maybe he was interested in her as a person. Had he sought her out? Was he looking for her now? Or was he also avoiding her? But because she steered clear of him, she didn't know.

It's better this way, she reminded herself. *If I actually talked to the guy again, I'd be a goner.*

§§§§

The following week, Stephen walked back from the House side of Capitol Hill, having finished a late-morning press event in the Cannon Caucus

Room. Enjoying the nice day, he took his time as he strolled along. His mind was on the sunshine rather than his long day ahead, yet his good mood hit a wall when he spotted Anne.

She sat in front of the Library of Congress's fountain, the *Court of Neptune*, reading a book. Stephen ranked the fountain the prettiest in the District. Neptune dominated the fountain, positioned in the middle, with his son Triton and two sea nymphs riding sea monsters at his side. The fountain's anatomically correct figures made it a highlight for many school children touring the Nation's Capital.

Since the day they talked in the copy room, Stephen avoided her presence at all costs; it proved to be easy because she was never around him anymore. And if she entered his thoughts, he pushed her aside, but seeing her from afar that sunny day made him stop. He pulled out his phone and surreptitiously watched her while pretending to check his e-mail. He told himself it would only be a minute and then he'd get back to work.

Though he stood across the street, he heard the water cascading in the fountain. While the world walked by, Anne kept her head in a book. The sun shone on her bare legs, crossed at the ankles and angled to the side. They were seductively ladylike underneath her pencil skirt, and he wasn't the only man noticing her. A young guy with a dog walked up and began talking to her.

Stephen didn't know him, but he knew the dog. It was Senator Henry Wilson's English bulldog. Like many members of Congress, he kept a pet in his office. An elderly Republican from the South, Senator Wilson hated Communists and his foreign policy was steeped in the Cold War. He'd owned bulldogs for the last fifty years and usually named them after a Communist leader of the day or a perceived enemy of the United States. His lingering hatred of Russia showed in the name of his current dog: Putin. Stephen guessed the guy walking the dog was one of Wilson's interns.

Though he couldn't hear their conversation, Stephen was bothered simply by the fact they were talking. He studied the intern and admitted he was an okay-looking guy who was close to Anne's age. Stephen didn't like that. Remembering the intern worked for Senator Wilson, he felt a little better because the intern most likely shared his boss's view of the world. Surely Anne wasn't interested in a right-wing lunatic who thought Castro still had nuclear weapons pointed at the US?

When Anne shook her head at the intern, Stephen smiled and waited for him to leave. After another minute of conversation, the intern shook her hand. Anne also said good-bye to the dog, who repaid her pat on the head with a slobbery lick on her cheek. She cringed, and as the intern walked off, she splashed her face with fountain water.

Stephen chuckled at Anne's reaction to the dog. He didn't know many women who would wash their face in a public fountain. He looked at the water coming from the fountain and saw the statue of the sea nymph above

Anne. It was a beautiful nude of a woman riding a sea monster. The woman's head was tilted back in a somewhat erotic pose with her breasts prominently displayed. Something about the sculpture lulled Stephen into a midday fantasy of skinny dipping with Anne in a mountain lake.

It was during Stephen's fantasy that Anne sensed someone looking at her. She glanced at the people on the sidewalk, but they were all occupied with their own lives. Just as she was about to return to reading, she spotted Senator McEvoy across the street.

His eyes were fixed on her, and she stared back, wondering what he was doing. Why was he watching her? After a moment, he waved—a brief movement of his hand from left to right. She smiled as she hesitantly waved back, and a small smile appeared on his face in return.

She couldn't believe it. The whole silent exchange felt odd, but also exciting, and his warm expression made her ignore her better judgment. She pointed to her chest and then pointed to him, silently asking if he wanted her to come over.

Despite the distance between them, Stephen understood her question. He wanted so badly to nod his head and go on a walk with her. He wanted to talk, to see what she was reading, and maybe ask her about her favorite time of year to ride in those mountains she mentioned the first day. And he really wouldn't have minded finding a secluded area to give her a kiss.

But he didn't do any of that; instead, he mocked himself. He thought he could also ask Anne about her being an intern in his office. They might talk about the great political scandals involving interns—scandals that had tripped up many a politician before him. He could ask about her being ten years younger than him. Finally, he could ask about what it was like to grow up in a prominent Republican family.

He thought of everything at stake: a Democratic senate seat, his family's legacy, his career, her career. It was too much. Instead of saying yes to Anne, he shook his head and walked to his office, dejected.

As he left her sight, Anne kept her face completely composed, but inside she fell to pieces. She couldn't believe how foolish she was. She must've imagined what happened between them in the copy room. It was just a silly fantasy that they'd been avoiding one another. In reality, it was all one-sided, and she told herself he must know she had a crush on him. *How embarrassing. Why would he ever want to be with me? What was I thinking?*

Chapter 4

"Who wrote this piece of shit memo?" Senator McEvoy grumbled as he strode through the office.

Like every other subordinate in the office, Anne's head instinctively bowed. She hadn't written the memo, but she felt for whoever had. In the past few weeks, the senator had become sullen and irritable. Everyone tried to stay out of his way.

Humiliated by their last encounter in front of the Library of Congress, she continued to avoid him, though she had run into him once. He'd given her an uncomfortable smile and a short "hello" before hurriedly moving on. Anne had assumed he'd brushed her off because he knew she had a crush on him. She was mortified.

Indeed, Stephen avoided Anne, but he couldn't ignore her. Seeing her gave him a bout of regret and disappointment that wasn't easily dispelled. Despite those feelings, he wanted to make her smile, yet his presence seemed to have the opposite effect. She always said hello, but immediately looked away, and if she was smiling, she stopped at once after she saw him.

"Where the hell is Greg? I need to talk about this memo," he grumbled to Megan, who stood at his office door.

"He's on the House side for a caucus meeting."

"Tell him to come in when he gets back." As he moved past her he muttered, "And close the door behind you."

Shutting the door on her little brother's pissy mood, Megan turned to see Patty.

"I need to talk with Stephen," Patty said, pointing to the door.

"Believe me. You don't want to talk to him right now." She motioned toward her office door with a nod. Patty followed her inside, and with befuddled faces, they sank down on the couch.

"He needs to get laid," declared Patty. "That's got to be the problem. He hasn't been with anyone since he broke it off with Jennifer and Helen."

"But he *is* seeing somebody."

"Who?"

"Diane Schultz."

"She's pretty," said Patty. "But I'd rather watch paint dry than carry on a conversation with her. I sat beside her at a fundraiser last year. She was pedantic—just had to show us she was the smartest person in the room."

"I know. Stephen thinks she's tedious, too. He says they don't have much in common."

"He needs to find someone new. He'll be happier."

"That may be the problem." Megan eyed her sister. "He's found someone new, but he can't be with her."

"Who? The intern?"

"I think so."

"Anne Norwood is not an option. Period. End of discussion." Patty kept shaking her head while she spoke, unconsciously emphasizing her point.

"I agree." Megan closed her eyes and leaned her head back against the sofa. "But I feel for him. I think he really likes her."

"Are you serious? He barely knows her."

"It's just a guess. She's his type—cute, outdoorsy, smart—all rolled into one."

"Well, it's not possible. Even if she didn't work here, he can't have a girlfriend in college. It doesn't look good—especially compared to Langford's perfect little family. Not to mention what happens when Elton Norwood hears his daughter's boss took advantage of her." She shook her head again. "It's not happening."

Megan was quiet for a moment as she stared at the ceiling, looking for an answer. She raised her head with an idea. "Can't he at least talk to her? This could all blow over if he got to know her."

"Talk? I don't know . . . I don't trust him. If he wants to see her after he gets reelected in a year, that's okay. She's so young. It's not ideal, but at least she'll be out of college." Patty jumped up from her seat. "That's my take. I need to run. I'm having lunch with Mom."

Megan sighed as she watched her sister straighten her shirt. "Patty, how is it that you look so good in just a white shirt and pinstriped pants?"

"Thanks, sis." Patty preened. "I may cuss like a sailor and have a mean streak a mile wide, but God blessed me with a porn-star body."

"Well, you lucked out."

"Please. Marco loves you. I have no one in sight."

"That's because you're picky," said Megan with a wave of her hand. "I liked Heather. She was nice."

"Too high maintenance."

"Whatever. You just need to compromise."

"No way." Patty guffawed.

§§§§

That afternoon, Keith and Anne walked back from lunch at a Mexican restaurant not far from the Senate. As they approached the large building of the conservative think-tank, The Heritage Foundation, Anne stopped walking when she noticed a group of men coming out its doors.

One of the men in a cowboy hat and boots noticed her and smiled, saying to his friends, "I'll meet you at the restaurant. I need to say hello to this little lady."

Keith's eyes widened in fear, and he whispered, "That's Dan Langford."

"Yes, it is," she said regretfully. "And he's coming over here."

"You know him?"

"My dad does." She nervously clenched her purse. "Langford doesn't know who I'm interning for."

"Oh, shit."

" 'Oh, shit' is right."

Dan Langford approached them and called out, "Hello, Annie. I'm surprised to see you here. Why aren't you in Boulder?"

"Hi, Mr. Langford. Um, Dan Langford, this is Keith Jones. He's also from Colorado."

Langford gave Keith a perfunctory handshake and nicely, but he quickly returned his attention to her. "So, Anne you didn't answer my question. What are you doing in Washington?"

"I'm here for an internship." Smiling, she teased and tried to volley the conversation back to him. "I could ask the same of you. What are you doing here?"

"I'm on a fundraising trip, and I've got some meetings. So where are you interning?"

"The Senate." She said it firmly and plainly. "With Senator McEvoy."

"Excuse me?" He leaned in as if she'd mumbled her words.

"I'm working for Senator McEvoy." She smiled again, hoping to defuse things. "I'm the black sheep Democrat in the family."

Langford straightened his stance and said in a clipped tone, "Anne, I'd like to speak with you . . . alone."

"Okay." She looked at Keith, who raised his eyebrows as if to ask silently whether she wanted to be alone with the man. She nodded. "Can you give me two minutes?"

"Sure, but we should get to the office." He walked ten feet away and began tapping on his phone.

With more privacy, Langford began his interrogation. "Now, Annie, what are you doing? Why are you working for Stephen McEvoy? And for God's sake, does your father know?"

"I'm sorry if you're offended, Mr. Langford, but like I said, I'm a

Democrat. My father knows what I'm doing."

"Well, I'm disappointed in you." He shook his head. "I can't believe your father is happy either."

"Frankly, I don't think he considers it a very big deal. I'm his daughter, but I'm also an adult," she reminded him. "I make my own decisions, even if he doesn't like them."

"I doubt your father actually thinks that way."

"Actually, I know my father pretty well," she said in irritation. "My parents raised me to think for myself."

"Well," Langford huffed. "I hope you watch out in the office. The McEvoys aren't decent people. That oldest girl is supposed to be a lesbian, the middle one is married to a foreigner, and well, you know McEvoy's reputation. I bet he'd take a liking to a young lady such as yourself. You're not safe there."

Her lip curled at his offensive talk. She didn't know where to start, so she kept it simple. "That's nonsense, and regardless, I can take care of myself."

"I don't agree, if this is the choice you've made."

"I need to get going, Mr. Langford." She extended her hand. "It was good seeing you. I'll tell my father I ran into you."

"I hope you do speak with him, because I certainly will. Have a good day," Langford snarled. With a tip of his hat, he walked away.

Keith appeared again at Anne's side, and they started in the opposite direction from Langford. "Let me get this right. He knows your dad, and he's pissed you're working for McEvoy?"

"That's pretty much it."

"Are you going to tell somebody in the office? He was pretty offensive."

She cringed as she contemplated it, but she knew she should say something. "I guess so . . ."

§§§§

Later that afternoon, she gave Greg a brief rundown. He asked at once, "Do you mind telling Senator McEvoy this yourself? I think he'd be interested."

"Okay," she replied in a small voice. Inside, she was excited to see the senator again, but she also dreaded telling him everything. She made light of it. "I don't mind. There's not much to say other than he's a stupid asshole, and I hope he loses."

Greg led her into Stephen's empty office, saying he'd go find him, and Anne took a seat on the sofa and studied the quiet room. She was impressed.

It was different from every other politician's office she'd been in. It didn't have a "me wall", with awards and photos of Senator McEvoy with famous people; nor did it have patriotic knickknacks. There were no American flags or models of fighter planes or reproductions of the Constitution. Instead, bookshelves and photography covered the walls. The books showed signs they'd actually been read, and the art was impressive. Ansel Adams photographs of Colorado hung most prominently, but there were other photos Anne guessed were done by a talented amateur.

While Anne waited in his office, Greg told Stephen and Megan snippets of what he knew. As they entered the office, Anne looked up with wide eyes that bore a hint of resolve. Stephen thought her cute sitting alone in the middle of the couch, her legs crossed to the side. Somehow he'd been blessed with the opportunity to speak with her again, and it made him smile.

After Greg shut the door, Stephen announced, "Thank you, Anne, for agreeing to talk. You know you don't have to do this."

"It's okay. It's not that big of a deal."

"Well, we do appreciate it," said Megan as she took a seat next to Anne on the sofa. She side-eyed Stephen, as if she picked her spot intentionally.

He smirked, nabbing the chair next to Anne. "Well, thanks again," he said. "I've barely spoken to Langford. I'm just curious as to how his mind works."

"Well, his mind doesn't really work. He's not very smart." Her eyes connected with Stephen's, who laughed heartily.

As his laughter slowed to a chuckle he asked, "So where were you?"

"After lunch, Keith and I ran into Langford in front of The Heritage Foundation."

"But of course." Megan giggled.

"Yeah, the perfect place for him." Anne snickered. "Anyway, he scolded me for working for Senator McEvoy and said he was going to talk to my dad." She rolled her eyes. "Whatever. My dad won't care, though I should probably warn him."

"Probably a good idea." Greg nodded.

"Did he say anything else?" asked Stephen.

"Oh, he insulted you and your family," Anne said with a wave of her hand. "What you might expect."

"How so?" asked Megan.

Anne grimaced. "He said you weren't decent people. You've got to understand. He's really backward."

"Did he mention Patty?" Stephen asked with a sneer.

"Or Marco . . ." Megan said as her eyes narrowed.

"He did." Anne shook her head. "He's a bigot."

"Asshole," snarled Stephen. "What did he say about me?"

Anne frowned and spoke slowly. "Senator, it wasn't complimentary of you . . ."

"Well, I would expect that."

"Do you really want to hear this?"

"Yes. I don't know him. I've heard about his ways, and I'm curious about what he'd say in more . . . unguarded moments."

"This is a little hard, Senator, because I have a lot of respect for you."

"It's okay." He nodded to give her confidence. He wanted her to know she was safe regardless of how he ranted in the office. His outbursts weren't directed at her; in fact, they were the result of his avoiding her.

Gazing into his eyes, she waited a moment and took a breath. "All right, I'll tell you what he said because he may use something like this against you in the campaign."

"Whatever he said, it's not true, so it doesn't matter. I only want to understand what he's thinking."

"Well, he commented on your reputation with women and said I wasn't safe here. I told him it was nonsense."

At that moment, Stephen's annoyed dislike of Langford transformed into hatred. The man mortally wounded any chance he might have had with Anne. Langford had ensured that in the back of her mind, Stephen was only interested in sex with her. It would now be the proverbial elephant in the room.

Finding his voice, Stephen searched for some connection with her. "I can't apologize enough for you having been put in that situation. Of course it's nonsense, but thank you for enduring the uncomfortable position of having to tell me. I now know what the man is thinking and is liable to do."

The chirp of a phone sounded from Greg's pocket. "I've got to go to the Majority Leader's office," he announced. "Anne, I'm sorry I have to run. You've gone above and beyond the call of duty. We really appreciate it. I'll catch up with you later."

"Thanks, Greg." Anne smiled. "Like I said in the beginning, it's not a big deal."

"You've been great, Anne," Megan said, patting her on the leg. Her eyes flew over to Stephen with a sharp look. "We should probably leave Stephen to his work. Don't you have a meeting with Congresswoman Schultz?"

Stephen stared at Megan. He was fully aware she was sending a message that he should leave Anne alone, but he wasn't going to listen to his sister. He wanted to show Anne he was a decent guy. "No. I don't have a meeting." Turning to Anne, he asked, "Do you have a moment?"

"Sure," she squeaked.

Megan's phone rang, and her eyes widened as looked at the caller ID. "It's *The New York Times*. I have to take this." She glared at Stephen as she walked to the door. "I'm leaving the door open, okay?"

Stephen nodded before leaning back in his chair. "So, Anne, can we talk about something else? Maybe something a little less sordid?"

"Um, sure."

"Good. How's your thesis coming along? Jefferson and Sally Hemings, right?"

"Uh . . . working on it, but I've been distracted studying for the LSAT."

"When are you taking it?"

"In three weeks. I need to work on the logic problems. I'm taking a prep class, but it's not helping me. I guess my mind is illogical."

"There's no evidence of that. In fact, everything I've seen of your work indicates the opposite."

"Thanks." She looked down and smiled.

In the few seconds of silence that followed, an idea popped in his head. He knew he should clear it with Megan and Patty, but he didn't have time. The moment was now.

"So are any of the other interns taking the test?" he asked.

"Yes. Let me think . . . Keith, Sam, maybe Alicia. I can't remember."

"You know, it wasn't that long ago I took the LSAT, and I actually liked the analytical reasoning part of the test. I'd be happy to help everyone study for it. I should get to know everyone."

"Wow. That would be great and very generous of you, considering your schedule."

"Are you kidding? I'd much rather skip another lousy reception to play around with logic games. And it's the least I can do, considering all the work interns do here without pay."

"Well, that's wonderful. Thank you."

"Good. I'll set it up with my assistant. If I'm not flying home, Thursday evenings are good for me."

"Okay, I'll tell the other interns."

He was pleased his plan might work. "Well, if you'll excuse me," he announced, standing up from his chair. "I have to go call an irate mayor now. Thanks for everything, Anne."

"No problem." She chuckled. "I guess I should call my dad."

"Will that be bad?"

"Nah. He'll be more annoyed than anything," she admitted. "Frankly, he doesn't really like Langford."

"Funny. I don't either." His blue eyes shone as he smirked, and she laughed with him.

"Have a good day," she said as she rose from her seat. "I'll see you in study hall."

"Absolutely. I'm looking forward to it," he replied, and grinned as she walked out the door.

§§§§

Later in the day, Stephen told Megan only the bare facts about his plan to tutor the interns on the LSAT.

She closed her eyes and shook her head. "You've got to be kidding me?"

"Nope."

"Well, I guess there's nothing wrong with it. It is for a group. And frankly, after the last few weeks, your whole staff could use some more kindness and conversation from you."

Stephen had to agree. He knew he'd been a jerk to his staff. They were all dedicated and hard workers who deserved better. "You're right." He decided to press her further. "But what if I wanted to spend some time with one person going over things a little more?"

"Pfft. You're relentless." Megan snickered. "I'd say the door needs to be wide open at all times, and the rest of your staff needs similar access to you."

He frowned in silence. It wasn't very appealing.

"It's hard seeing you so unhappy," she said with a sigh. "You like her, don't you?"

Her eyes held such sympathy he looked down and shrugged. After a moment, he mumbled, "It doesn't matter."

"I want to help, Stephen, but I've got to walk a line here," she said as she crossed her arms. "Maybe you could talk privately if someone else was nearby . . . Patty or Greg or me, for example. It might be okay."

"I like that idea . . . a lot . . . with the exception of Patty." He grinned.

"Well, you know I'm going to tell Patty."

"Okay," he grumbled.

"And I hate reminding you, but no intimate talks with whoever it is you plan on talking to." She smirked for a second, but her voice became serious. "And no physical contact."

"Thanks for bringing me down to Earth," he muttered. After a moment, he looked up with a change of heart and smiled. "But thanks for helping me out, also. I'll let you know when I need you."

Chapter 5

When Anne arrived home that evening, she called her father to tell him about her run-in with Langford.

"Anne," Elton responded in his booming voice. "Didn't I tell you that you'd get a lot of questions if you worked for McEvoy?"

"I know, and they've been easy to handle up 'til now." She frowned and nestled into the pillows on her bed. "I just never expected to talk to Langford."

"Well, politics is a small world."

"He said he was going to have a word with you."

"Why? He's going to call me because my daughter is interning for a Democrat?"

"That and—"

"He needs to be worrying about his poll numbers, not you."

"That's true." She laughed at her father's keen ability to prioritize life's problems.

"He can go right ahead and call. I'll defend my daughter's right to make her own decisions. How else are you going to grow up if your mother and I hover over you?"

"Well, Mark and I appreciate you for it," she said, referring to her brother, who'd also benefited from their parents' long leash. "But aren't you worried you may hear about it from other people in the party?"

"No. I've been in office for twenty years. What are they going to do? Give me a primary challenger over my daughter's internship?"

"I guess not. I've got to say I was surprised Langford was so rude to me."

"Oh, that's his way," he said dismissively. "Even for a politician, he's not good at hearing things he doesn't like."

"He was pretty offensive. He said the McEvoys weren't decent people, and he brought up Patty McEvoy being a lesbian." She knew that would get a rise out of her father. His beloved sister, Aunt Jean, had a longtime companion.

"Typical," he muttered, disgust clear in his tone. "Why does he care?"

"I don't know. He also said Megan McEvoy was married to a foreigner."

"She is?"

"No. He's just Hispanic."

"He better not say anything that stupid on the campaign trail."

"I agree." Knowing she had to tell him the worst part, she winced. "And he told me I'm—and I quote—'unsafe' in Senator McEvoy's office because of his reputation with women."

"Unsafe? What does he think is going to happen to you? McEvoy will attack you?"

"I told him I can take care of myself."

"Of course you can," he said with pride. "And Langford better not be thinking he's going to win this election simply because Stephen McEvoy gets around. Hell, I didn't agree with his dad very often, but Patrick McEvoy was a decent man and a smart politician. His son seems to be the same. He's not going to chase after women in his office, especially when he's trying to get reelected."

"Yeah," she said with a small sigh. She hated having to admit he was right. "From what I know of him, I don't think he would either."

§§§§

The following Thursday night, Senator McEvoy's secretary ushered the group of interns toward his open door and announced, "He wants to see everyone in his office first."

"I'm stoked. It's really cool that he's doing this." Keith grinned before whispering in Anne's ear, "Especially considering what an asshole he's been to everybody lately."

"Well, at this point, I'll take any help I can get." She refrained from agreeing the senator had been a jerk.

As the four interns took their seats, Keith babbled away about the test while Anne's eyes wandered once again around the beautiful office. The antique furniture didn't appear to be the standard, government-issued office suite; she guessed it had belonged to Patrick McEvoy at one time. The expansive bookshelves held hundreds of books, and crammed in between The Almanac of American Politics and Black's Law Dictionary sat a tattered copy of Wallace Stegner's Angle of Repose. She loved that book. She wondered if the senator had read it or if it was a leftover from his father, like the furniture and Ansel Adams photos.

An arrangement of smaller color prints that hung off to the side of the bookshelf caught her eye. She wished she could walk over and see them because she thought she recognized some of the places in the images. She had a hunch he'd taken them himself, and at that moment, she felt like her heart was sighing—he's such an interesting person.

As he walked in, rolling up his sleeves, Stephen greeted the room, "Thanks so much for staying late today and indulging me."

The interns all returned the thanks, saying he was indulging them.

When he sat down, he asked each of them about their interest in law school and any worries they had with the test.

Anne listened to her peers' answers, but she was more intent on staring at the senator's arms. Even from his forearms, she could tell he was muscular, and the black hair on his arms matched the hair on his head. She abruptly looked away when it occurred to her that black was probably his hair color everywhere.

While the other interns answered his questions, Stephen listened to their answers, but occasionally glanced at Anne. He couldn't catch her eye, though, because she seemed to stare at something behind him. He decided it would be too obvious if he turned around and looked. When it was her turn, he finally saw her hazel eyes again.

"So, Anne, what's your interest in law school? Are you like Keith, looking to avoid job hunting during a global economic crisis?"

"That wasn't my reason, but since he mentioned it, I think it's a pretty good one."

"Yes, it is." He chuckled. "So what was your original reason?"

"I'm interested in environmental law. Growing up in the country, I've seen how much it's changed—how much has been lost. I want to do what I can to preserve what's left."

Stephen nodded, but he questioned himself whether or not the study session was a good idea. Her answer made him want to talk to her alone for the rest of the night.

He wondered if she had any idea how much they shared in common. She must have seen the Ansel Adams artwork he had taken from the family collection in Denver. Did she notice his own photography of the places he loved? Did she know what she said was important to him, too? He grumbled to himself that she probably knew nothing about him; he hoped he could find a moment to speak with her in private.

His study hall went as he planned. Just as he had promised Megan, he gave every intern an equal amount of attention, though he joked a bit more with Anne. After the session ended, the interns scattered in different directions for the evening. Only Anne and Keith followed him out of the room. Keith began texting his girlfriend as they walked and soon fell behind, which left Anne and Stephen walking alone.

Grasping for conversation to avoid an awkward silence, Stephen was about to ask her the date of the LSAT when she spoke first. "I saw the photography in your office. The Ansel Adams photographs are amazing, but what are the color prints? They looked familiar."

"I took them." A satisfied smile crossed his face. He couldn't believe his luck. "They're places I like to go. When I look at them, it takes my mind off work."

Remembering Megan sat in her office, Stephen took a leap of faith. "I can show them to you, if you like."

"Oh, thanks," she said with a hesitant smile. "That would be great."

As they approached the cubicles, Keith grabbed his bag. "I'm out of here," he said with his phone pressed against his ear. "See you tomorrow."

Anne told him good-bye and dropped off her notebook while Stephen walked down to Megan's office to alert her. In a voice low enough so Anne couldn't hear, he interrupted Megan's typing. "Anne asked about my photography. We'll be in my office."

"Okay." Her simple answer carried a stern admonishment, but he smiled and left her office door wide open.

As Anne walked into his office, he was checking messages on his cell phone. The butterflies in her stomach left her not knowing what to do, so she examined his photographs. They varied in size and composition, but were all images of places she either knew or had a pretty good idea where they might be. She concentrated on identifying landmarks in the photos, trying to place them.

"What do you think?" he asked.

She startled at his voice.

"I'm sorry," he said in a soothing tone. "I didn't mean to scare you." His voice wasn't the only surprise; he also stood closer than before.

She decided to take a half step away for some breathing room. Even at that distance, she noticed the pleasing smell of soap. "It's okay. I'm not scared," she said with a smile. "I was just figuring out which photos I knew and which I didn't."

"And?"

"Well, this one is definitely Willow Lake. I've been there many times."

"You're right. Good eye."

"Thanks," she said in a soft voice. Even the smallest compliment from him made her happy. She wanted to know more. "What were you doing there when you took this photo? My dad hunts around there."

"I was on a long backpacking trip. Do you backpack?"

"Not very often." She shrugged. "I don't like death marches."

"I don't either. I'd rather find a couple of spots along the way, camp for a few days, and then take day hikes. I don't like lugging my gear all the time."

"That's why I go out on my horse. He carries everything, so when I find a nice spot, I've got everything I need."

"Who do you go horse camping with?"

"I don't know. Friends. My brother. Sometimes I go alone."

"Really? You do overnights by yourself? Not that many women go out alone."

"Ah, but it doesn't feel like I'm alone if I'm with my horse."

"Good point."

"The only problem being without other people is I feel weird sleeping outside. You're so exposed. I sleep in my tent, which I don't like because I get claustrophobic. I'd rather sleep under the stars."

"I would, too."

She tried to imagine him grungy from camping. He had a heavy five o'clock shadow, and she thought he'd have a full beard after only a few days away from a razor. He'd be an interesting person to talk with on a hike, especially during her favorite time when only the moon and stars shed light. He might be a different person out there—more like the one standing with her at that moment, rather than the hurried one in the office. She thought of being together outside, and she looked away as her eyes widened. Lots of nudity in the good old outdoors. Lots of time with nothing to do.

"But you probably don't get out much," she blurted out to clear her thoughts.

"I don't." He sounded wistful. "I can do day hikes here and there and go out for a night occasionally, but I only get a week in August to take a longer trip. Not next year, though."

"Oh, the campaign."

"Right."

"Well, it means you'll have a job for the next six years," she joked. "That's important."

"Good way of looking at it." He smiled and nodded at the photographs. "So what do you do out there?"

"Well, when I was little I'd play in the water, chase frogs, or play hide and seek with my brother, things like that. Now I find a rock to sit on and read. It's probably one of the things that turned me into a bookworm."

"I often take a book outside myself, usually long ones so I have a lot to read."

"I notice you have Angle of Repose on your bookshelf. That's a wonderful book."

"Yeah, it's one of my favorites."

Megan's voice came from the direction of the open door. "Hey, I'm off to pick up Marco at the airport."

"Okay." He checked his watch. "It's getting late."

"I need to get something from home first, though. Anne, would you like a ride?" Megan asked.

"Oh, thanks. That would be great, but I live in Adams-Morgan. Is that out of your way?"

"Not at all. I live in Dupont," Megan replied.

"Great. I'd love to skip the Metro tonight. Let me just get my stuff."

Turning to Stephen, Anne wondered for a moment how to say good-bye after he'd been so friendly with her. Calling him "Senator" seemed odd. She remembered her place, though, and addressed him properly. "Thank you, Senator McEvoy. Study hall was very helpful, and thank you for showing me your photos."

"It was my pleasure," he answered with a warm smile. "It was good talking with you."

His smile caused her to blink a few times as she took it in. She tried to explain it to herself and decided he simply wanted to be friends. *He's just a nice guy.*

Chapter 6

After learning where Anne lived in Adams-Morgan, Megan pulled onto Massachusetts Avenue and started her investigation. "So do you have plans this weekend, other than studying?"

"I'm going to a fundraiser on Saturday night. I think it's cocktail attire. Am I right?"

"The DSCC one?"

"Yeah, that's it."

"I'm going, too. I'd wear a cocktail dress to be safe. I usually do." Megan didn't mention Stephen also planned to attend the Democratic Senatorial Campaign Committee fundraiser that night. Instead, she used it as an opportunity to probe. "So, do you have a date?"

"No, I'm just going with a group who got some comp tickets."

"You're so pretty. I assumed you'd have a date."

"Hardly. I'm definitely average. I grew up with a bunch of gorgeous girls who could out-ski anyone."

"Hmm. Well, you know what they say . . . 'Washington, D.C. is Hollywood for ugly people.' Everybody in D.C. is a geek. Being pretty and smart in this town makes you unique and desirable. "

"That's very nice of you, thanks. But I think I identify more with the geek part."

"Don't thank me. It's true. So what are your plans for the summer if you're going to law school in the fall? Backpacking through Europe?"

"Europe? I wish. Actually, I'm waiting a year to apply. I want some time off, and I need to make money. My dad's only willing to pay for part of law school. He's got this whole self-sufficiency thing with us. I want to stay in D.C., though."

During the rest of the car ride, Megan learned about Anne's plans for

Thanksgiving and Christmas (she planned to stay in D.C. for one and head to Silverthorne for the other); when Anne planned on ending her internship (April 1, so she could concentrate on her thesis due in May); and if her family would visit her while she was in D.C. (no, because Elton hated it).

At the end of the ride, Anne thanked her profusely, but Megan wouldn't hear of it. "Honestly, it was my pleasure. I feel like I know you more now." She smiled because she liked Anne and because she couldn't wait to tell Stephen about her.

§§§§

It was impossible to miss the late arrivals to the fundraiser the following Saturday night, especially when one such latecomer was Senator McEvoy. Anne saw him and Congresswoman Schultz as soon as they walked in the door. Even in a conservative shift dress with pearls, the congresswoman was attractive, with her red hair shining against the black of her dress. The senator looked even more dashing than usual in a dark gray dress suit and a white shirt with French cuffs. But as soon as she surmised he was on a date, Anne couldn't bear to look at him any longer. She felt as if she'd been punched in the gut.

The giant ballroom at the Washington Hilton held close to 500 people, but Stephen spotted Anne not far away. Her table was rowdy with laughing Senate staff, while his dinner companions of lobbyists and donors never said anything remotely humorous. When he saw Anne laugh, he wondered what she thought was so funny.

Noticing her strapless dress, he thought she looked lovely—and probably even lovelier with the dress off. He swallowed his envy of Keith, who sat beside her and moved closer when they spoke. Stephen was so preoccupied observing Anne that he ignored his date. When Diane noted his silence and asked if something was wrong, he lied, saying he had a headache.

After dessert, there was movement around the podium as the various speakers got ready for the night's program. He watched as Anne left her table, no doubt for the ladies' room. Somewhere in the building, she was alone, and Stephen acted on impulse. Waiting a few minutes so she could use the facilities, he excused himself and went to find her.

The Hilton's cavernous basement proved to be a maze, but when he finally found her, he was pleased with his luck because they were out of the way. Though people milled around further down the hall, no one could hear or tell who they were.

Anne's eyes widened when she looked around, and he guessed she too must have realized they were virtually alone. He stared at her freckled skin, which was rosy against her pink dress. The form-fitting silhouette showed off her svelte figure and cleavage.

"Good evening, Anne."

"Good evening, Senator."

"You look . . . lovely," he said in a rough voice.

As he spoke, Anne realized why she felt so crushed when she saw him with Congresswoman Schultz. Anne didn't have a claim on him, but she wasn't crazy. *I don't know what he's thinking, but something is happening between us. Something is going on here, right now.*

"Thank you, Sen—"

"Please . . . don't call me that. Not when we're like this. Please, call me Stephen," he said softly.

"Okay." Proven right, she smiled and became more self-assured. "Thank you, Stephen."

"That's a pretty dress."

"Oh, this one?" She looked down and shook her head. "Ironically, the last time I wore this was at Dan Langford's daughter's wedding."

"Really?"

"Yeah, it's kind of a crazy story . . . well, the dress isn't, but the night was. It was a mess, or I was mess."

"Tell me about it." He smiled and leaned against the railing on the wall.

"I don't know." She laughed. "I wasn't on my best and brightest behavior."

"Oh, God." He chuckled. "I've spent most of my life not on my best and brightest behavior. Tell me your story. I'm intrigued Langford is in it."

"Well, I guess I can." She hoped he'd find it funny. "It was two years ago. My brother, Mark, was home from med school, and it was the day of the wedding. Without telling us, my mom had RSVP'd for the whole family. My brother and I were irritated, and we argued with her. Mark finally agreed to go, but he filled his flask with vodka beforehand."

"Uh-oh."

"Yeah." She giggled. "Anyway, it turned out there wasn't any alcohol at the reception because Langford's family doesn't drink. Both my mom and dad grumbled about not believing in weddings without a real toast, but Mark kept smiling and patting his suit jacket like he was prepared. At the dinner, we were stuck at the table with the minister and his wife, and they started asking us if we've been saved, where we go to church, and all that. My mom tried to be polite and told them her father was a Presbyterian minister, but my dad wouldn't even talk to them. He hates evangelicals—he thinks they invade his privacy. Meanwhile, Mark was in the bathroom getting drunk."

"Sounds like he had the right plan."

"I know! I finally couldn't take it anymore. I found Mark and made him give me a few swigs. We left the reception early and met up with friends at a local bar that never cards so I could get it in. He left after an hour or so, but I stayed and got really drunk."

"This doesn't sound so bad—"

"Well, when we left the bar, I barely could walk in my heels. I fell on my ass right in front of a cop and got arrested for public intoxication and being a minor under the influence."

"Oh, not good." He winced. "What did your dad do?"

She rolled her eyes. "Well, Elton Norwood, District Attorney, was pissed. I mean really pissed. I was in the friggin' jail, and he came down to give me a speech about how he wouldn't use his influence to get me out because it was his duty to enforce the law in Summit County. But as my father, he'd pay my bail and stand by me at my trial."

"Are you serious?"

"Oh, yes. Luckily, the sheriff on duty that night took pity on me when he learned I was turning twenty-one the next month. He let me go."

"So that's the story of this dress."

"That's right." She smiled.

"I can't believe your dad didn't get you out. My dad always did."

"Maybe that's the difference between having a Republican versus a Democrat dad."

"Maybe so. Though I've been in trouble more than just once."

"Well, you're a lot older than me." She laughed, but stopped when she noticed he wasn't smiling. "I'm sorry. That was really rude. Please forgive me."

As her earnest eyes pled with him, Stephen was quiet for a second. He wasn't upset with her; he was upset with his predicament. He'd just enjoyed a nice chat, but now he faced one of the realities dividing them.

"Don't worry about it." He smiled to make her feel more at ease. "I believe I'm ten years older than you. That's a fact."

"Well, thirty-two doesn't sound so old to me," she remarked hesitantly.

"And twenty-two doesn't sound so young to me."

They gazed at one another in silence as if they played a game of chicken. After a while, she looked away. "I should get back."

"Yes." His face fell. "I suppose you should."

"You're here with Congresswoman Schultz, aren't you?" Her voice was pointed.

He wasn't sure how to respond. He couldn't lie and say Diane was only a friend—he'd spent too many nights in her bed. "Yes, I am." Without thinking, his body overrode the tight control he had over his feelings for Anne. He raised a hand to stroke her shoulder. "But I wish—"

"Stephen, can you help me out here?" The bass of a masculine, southern drawl boomed through the hall.

Dropping his hand at once, Stephen turned to the voice he knew well. "Of course, Grayson."

The elderly Senator Grayson York had represented the state of Georgia in the Senate for the last forty years, and for the majority of those years, he'd been best friends with Patrick McEvoy. If anyone outside his family had to see him touch Anne, Stephen was glad it was Grayson. Indeed, as Patty's godfather, he was family.

As Grayson ambled their way, Stephen welcomed him, "Grayson, I'd like to introduce you to Anne Norwood. She's interning in my office."

"Miss Norwood, it's a pleasure to meet you," Grayson said as he extended his hand. Stephen smiled at Grayson, who showed off his good manners and didn't call out an awkward situation. Instead, he pushed ahead with his southern charm. "Anne is a name that runs in the York family. My daughter, Cynthia, almost named my grandchild Anne."

"Good evening, Senator York." She shook his hand. "And what name did she choose instead?"

"Elton . . . turned out to be a grandson rather than a granddaughter."

"That's actually my father's name."

"There aren't too many Eltons in the world. What does your father do?"

"He's a district attorney in Colorado." She smiled sheepishly. "He's a Republican."

"Aw, don't worry about that. Sometimes it seems like everyone in Georgia is a Republican except me."

Both she and Stephen broke out into laughter. When the chuckling died down, Anne shook her head. "I'm sorry, but I should get going. It was nice meeting you, Senator York."

"Have a good evening, Anne."

She turned to Stephen. "And it was good to talk with you, Senator McEvoy."

Stephen said good-bye, and their eyes lingered for a few seconds. He felt as if she was asking him if their conversation really happened. He gave her a slight nod to acknowledge that it had.

As she walked away, Stephen admired her bare shoulders before he quickly turned to Grayson. "You asked if I could help you, but I believe your question was aimed at helping me."

"Why don't we sit?" Grayson pointed at two Queen Anne chairs off to the side in the hall. "At my age, you get tired standing."

Stephen looked around to make sure they were still alone before taking a seat.

"So who is this Miss Norwood?" Grayson asked as he settled into his chair.

"As I said, she's an intern in my office." He sighed. "Nothing has happened."

"I didn't ask if anything had happened." Grayson chuckled. "But now that you mention it, I've been around a while, and I know you. Something will happen. You should stop while you're still ahead. This looks like your garden-variety intern infatuation."

"You're right. I should stop while I'm ahead, but it's definitely not garden-variety." Leaning onto his knees, Stephen rubbed his hands together in thought. "This is different."

"How different?"

"I've never felt like this before, and yet I barely know her. Do you think it's possible to feel strongly about someone you hardly know?"

"I'll tell you. Fifty-seven years ago, I decided I wanted to marry Laura really only knowing she was Protestant, she was clever enough to make me laugh, and there was no place I wanted to be more than up her skirt. All of those things are still true today."

Stephen laughed and shook his head at the man who was both his colleague and substitute father figure.

"Are you sure she's special?" Grayson asked, taking a handkerchief out of his pocket. He wiped his brow and chuckled. "Now don't be offended, but in the South, we'd say you're a hard dog to keep on the porch."

"I don't think that would be a problem with the right woman. I've always wanted to settle down eventually."

"Well, even your father settled down . . . eventually. Listen, if you're thinking seriously about that young lady, you need to hear this. I've got a daughter whom I love dearly. I bet Elton Norwood feels the same way about his little girl; they'll always be our little girls, in a way. I'm warning you, if someone such as yourself—with your power and privilege—took advantage of my young daughter . . . well, I would . . ."

"You would what?"

"Cut his balls off."

"I won't take advantage of her." He shook his head. "At this point, I'd just like to get to know her. Tell me something. I keep trying to think of what my father would have done in this situation."

"Patrick? With Lillian? Aw, hell, thirty years ago he wouldn't have blinked an eye. He'd have pursued her the moment she walked in his office. Now things are different. An elected official can get crucified for messing around with an intern."

"Yeah. I know that," Stephen said sarcastically.

"So what would Patrick do today? I'm not sure. He was as devoted to Lillian as I am to Laura, but . . . he valued his family's legacy, public service, and had impeccable integrity. I don't know if he'd jeopardize it."

"That's not really helpful."

"I can't speak for the dead." Grayson smiled in sympathy. "And this is your life. You have to make your own way."

Rubbing his brow in confusion, Stephen nodded.

"Now, I know you came here with Diane Schultz tonight. She's a wonderful woman, and you need to attend to your date. Let's go back to that dreadful dinner. You'll be able to honestly tell her you were talking with me."

When he entered the banquet hall and saw Anne's empty table, he grimaced. He assumed they had gone out to a bar for some fun, as most of the younger staff did after a dinner. Looking over to Diane, he noticed she was deep in conversation with a lobbyist.

While he and Diane only dated casually, he knew they both expected to share a bed once the evening was over. With his conversation with Anne fresh on his mind, he decided he couldn't do it. He didn't want to be with

Diane. Anne was the one for him, but he couldn't have her. He shook his head at his predicament; he had no idea what to do.

Chapter 7

On Monday morning, Anne walked into the office with trepidation. She told herself she shouldn't be nervous, but the butterflies from her encounter with Senator McEvoy reemerged. Both worried and hopeful she might see him in the office, she buried her head in the Federal Register to keep her thoughts on work. But when she came back from lunch, she was so self-absorbed she ran straight into his path.

"Good afternoon, Anne." His smile twitched as if he held back a chuckle.

"Good afternoon," she blurted out, not certain how to address him. *What am I supposed to call him now?* He stood before her dressed in his usual suit and tie, which would call for "Senator McEvoy." Yet they were alone, and his blue eyes danced, so she wanted to call him "Stephen."

"Did you enjoy the rest of your Saturday evening?" he asked, crossing his arms. "I noticed you left early."

"Um. Yes. We went out."

"I called it an early night to get some sleep. I had to work yesterday."

She processed his comment as he stared into her eyes with intense sincerity. *Is he trying to tell me he wasn't with Diane Schultz Saturday night? That he didn't sleep with her?* She searched his eyes for an answer, and his happy gaze made her think she was right. She smiled and remarked, "Your schedule must be difficult right now."

"It comes with the job. We'll still get to have a prep session this week." His smile grew. "That will be fun."

"You're generous to do it."

"Well, I enjoy it."

Patty's voice echoed through the hall. "Stephen, we have a meeting."

"I'll be right there," he said, sounding a little amused.

Anne looked at Patty for a moment as she stood checking her phone.

After a few seconds, Patty glanced at them with a suspicious glare. Anne turned to Stephen again, wondering what things were like between the siblings.

"Excuse me. I have to go placate my sister." Stephen rolled his eyes.

"I'm guessing you've had to do that your whole life." She laughed. "Has it gotten worse since you took office?"

"Absolutely. It *should* be easier now—because we're adults." He shook his head. "But because of my job and the fact that we're all working together, it can be worse than when I was twelve."

"That must be really annoying."

"Believe me it is." He nodded toward Patty. "I should go now. Have a good rest of your day."

"You, too."

They parted ways, and Anne went back to her desk bewildered—yet again.

§§§§

When Stephen sprinted out of the room after Thursday's study session ended, Anne was disappointed. She'd hoped they could talk again like the week before, but he obviously had plans. She frowned to herself thinking they might be with Diane Schultz.

As she passed by his office door, Greg called her name. She poked her head in, and saw Megan kicked back in a chair while Greg sat with his feet up on his desk.

"Hey, do you want to have dinner with us?" he asked. "We're just going to the brew pub down the street."

Anne glanced at Megan to make sure she was welcome. Megan shrugged with a smile. "Come along. It'll be fun."

"Great. Thanks for asking."

Stephen's voice came from behind her. "I'm ready to go when you are."

Anne looked over, her mouth agape in surprise to see him beside her.

"Are you joining us?" he asked.

"Yeah," she said slowly. "Greg invited me. Let me get my bag."

Anne flexed her hands as she walked to her cubicle. *It's a perfectly normal thing to go out after work. Do not make more of it than that.*

She stuck close to Greg as they walked the few blocks to the local brew pub. The loud and boisterous restaurant eased her fears of an awkward intimate dinner. Instead, the mood was fun. Everyone laughed as Greg and Anne told silly stories of growing up in Summit County, with its odd mix of ranchers, hippies, tourists, ski bums, and wealthy part-time residents.

When Megan excused herself to the bathroom, Stephen followed along. The moment they were out of earshot, she snapped. "You duped Greg into this, didn't you?"

"Maybe." He smiled. "I simply suggested it might be nice to continue to make Anne feel welcome in the office."

"Huh. A likely story."

"Well, it's true," he stated matter-of-factly. "Oh, and I'll take everyone home."

"Wait." She pulled him aside for an even more private conversation. "In what order are you dropping us off?"

"Greg first, of course, because he lives on the Hill. Then you, and then Anne. She lives in Adams-Morgan, right?"

"Yes, but I should be last."

"No, you live on the way up to Adams-Morgan, and I can get home quicker by taking Connecticut after dropping Anne off." His reasoning was sound; she couldn't dispute it was the shortest route around the city. "And there's nothing wrong with it. I always take Greg home after something like this. If Anne was a guy, you wouldn't even question it. Besides, Jim will be driving. We won't be alone." He smirked as he said the last sentence.

Jim had also been his father's driver, and he remained intensely loyal to the family. Stephen didn't think his sister needed to know Jim always listened to the radio through an ear bud while he drove. He never turned to look in the backseat no matter what went on behind him.

"Patty *will not* like this," she warned.

"We don't have to tell Patty. And if she does find out, it's not a big deal." He shrugged. "Come on, Meg. Give me a break. I'm not going to touch her. I just want to get to know her better. This is harmless, and it's ten minutes tops we'll be alone."

"Well . . ." Megan shook her head. "Okay. I'll cover for you, but you owe me."

When Anne learned of the ride home, she was happy to avoid the unreliable late-night Metro. Greg was also happy to have the ride, saying he was pleased to get home sooner to his wife. It was only after they dropped him off that Anne learned she would be the last person in the car with Stephen.

Anne gulped. While things had been easygoing between them, she didn't expect to end the night alone together. It would change everything. Something didn't feel right about it—like it was a setup. As they drove first to Greg's house and then to Megan's, Anne tried to calm herself down, but she wondered what he wanted.

When Megan left the car at her beautiful home on Swan Street, Stephen switched from the front to the now-open backseat. "So where do you live?" he asked as he sat down. "I'll tell Jim the address."

"Um. Kalorama, just off Eighteenth Street."

Stephen tapped Jim. Removing his ear bud, Jim leaned to hear the address. Afterward, he nodded, replaced the ear bud, and drove on without saying a word.

Anne crammed the left side of her body into the car door. She wanted to be as far away from the senator as possible. Her head down, she focused on her coat buttons as she calculated the driving time to her home. Curiosity soon overtook her, and she glanced at Stephen, who stared at her with a furrowed brow. She didn't know what to say, so her focus went back to her buttons.

"How's your horse?" His voice broke the silence.

"My horse?" She raised her head and smiled hesitantly. "He's good."

"Do you have a picture?"

"Yeah." She fumbled around her purse and found her phone. After a few taps, she pulled up a photo of a well-fed black beauty with snowy mountains in the background. "Here he is."

Stephen smiled. "He's beautiful. With a nice, thick, winter coat."

"He's my boy." She smiled and returned the photo to her bag. "I miss him."

"You know, there are lots of places to ride in Virginia."

"Don't they mostly ride English there?" She shrugged, not waiting for an answer. "I don't really like it. It feels uncomfortable."

"I prefer western, too, and actually bareback even more, if I know the horse."

"Yeah, me, too." She examined the gaze of his bright blue eyes. *He has to be the smoothest operator on Earth if he's pulling this stuff out of thin air to impress me.* She grasped for something she could ask to test his abilities at impressing women. "So, *Senator McEvoy*, what are you reading these days?"

Instead of immediately answering, she was surprised when his brow furrowed again. His expression became earnest. "Please, when we're alone, I want you to call me Stephen. I'm sure it's confusing, but I . . . I feel like I won't get to know you if you only think of me that way.

"I mean . . ." His voice became stronger as if he was backpedaling. "When you call me Senator McEvoy, you might as well be talking to my father."

"Right . . ." She nodded, although she was curious what he meant by *get to know you*.

"And I'm not answering your question until you tell me what you're reading." He chuckled.

"Why?"

"Because my current book is a little embarrassing."

"Okay. But actually, mine is embarrassing, too—because I've read it at least three times already. It's *Jane Eyre*. I picked it up again last night when I couldn't sleep." She cocked her head. "All right, *Stephen*. Now it's your turn."

He smiled and shook his head. "You'll see why it's embarrassing. I'm reading *Master of the Senate*."

"The LBJ book? I read it last year in a poli-sci class. Is it the title that's embarrassing?"

"I suppose so. In no way do I aspire to be the master of the Senate. It's a good book, though."

"It is. I really liked reading about Lady Bird. She was such an interesting woman."

"And LBJ was a fascinating man. Really impressive."

"Thanks in large part to Lady Bird," she muttered without thinking about who she was talking to. "Lady Bird was amazing, and he treated her like shit. She helped his career every step of the way, and he practically flaunted his affairs in front of her."

His eyes were wide by the turn in the conversation. "Um. Well, at that time—"

"At that time? You have got to be kidding me. Like it doesn't happen *all* the time. Arnold Schwarzenegger, Bill Clinton, Mark Sanford, John Edwards, Eliot Spitzer—"

"It wasn't like that for my parents." His voice was soft, but his body was rigid, looking uncomfortable by the subject.

She could sense she'd struck a nerve, so she steered them away from the topic. "No. I'm sure it wasn't. Your father was a good man in addition to being a good politician."

"He was." Stephen was silent for a moment as if he were debating what to say next. With his focus entirely on her, he said, "I've always looked up to both my parents, though. They had a great partnership. That's something I want one day."

Nodding at first, she soon turned away from the intensity of his stare; she had nothing to say in reply. She'd entered completely uncharted territory. Luckily, they were only two blocks away from her house, but the minute of silence was deafening.

By the time Jim pulled up in front of her door, she was composed once more. "Thank you for dinner and the ride, and especially the conversation. I always like talking with you."

"It's my pleasure, and I always like talking with you, too." His smile faded a bit as he muttered, "If only . . . well . . . never mind."

"If only what?"

"There are a lot of 'if onlys' in my life," he said with a wistful chuckle.

"Maybe you should give up on some of these 'if onlys'. Maybe you'd be happier if you let it go. Some things aren't meant to be."

"And some are." He stared her down. "I've become sure of that."

He'd spoken so quickly and with such conviction that she was taken aback. More seconds passed as she returned his intense gaze. *Is he talking about me? But he can't be. What do I say?* She searched her mind for generic advice and offered, "Then it will happen, regardless. Things will come together."

"That's usually the way it works, right?" he asked as a smile crossed his face.

"Yeah." She also smiled—about what, she wasn't sure, but his expression made her want to return the feeling. She opened the car door and stepped out. "Good night, *Stephen.* Get some rest."

"Good night," he said, his smile brightening even more.

§§§§

The following morning, Anne stood in the copy room, assembling media packets for a press conference later that afternoon. Like many of her daily tasks, it was mindless work. Whatever the job, it was usually more interesting than her classes, but that day she would've preferred sitting through a lecture. The mundane office work left her to speculate about Stephen.

Parsing his words from the prior night, she couldn't find anything strange —except him saying he wanted to get to know her. That was very out of the ordinary for a senator to tell an intern. And when she considered how he looked in her eyes as he spoke, something did feel odd. *Like he's speaking in code.*

"Morning, Anne," he said over her shoulder.

She'd hoped sleep and time would create some distance—some clarity for her with the man. But by her reaction to seeing him, she knew it hadn't happened. She slapped a pile of folders onto another, wanting the noise to counter her unease.

"Good morning." She smiled, happy again to have avoided the confusion as to what to call him.

"Did you finish your book last night?"

"No. But does it really matter if you ever finish a book you've already read?"

"I suppose not."

As she admired his bright smile, she noticed for the first time that while he was tall, he was the perfect height for her. The twinkle in his eye made her want to tease him. "And did *you* finish your book, *Master of the Senate*?" She was proud of her play on words.

"As a matter of fact, I did." He leaned against the counter with a smirk. "Maybe now I should locate one of my mother's multiple copies of *Jane Eyre*."

"Er . . . it's a really dark book." *Dear God, don't let him read it.* She dreaded a conversation about a story of a young woman in love with her rakish, older employer. "You probably won't like it."

"I don't know about that." He shrugged. "It's a classic. I probably should've read it before. And it can't be that dark. There's a happy ending, right?"

"Well, yes, there's a 'happily ever after,' but it takes a long time to get there . . . and not until the very end. A lot of people don't like it."

"So it's a romance?" He cocked his head. "But it takes until the end of the book for the couple to get together?"

"Pretty much."

"And what do you think of the . . . delay?"

"I think it's realistic, especially given the challenges they face." She met his warm, intense gaze—so intense she was quite certain they indeed spoke in code, and the subject wasn't *Jane Eyre.*

"Given their struggles, do you think their relationship was worth it in the end?" He followed up with a more pointed question. "Do you think that's the way it really is?"

She no longer trusted words; she couldn't take them at face value when they talked. She gave him a quick nod and left it at that.

"That's good to know," he said softly. Pushing off the counter's edge, he straightened his stance and smiled. "I need to run. I leave for Denver in a couple of hours. Have a nice weekend."

"You, too," she squeaked with a small smile, as he walked out of the room.

Turning her back to the door, she placed her hands to her temples and tried to calm down. She played devil's advocate to talk herself out the notion that he wanted her, but she failed. There'd been too many conversations—too many awkward conversations—to think there was nothing going on. Her mind rummaged through what he'd said during the last few weeks. Telling snippets stuck with her: all the compliments he paid her, how he sought her out to talk, the tension between them—particularly the night of the fundraiser—and finally, his asking her if a good relationship was worth any wait or struggle.

Faced with the evidence, she laid her hands on her cheeks as they reddened. Her crush had grown into strong emotions, but the feelings were based on mundane things. It wasn't because he was a handsome, powerful man—at least not only that. She liked that they shared so many interests, that he knew something about horses, that he was a thoughtful person, and that he could make her laugh and blush. Ultimately, his underlying sadness drew her in. She still didn't know what it was about, but she felt special because sometimes she could coax him out of it.

Despite the feelings welling inside of her, she knew she had to put a halt to them. It was an impossible situation. He was a senator; she was an intern. It would ruin them both and hurt their families. Nothing was worth that.

For the next week, Anne went back to avoiding Stephen. She didn't take the drastic measures she had in the past, yet she still managed to limit their interactions. He often seemed disappointed when she'd run off after only a few words. She told herself she was doing him a favor. Obviously, he wasn't thinking clearly about the risk. She needed to be smart for both of them.

Chapter 8

The following Thursday was the last study session before the LSAT. When she entered the room, Stephen grinned so widely she couldn't help but give him a bashful smile. She found her seat and resolved to keep her mind on her work rather than flirting with a dashing senator.

It proved to be easy. As Stephen worked through logic problems, Anne's stomach began to gurgle in pain. Against her better judgment, she'd eaten the sketchy chicken tikka masala at the Indian buffet lunch. Keith encouraged her, though he admitted he had a stomach of iron and never got sick. She was just the opposite; if someone was going to get sick from a food, she was the one to do it.

When Megan brought in a surprise dinner of pizza, food was the last thing she needed to see or smell, so she kept her head down. She glanced up once and accidentally caught Stephen's eye. He looked concerned, but a whiff of pepperoni made her turn her head away.

"Anne, do you want a slice?" he asked.

"No, thank you," she answered, forcing a feeble smile. She resumed staring at her paper.

As the clock neared seven, she couldn't control herself any longer. Without making eye contact with anyone, she quietly excused herself and hurried to the bathroom. She barely made it into the first stall. Afterward, she washed her mouth out, and searching for some solace, she leaned across the large vanity and pressed her hot cheek against the cool porcelain counter.

The tap, tap, tap of heels made her open her eyes.

"Anne, are you okay?" Megan asked.

"Yes . . . no . . . I guess . . . not really."

"All of the above?" Megan chuckled. "Don't worry, I understand."

"Thanks." She winced. "My lunch didn't agree with me."

"Do you want me to help you to the office?"

"No." She closed her eyes again. "I'll be okay in a couple of minutes. I just need to catch my breath."

"Okay. Do you want some Seven-Up or water?"

"Water. In a little bit."

"Well, come back when you feel up to it, and I'll get you some."

When Megan returned, the study session had ended, and Stephen was talking football with Greg and Keith. She tugged on her brother's shirtsleeve.

"How is she?" he asked, stepping aside from the men. He wanted to know the result of the mission he'd sent her on.

"She's got a stomach thing. She looks horrible."

"That's too bad." Stephen frowned.

"If I could, I'd drive her home, but I can't. I have to meet Marco at the German Embassy in twenty-five minutes."

"That's okay." Stephen smiled. "I'll take her home. I already offered a ride to Greg and Keith."

"Pfft." Megan rolled her eyes and said under her breath, "You're the luckiest bastard on earth. Opportunities just happen for you."

"Given how unlucky I am in this situation, I could use an opportunity," he whispered.

"Whatever. She's so sick nothing is going to happen."

Keith's voice rose above them all. "Whoa, Anne, you don't look so good."

"Um. Yeah." Standing in the doorway, Anne smiled weakly and shrugged. When she saw Stephen staring at her, she became mortified. She ran a shaky hand through her hair. *Great. I look as crappy as I feel.*

"Poor Anne. Let me get that water for you now," said Megan as she left the room.

"I'm giving these two a ride home," said Stephen, nodding to Keith and Greg. "I'll drop you off, too."

"Oh, no, it's okay. I can get a cab." She worried about the very real possibility of puking in front of him.

"That's ridiculous. I'll take you."

"But—"

"Don't worry about it." He pointed behind her. "Megan's got water for you right here. Why don't you sit down and have some before we leave?"

Too exhausted to object, she took the water from Megan and sipped quietly while everyone conversed around her. When the crew made it to Stephen's car, Anne climbed in the back with Greg and Keith, while Stephen sat in the front with his driver. She was happy to hear Keith lived near Greg on the Hill, thinking it would get her home quickly. Then she remembered it also meant she'd be alone with Stephen for at least fifteen minutes as they made their way to her place.

If she hadn't been so sick, she might've panicked. Instead, she stared out the car window and repeated a simple mantra: *I will not puke in Stephen's car. I will not puke in Stephen's car.*

Unfortunately, the mantra wasn't effective. When Jim pulled up in front of Keith's house, she whispered, "I need to step outside for a moment," and ran off. As soon as she was around the corner, she grabbed a wrought iron fence for leverage and retched what was inside of her stomach onto the outside world.

"Are you okay?"

The sound of Stephen's voice made her pause for a moment. *Why, God, is this happening to me? Why does he have to see me like this?* Her stomach didn't agree with the pause, and she heaved again. When she caught her breath, she answered him, "No. Not okay. It's nothing you want to be around."

"Don't worry. It's nothing I haven't seen or done myself." He chuckled. "I've got some water for you when you're done."

After her final hack, she waited a moment before turning around. She hardly looked at him as he handed her the water. "Thank you." She took a few swigs, washed out her mouth, and spat onto the ground. "Very ladylike, I know," she joked.

"Very human." He nodded to a short brick wall a few feet down. "Let's sit here for a minute. I don't think a car is the best thing for you right now."

Sitting beside him on the wall, she felt the need to explain herself. "I'm sort of a slippery slope when it comes to nausea. Once my stomach starts churning, it just keeps going."

"You're doing pretty well, all things considered. I'm a baby when I'm sick. I start whining as soon as I get a stuffed-up nose."

"That's exactly the way my brother is." She chuckled and took a sip of water. "I hope you know it's incredibly annoying to the women around you."

"And that's why men don't bear children. We couldn't handle it."

"That's true." She smiled at him, but quickly turned away when she saw how kindly he looked at her. After a moment of awkward silence, she declared, "I think I can go now."

When they returned to the car, she observed as Stephen spoke to Jim out of earshot. Greg asked her how she was doing. "Okay, but a little wiped out," she replied.

"Let's get you home, then. My house isn't far. You'll be home in no time," Greg said.

She agreed and climbed back in the car. Needing something to support her, she rested her head on the window.

Even before Greg got out of the car, her eyes drooped. At first, she fought to keep them open, but she soon reasoned it made sense to keep them closed. It felt better, and if they were closed, she wouldn't have to make conversation with Stephen when she looked like crap and had vomit breath.

She never expected to fall asleep.

"Well, hello, sleepyhead," was the next thing she heard.

She blinked a few times trying to place herself. Across the seat, Stephen sat respectably on his side of the car with a happy grin. She was hesitant. "How . . . long did I sleep?"

"Your eyes were closed before we left Greg's. We only got here a few minutes ago."

She looked at the empty front seat. "No Jim?"

"He went to get coffee." Stephen shrugged. "I hope you don't mind. I didn't want to wake you up."

"No, I don't mind. It's fine." She nervously touched her tousled hair.

"Here . . . have some more water." He held the bottle out.

"Thanks." She glanced outside. Despite the car's dark windows, she saw they were parked a few houses down from her own.

"You look a lot better," he said.

"Yeah, if I looked how I felt, I must've been pretty scary."

"I didn't mean it that way." His brow furrowed. "You just looked ill."

"Well, at least I didn't make a mess in your car. I was worried about that."

"I wasn't."

"You weren't?"

"No. We weren't driving far. Plus, I witnessed you deposit every last bit of your lunch on those nice people's rose bushes." He smirked. "It sounded like you got it all out."

"Hey! You said you didn't mind. What was I supposed to do?"

"I'm not saying you had a choice. You *were* really bad off. I'm simply saying those people were unlucky."

"Okay. That's true."

"I hope there's a good rain soon, or they won't be able to enjoy their garden."

Without thinking, she laughed and pushed at his arm. "Now you're being mean."

"No, I'm not. It's a fact that it smells a little around there right now."

"What?" She gave him a good punch.

"Hey!" He laughed and batted her off. "I believe physical violence against a government official is a federal offense."

"I'm only defending myself from your teasing."

The two playfully scuffled, until she realized what they were doing. They were touching. His suit coat was wool, but soft, and his hands were warm. When she realized she wanted to touch them more, she froze. His smile faded into a serious stare. The intensity of the moment was unbearable; she couldn't live in the unknown anymore.

"Am I crazy?" she asked in a voice that gasped with exasperation. "Or is something happening here? Is there something happening between us?"

"I don't know," he replied slowly. "Something is for me."

"And what is it?"

"Right now, I just wish I wasn't a senator and you weren't an intern in my office."

His face remained placid and full of honesty. What little resolve she'd had left began slipping away. She kicked herself for giving in but decided to test the waters to see exactly what it was he wanted. "Why is that?"

"Because I'd really like to ask you out." A hesitant smile formed again as he said it. "What I don't know is—if we weren't who we are—if you'd say yes."

She smiled at his answer. No matter how much she wanted to kiss him at that moment, the fact he didn't try something physical meant a lot. "If things were different, I'd definitely say yes."

They shared a quiet smile, though he soon sighed. "Now what?"

She felt the weight of their circumstance take over the car. The impossibilities of a relationship with him flooded her mind, and she swallowed hard. "Nothing can happen. There's too much at stake for you. If . . . *when* it came out . . . you'd have to lie or make up a stupid nondenial denial. I don't want that to happen to you."

"There's too much at stake for you, as well." He shook his head. "It can't happen to you either."

Hearing aloud what she'd already told herself for weeks was painful, especially when they'd just admitted how they felt. She grasped for a solution.

"We could be friends."

"We could." His smile appeared again. "But there are limits on how friendly we can be."

"*Friendly?*" She snorted. "I'd say the limits are pretty obvious, but how long do you think there would be these . . . restrictions?"

"Well, if Patty had her way, nothing could happen between us until after I win reelection next November and get sworn into office in January. Until then, we can only be friends—in the most platonic sense of the word."

"Um, you've talked with Patty . . . about me?" She was shocked she'd been a topic of discussion with Patty, who Anne was sure breathed fire.

"It's one of the worst downsides of my job. I've got to be managed for a lot of things—my work, my schedule. And with my . . . er . . . personal life, I've got to be open with Patty and Megan so they're not blindsided if something comes out. Patty always says, 'I can't protect you if I don't know what to protect you from.' So yes, they both know something— Megan more than Patty."

"Well, Megan's friendly, but Patty always seems to look at me suspiciously."

"Megan likes you. She's been walking a fine line trying to help me out."

"She sounds like a nice sister." She grimaced, thinking about his other sister. "But Patty's right. I'd only be trouble for you."

"Even if you didn't work in my office, it would be a problem if it were to come out I was friends with a gorgeous college student." He smiled and raised his eyebrows.

Her face warmed hearing the compliment, and she shook her head. "Hardly."

"The story would be I'd seduced a pretty young thing. You'd be a joke—not what you really are," he said with a frown.

"What's that?"

His voice softened. "The clever, funny, and beautiful woman with whom I share so much in common."

"Oh, Stephen," she said under her breath, taking in his sweet words.

"Not to mention, your father would kill me." He chuckled.

"Ha! You don't know my dad very well. He'd hate you, but he'd kill me. I'd be the one who let him down."

"Even worse." His smile soon disappeared. "And the fact that Dan Langford knows you work in my office is a red flag, too."

Anne nodded. Everything he said made sense and only confirmed what she already knew. They were in an impossible situation. When she didn't speak, he broke the silence.

"Despite all of that, I don't want to stop talking to you . . . getting to know you."

"Me neither." She smiled shyly. "It would be nice to continue. Maybe a little frustrating, but—"

"Only a little frustrating?" He laughed.

"Okay. More than a little." She winked. "A lot."

Their eyes locked as they shared each other's thoughts for a moment. She was sure she'd stopped breathing. *Oh my God. He's going to kiss me.*

"You know I want to kiss you right now, don't you?" he said, arching his brow.

"Oh, you do, do you?" She giggled nervously.

"I'm trying to be good."

"Yes, we're in public." She nodded toward the street.

"Well, yes, but we've also got a lot to think about and more to discuss." His voice lowered. "And I want to kiss you . . . very much, but not here, not like this."

"We'll see if you get a second chance."

"I'll be happy if I just get to speak to you in private again." He frowned as he checked his watch. "I'd like to stay and talk with you as long you'll have me tonight, but I've got to leave for Denver in a couple of hours. I'm late actually, and I won't be back until Tuesday."

"Well, have a safe flight." She smiled, though she was sad their time together was ending. "I'll see you next week."

"Good luck on your test on Saturday. You'll do great." He reached for her hand, and after admiring it for a moment, he looked into her eyes. "Good night."

"Good night." She squeezed his strong hand in return and left the car—stunned.

§§§§

The next morning the office was shorthanded again, and Anne sat at the reception desk to cover the phones. It was a busy call day, which she hoped would distract her from thoughts of Stephen. But when she had to answer every call with "Good morning, Senator McEvoy's office," she was reminded of her predicament.

Wanting to clear her mind, she decided to spend time at her newfound quiet space on the Senate side of the Hill. Her Fridays always ended early at two o'clock, and she made her way to a small brick structure surrounding a fountain. With its aged walls and arches, dark green plants, and gurgling water, it felt like a hidden grotto in the middle of a city. When she walked through its gate, she was surprised to find someone else there.

An older woman sat on one of the benches dabbing her eyes with a handkerchief. Well dressed in the understated suit of a "lady who lunched," she bore striking white hair and a lined face which still held the loveliness of its youth. She looked familiar, and Anne guessed she was a senator's wife upset with her husband. Feeling like she was intruding on a personal matter, Anne turned to leave.

"No, dear. Don't worry. Please stay." The woman's lips turned up into a smile. "These aren't tears of sadness—well, maybe a little. I was only remembering how I sat here with my husband. He's passed away."

"Oh, I don't have to stay. You probably want to be by yourself."

"It would be nice to have some company. Not too many people spend any time in this place. It's called Summerhouse. Did you know that?"

"I didn't. What was it used for?"

"Back when people rode horses it was very popular as a watering hole."

"I hadn't heard the history." Anne looked around at the rough-hewn stone. "I think it's beautiful, but I suppose it's sad the place is so quiet. More people should enjoy it."

"I feel the same way." The woman patted the bench. "Please, come sit here."

"Thank you," Anne said, taking a seat.

"I'm Lillian McEvoy," the woman declared with a broad smile. "What's your name, dear?"

Chapter 9

Anne wasn't sure if she successfully hid her shock as she sat beside Lillian McEvoy. She wasn't just Stephen's mother; Lillian McEvoy was the country's most famous political matriarch—much better known than her senator son. Anne's own mother and father would be impressed to meet her.

Anne sat a bit straighter. "My name is Anne Norwood, and actually, I'm interning in Senator McEvoy's office."

"Well, what a coincidence." Mrs. McEvoy's face lit up as she turned toward Anne.

"Yes, it is." Although she was rattled, Anne maintained a calm smile. "It's been a great experience so far."

"Oh, that's wonderful to hear." Mrs. McEvoy gave her a once over. "So are you a senior in college or in graduate school?"

"I'm a senior at Boulder. I'm studying at Georgetown for my final year while I'm interning."

"And what do you plan to do next?"

"Law school, eventually." She wrinkled her nose. "It sounds boring, doesn't it?"

"No, not at all. There's nothing wrong with being a lawyer." Mrs. McEvoy cocked her head. "Where in Colorado are you from?"

"Silverthorne."

"Oh, really?" Mrs. McEvoy raised a perfectly penciled eyebrow.

Anne knew what she was getting at, so she decided to get her family baggage out in the open. "My father is Elton Norwood—the district attorney."

"Yes, I know of your family." Mrs. McEvoy's voice became cautious. "Your grandfather was a Republican attorney general."

"Yes, that's my grandpa."

"So why are you working for my son?" Her tone was one of friendly interrogation, and she didn't blink.

Meeting the woman's steady gaze, Anne held her ground. "Well, I'm a Democrat, despite my family."

"What do your parents say to that?" She raised an eyebrow. "Especially your father?"

"My dad says he has more important things to worry about than where I'm interning my senior year of college. My mom just wants me to be happy."

"So you're the little black sheep of the family?" Without waiting for an answer, she smiled, which put Anne at ease. "I like that."

"I guess I am. My brother doesn't have any interest in politics. He's in med school—though he is a Republican."

After a moment, Mrs. McEvoy brushed some dust off her suit jacket as if she was contemplating something. "Hmmm. Well, your family is known to be moderate—more reasonable than the right wing that's taken over that party."

"Believe me, my dad is plenty conservative, but he's not a social conservative. He really only cares about crime and overregulation. Oh, and taxes, especially taxes."

"Why has he never run for a higher office? A moderate Republican can do quite well in Colorado."

"Oh, no." Anne shook her head. "Neither of my parents wants to be under the microscope of a statewide campaign."

"Very smart of them. Things are different today than when Patrick first ran in the sixties. I think Stephen is having a hard time adjusting to the scrutiny." She regarded Anne again for a moment. "So, what do you think of the new Senator McEvoy?"

"Um. He's . . . Senator McEvoy is very nice . . . impressive, really." She kept her smile frozen. *Shit. I almost said Stephen.*

"That's good to hear. As the only child in the entire McEvoy family interested in elected office, he's very driven, but he's still my sweet boy. I'm glad you think he's a nice person."

"He is." Certain the conversation would only become more uncomfortable, Anne decided it was time to leave.

"Mrs. McEvoy, it's been wonderful talking with you. I appreciate you sharing your story."

"Please, call me Lillian. I've enjoyed our conversation immensely. You cheered me up. I'll stop by the office one day and say hello."

"Thank you. That would be very nice." *But what on earth will Stephen think? I need to get out of here.* She looked around the empty benches. "Did you come here alone? Can I walk you somewhere? I'm going to Union Station."

"Oh, no, dear. That's not necessary." She patted her on the knee. "My driver is waiting in the car nearby. I can make it there myself. Thank you again for a lovely visit. I'm so glad I met you."

§§§§

On Sunday morning, Stephen taped an interview for a news program with the Denver ABC affiliate. The piece was scheduled to play back-to-back with a similar interview featuring Dan Langford. As Patty, Megan, and Stephen exited the elevator of the television station, Dan Langford entered with his campaign manager, Trey Johnson. The two rivals locked eyes for a moment. Stephen cast a quick glance at Megan and Patty to make sure they saw who approached them.

"Hello, Dan." In order to take the high road, Stephen was the first to extend his hand. "It's good to see you again."

"Yes, you, too," Langford replied awkwardly.

Stephen liked that he seemed to have disarmed him. He pushed it further. "Have you met—"

"Yes, we've all met before," Patty snipped. "Stephen, I think it's time we got going."

"Ah, yes." Stephen didn't want to end on a negative note so he magnanimously gave Langford some advice. "The questions are all softballs—just watch out for the one on the differences between the House and Senate health care bills. Good luck."

"Er. Thanks . . . very much." Langford seemed ruffled. "Have a good day."

Stephen walked away, only to hear Langford call to him. When he turned around, Langford wore a suspicious stare. "I forgot to ask you about something."

"What's that?"

"I understand a friend of my family is interning for you right now."

"Really? Who?" Stephen knew exactly where Langford was going. Out of the corner of his eye, he caught Megan's cautionary expression. He guessed she wanted to make sure he betrayed nothing. Patty, on the other hand, glared at Langford.

"Anne Norwood," Langford answered with a smug smile.

"Yes. I know her." Stephen kept his practiced impassive face. "Her family is well-known. I believe her father is friends with my chief of staff's family."

"She's a pretty girl, don't you think?" Langford pursed his lips, raising his eyebrows.

"And?" Stephen knew better than to say anything to such a question.

"Nothing." He shrugged. "I just guessed you'd take a shine to a girl like her."

Stephen met his stare, but didn't reply. Instead, he turned on his heel and left the building with Patty and Megan following behind. All were quiet until they got into the car when Patty erupted.

"What the fuck? Why did you even talk to him? All you had to do was say 'hello' and move on."

"It was the right thing to do," he answered tersely.

"He's right," agreed Megan. "Stephen is the incumbent, and we're leading in the polls, if narrowly. We can't have stories where Stephen is anything less than cordial and gracious to Langford."

"Agreed, but you gave him an opportunity to needle you."

Staring out the window, he ignored his elder sister in the backseat, but he still heard her mutter, "And he better not be right about Anne."

Stephen glanced at Megan, who frowned and shook her head.

§§§§

Anxiety kept Anne on edge for days. Naturally, she was a little uneasy over her performance on the LSAT, but she was mainly anxious about Stephen. Would he regret opening up to her? What would he say about her conversation with his mother?

She kept her eyes and ears open for signs he'd returned from his trip, but there was nothing. It all made her feel strange and sad. *How can I be involved with someone when we have no communication?*

When he tapped her shoulder on Wednesday morning, she jumped from her seat in surprise. She'd been listening to her iPod as she read through some constituent mail. Startled, she pulled out her ear buds and looked up. A shy smiled spread across her face.

"Hi," she said.

"Hello. How are you?" He smiled.

"Good, but you snuck up on me again." She was too tickled not to flirt.

"I don't mean to, but it's kind of fun to see your reactions."

"Oh, thanks. I wish I could do it to you."

"That makes two of us," he whispered with a smirk.

Her jaw dropped, and she shook her head.

"Senator, I'm sorry to interrupt."

Anne and Stephen turned as his secretary stood before them. Stephen shrugged. "It's fine. What do you need?"

"For security, the White House needs the name of your companion for the state dinner next month. I was going to tell them you would be taking Congresswoman Schultz. Is that correct?"

Anne's heart stopped, and she glanced at Stephen before she quickly looked away. She didn't want to hear his answer. He needed a date for such an occasion, and it couldn't be her.

"No. I won't be taking Diane. I'll take Patty, or if she can't go, I'll take my mother."

"Oh. I'm sorry. I'll inform them right away." She seemed embarrassed for presuming too much.

"Don't worry about it. You can check with Patty when she's back on

Friday. She extended her trip."

As his secretary walked away, Stephen looked at Anne, who gave him an uncomfortable smile. In a low voice, he said, "Megan may need to talk with you later—probably after four." He punctuated it with a wink.

"Okay. I'll be here if she needs me."

Stephen left her with a smile. She turned around and grinned at the stack of letters. It was obvious he had no regrets, and he wanted to talk again which made her tingly. She checked the clock on her computer screen to see how long she had to wait until four.

§§§§

In between his meetings that day, Stephen slipped into Megan's office and closed the door. "I need a favor."

"I'm guessing the favor involves an intern."

"Yes. I'm sorry." He knew he needed to make amends. "I know I promised to tell you more. I've wanted to, but our trip was busy. I promise to talk with you and Patty as soon as she's back in town."

"Okay. You know, Mom wants us all over for brunch on Saturday. Maybe we can talk then."

"Yes. But not *at* brunch—maybe after. I don't want to talk in front of Mom." He dreaded having to tell his mother about Anne even more than talking to Patty.

"Well, depending on how far this goes, you're going to have to tell her at some point. She needs to know as much as Patty and I."

Stephen's mouth twitched, but he nodded in agreement. Even when his father was alive, nothing was done that might put the political position of the family at risk without conferring with his mother. Patty inherited her shrewdness from their mother more so than their father. "Okay."

"I just want a little information about what's going on."

"I want to be friends with her." He shrugged.

"*Friends*? Patty's never going to believe you." She rolled her eyes.

"Friends for now," he grumbled.

"Okay. And in the future?"

"Can we take this one step at a time?"

"So what can I do for you right now?" Megan asked.

"Would you be willing to ask Anne to come to your office and let us talk alone for a few minutes? I have a short break between four and four-fifteen."

"Alone? As in door closed?" She skewed her mouth in distaste. "That's not what we agreed to."

"Yes, I know, but I'd like some privacy."

The skeptical look didn't leave Megan's face. Megan stared him down, as if she was calculating the damage a fifteen-minute rendezvous could cause. "Okay," she declared. "But you better come clean with me."

"Fine."

"I'll bring her in here and make a call right outside the door."

"Thanks, Meg." He breathed a sigh of relief. "I owe you."

"Yes, you seem to have a running tab at this point."

§§§§

A minute before four, Megan arrived and asked Anne to help assemble some press packets. She was chatty as they walked, telling Anne about the weather back in Denver and a new restaurant she'd found over the weekend.

When she opened her office door, Anne was happy to see Stephen. Studying his phone, he half sat on the desk with his long legs stretched in front of him.

Before she could say hello, Megan said, "I need to make a call. I'll be outside for a moment."

As she looked over her shoulder at the closing door, she felt Stephen take her hands in his. When she turned around, he smiled.

"Hey." He squeezed her hands.

"Hi." She smiled and glanced around Megan's office. It was hard to believe they were alone together at work and Megan had arranged it.

"I don't have much time. I hate it when no one leaves me any breathing room in my schedule, and it's always the worst after being back in the state." He continued to hold one of her hands as he led her to the couch.

Anne was at a loss for words. Being alone with him was wonderful, but the situation was too strange. Smiling uneasily, she said, "This is different."

"I'm sorry." His brow knitted together in concern. "I can only imagine how awkward this is for you. I'd like to see you outside of this damn office. I'm not sure how to arrange it, though." He smiled and traced his fingers along hers. "And I can't even start because you haven't given me your phone number."

"Give me a pen." She giggled.

"Here." Taking a pen from the inside pocket of his suit jacket, he grabbed a pad of paper on the coffee table. "Write legibly, please. I might become suicidal if I finally get to call you and I get a wrong number."

"Oh, I'm sure you'll make do with whatever girl you get on the line."

"But I don't want to *make do*."

Letting his sweet comment hang in the air, she bit her lip and smiled. As she wrote down her number, they chatted about the LSAT. She knew she should bring up her conversation with his mother, but she had no idea how.

When he tucked her number into his shirt pocket, she said, "I have to thank you for all the study sessions. They really did help me. A few of the questions were exactly like ones you had worked out. Keith is grateful, too. Wait until you see him."

"I'm glad to have helped him." He touched her hand again. "But I only did it so I could spend time with you."

"You did?" She couldn't fathom he would go to such lengths.

"I did." Stephen smiled, but his face quickly became more serious.

"I'm glad," she whispered. She was more than glad, though. She was entranced by this wonderful guy who, for some inexplicable reason, had become taken with her. All her instincts willed her to throw herself at him. She wanted to kiss and touch him to show him how she felt.

If the warmth of his gaze was anything to go by, she guessed he'd like it. When he squeezed and gently caressed her hand, she knew he'd *definitely* like it. *Oh God. If he's thinking what I'm thinking, we shouldn't be alone in the same room together at work.*

"I need to get to my four-fifteen," he said reluctantly. He stood and held his hand out.

"I'm sorry your schedule is so tight." She took his hand and followed him to the door.

"It's an awful week. I won't be able to see you until the weekend. Are you free on Sunday?"

"Sure." She wondered where on earth they would go.

"Good." He grinned. "Like I said before, we need to talk—a lot, but I also need to speak with my family. This past weekend wasn't a good time. I needed to focus on work, and the conversations are going to be . . . complicated. After I talk to them on Saturday, I'll call you."

"That's fine," she said as her gut clenched. She couldn't believe she was going to be a topic of conversation for the McEvoys.

"And I'm sorry I'm not going to be able to talk with you much this week. I'm too busy, and well, I'm realizing . . ." He shook his head as if he couldn't articulate his thoughts.

"It's okay. I totally understand. Don't feel like you have to talk to me here." When he looked distressed by her comment, she said, "I know this is . . . strange for you, too."

"Strange?" He smiled and looked down at their joined hands. "Yes, but also very, very good."

"I agree." She beamed.

The sound of the door opening caused Stephen to drop her hand at once. In response, she took a small step backward.

"Stephen, your four-fifteen is waiting in your office," Megan announced from the door. "Remember to tell those union guys that we're not answering questions from the press on that legislation until we hear from all sides. I'm tired of them bugging me about it."

"Okay." He smiled again at Anne. "Have a good evening."

"You, too," she answered as he left.

Winking at Anne, Megan pointed to a stack of press packets on a table. "Now that you're done with the packets, can you take those folders out to my assistant?"

"Of course." She picked up the folders and turned to Megan with a big smile. "I'm always happy to help you."

§§§§

That night, Megan lay in bed with her husband, Marco Zamora, who'd returned from another long trip. He was a career diplomat at the State Department who specialized in only the thorniest of foreign policy issues. His Mexican-American heritage and street smarts, combined with his big heart, made him unique in the genteel Foreign Service. Megan was certain if Marco could orchestrate talks between warring countries, he could find some middle ground for Stephen and Patty.

As she snuggled against her husband, Megan told him the whole story. His brow furrowed as he listened. When she finished, he took a moment before giving his professional assessment.

"I should be there when he tells Patty. I feel for him—always having to talk with his sisters about his private life. Maybe having another man there will help. And the conversation shouldn't be at your mother's, for Christ's sake. Let's come back here. A mother in the mix will only make it worse. Plus with all his dad's things around him, he'll feel pressure to do whatever Patty demands rather than what's best for him personally." He paused for a moment and stroked her arm. "I have to say, I feel sorry for the guy."

"You feel sorry for Stephen?" Megan raised herself on her elbow. "Why in the world? He's got everything going for him."

"If he feels a tenth of what I feel for you for this Anne Norwood, he's in a terrible predicament," he said as he stroked her hair.

Chapter 10

On Saturday, the McEvoy siblings and Marco walked up the drive of the impressive Kennedy-Warren building.

"If you're free," Stephen said to Patty. "I'd like to talk with you after this."

"Sure." She fluffed her red curls. "About what?"

"Anne." He raised his eyebrows and nodded, acknowledging he dropped a bomb.

"What the fuck, Stephen? What is it with you and her?"

"I said, let's talk later."

"An *intern*?" She stopped walking and angrily shook her head. "You're a cliché."

"Patty, not now," Marco said under his breath. "The doorman's right there."

"Okay," she said, and shot a dirty look at Stephen. He simply shook his head in reply as the four walked through the doors.

Lillian McEvoy had a splendid apartment, replete with multiple terraces and formal spaces. Despite the grandeur of the dining room, she preferred to have most meals in the kitchen, which had a cozy eating area. She was always happy to cook for her children, and as they assembled in the kitchen, she wondered why there was a tense mood among them.

When they sat in silence eating the feast she had prepared, she recognized she would have to move the conversation along. She hated having tension over a nice meal.

"I met the most interesting young woman recently," she said in an attempt to break the icy mood. "She's an intern in your office, Stephen. I'm sure you know her. Anne Norwood? She's very nice, *and* she's Elt—"

After Lillian said Anne's name, simultaneous reactions sprung from everyone at the table. Stephen froze with a forkful of egg in his mouth. Megan munched her toast but turned immediately to her husband. Marco, on the other hand, continued to eat as if nothing had happened, though his eyes moved from person to person, studying everyone's reactions.

Patty was the only one who spoke. Placing her orange juice on the table, she snorted. "Oh my God!"

"Now, Patty. That's not nice," Lillian chided. "You can't help who your parents are. She seems like a nice person, even if she's from a Republican family."

"Oh, Mom, I wasn't laughing at *Anne*. I was laughing at Stephen." She snickered.

"Stephen?" Lillian cocked her head. "Why are you laughing at Stephen about Anne Norwood?"

"Because he doesn't just *know* her." She guffawed. "He's got *a thing* for her."

Lillian followed Patty's smug gaze to Stephen, who looked livid.

"Anne? Anne Norwood?" she asked her son. "The girl I met last week? You're interested in her? But she's an intern."

"Exactly," exclaimed Patty.

"And her father is a Republican elected official in your state." Lillian leaned in and eyed her son. "You're not serious, are you, Stephen?"

"Yes, he is. Thank you, Mom, for saying what I've said all along. Maybe he'll listen to you."

"Now, Patty, don't make more of this than it really is," Marco interjected in his calming voice. "Stephen, I hope you don't mind me saying what I see here. But as I understand it, Mrs. McEvoy, Stephen and Anne happen to have a lot in common and are just friends."

Lillian's eyes shifted between Marco and Stephen. *Since when is my son just friends with a beautiful woman?* She didn't want to add fuel to the fire so she simply asked, "Stephen, what's going on?"

The room quieted as everyone waited for him to speak. He stared blankly at the wall with his mouth set in a hard line. After a moment, he spoke in an almost monotone voice. "Anne and I are friends. I like her a lot. I want to get to know her more, but there are a million different problems with that happening. It's very frustrating."

"Glad you recognize that," Patty remarked. "There *are* a million different legal, political, and PR problems with that happening. So you should cool it until after the election. You can wait."

"That's over a year away," he snapped.

"If you're saying you want to date her right now, the answer is categorically no." Patty put her napkin on the table with a thump of finality. "Even *if* she quit her internship on Monday and was able to keep a secret, the story would slip somewhere. And with your reputation, it's a great story. The media will run with it. You have to be more careful than anyone."

"I don't understand how you can even consider her," Lillian said dismissively. Her mouth hardened, and she issued a maternal judgment. "You know better."

"Of course I do," Stephen spat, his eyes aflame. He tugged at his shirt collar as if it held him captive. "That's why this is a problem."

Lillian looked at her son. He was a man, but all she saw were the eyes of her little boy. And those eyes were sad and angry. She tried to determine what he saw in Anne that made him even consider her, given her age and liabilities. Yes, she was attractive in the way he always liked, but she was also more refined than your average girl. Like him, she was smart, political, and funny. All of those traits added up to someone who would catch Stephen's eye. She decided to reason with him. "You know your father always wanted what was best for all of you. He wanted his children to be happy. But he also was practical. If he were here, Stephen, I believe he'd ask if you thought having a relationship with Anne was worth the risk."

He shook his head. "When I think of everything at stake . . . the Senate seat, my future, *her* future, the family name, I can't say if it's worth it."

"Then why are even we talking about this?" asked Megan with a frown. "Why have you been pursuing her? Admit it. You really like her. It's okay to say it."

Stephen's expression spoke for him—he smiled and sheepishly nodded.

"Pursuing her? What?" Patty's head swiveled toward Megan. "And what do *you* know about this? Why haven't you told me?"

Megan shrugged defensively. "We've only discussed her a few times."

"I think our main goal here, as a family, is to support Stephen," declared Marco. "If keeping this Senate seat is important to this family—and that's Stephen's job, then we should support him."

"You're right. That *is* his job," said Patty. "It's his duty to his family and his party to keep it."

"Don't talk to me about duty," snapped Stephen. "Just because you chose a private life rather than running for office shouldn't mean I have to give up everything simply because I'm fulfilling a family role."

Patty slammed her hand on the table, causing the beverages to shake and the silverware to jump. "I *chose*? I *chose* what?"

"For Christ's sake, Patty, don't put words in my mouth. I didn't say you *chose* to be a lesbian. I said you chose to be a private citizen. If I were you, I'd do the same damn thing."

"It sounds like you *do* want to be a private citizen."

"Stop it," demanded Lillian. "Stop it now. I won't listen to you two bickering." With everyone quiet again, Lillian studied Stephen as he focused his anger at the food on his plate, rather than looking at his family.

While she was fully aware he'd been wild as a young man, she also knew he maintained a certain level of caution, especially with women. He was careful if something might adversely affect his career or the family, and that carefulness had only intensified since he took office. If he had already engaged in risky behavior—of any sort—with Anne, something was different about her. That worried Lillian, so she decided to pull him back.

With a brief touch of his shoulder, she said, "Now, sweetheart, no one forced you to take on this role. You've always wanted it, regardless of your sisters' decisions. It's true your father would've been very happy you took his seat, but he'd have been proud of you no matter what you did with your life."

Stephen nodded warily as his mother continued.

"I know the enormous pressure you faced to fulfill the remainder of his term. You hadn't planned on taking on that responsibility so soon." She glanced at Patty. "And we *all* appreciate what you've done for the family. Your father would recognize you've made some sacrifices."

Crossing her arms, Patty grumbled.

Lillian shook her head at her daughter's reaction before turning back to her son. "As Marco said, as a family, we should support you, and we do."

"Thanks, Mom," Stephen said, still somber.

Wanting to make an impact with her opinion, Lillian delayed her next statement as she ran her hand along the tablecloth's floral needlepoint. After a moment, she announced, "But I do not want you seeing Anne Norwood." She looked up and gazed at Stephen. "You will ruin yourself."

Stephen blinked a few times and remained stoic, while Patty grinned.

Lillian clasped her hands together so tightly the white of her knuckles showed, and she took a deep breath. "And yet, I can't stop it from happening. You're a grown man, and you're already pursuing her." Her voice carried bitter annoyance. "And we all know what happens once these things get started."

Her equivocal announcement quieted the room. Marco again took stock of everyone's expression. He leaned toward his mother-in-law. "Lillian, I appreciate what you've said and your thinking on this. It's very rational."

"Thank you, Marco," she said with a grim smile.

"I'm wondering if maybe there isn't a potential way out of this." He sounded like the career diplomat he was.

Stephen furrowed his brow and turned to him. "What's that?"

Marco shrugged. "The family could help . . . could be there. We could sort of chaperone, if you will, when you're with her."

"Chaperone?" Lillian asked as she imagined what that might entail.

"Huh?" Stephen asked. His worried expression stayed with him.

"Mom, please," Patty said. "I expected you to be on my side on this one. This is a political shit storm. You're not seriously considering we help him lose his seat? What do you think—"

"I've not said what I will do," said Lillian holding up her hand to stop Patty's tirade. "I'm only listening. Overall, my goals haven't changed. I'd like a happy son, and I'd like to win this election. Obviously, I'd like Stephen to give up on this silly notion immediately." She waited a moment to see if she was having any effect on Stephen. His expression remained resolved, so she sighed and gave Stephen a knowing look. "But I'm not stupid."

"Mom, Dan Langford knows Anne works in the office," said Patty. "Remember I mentioned the run-in with him last weekend when he was a jerk? He actually brought up Anne, saying she's just the kind of girl Stephen would like."

"Hmm. Langford was actually right about something for once," Lillian quipped in an attempt to lighten the mood.

"But it means he's already thinking of attacking Stephen about his past," Patty said.

"Well, of course he is," said Lillian. "We've discussed that. It's the whole reason Stephen's been so open with you about his personal life."

"But, but . . ." Patty began looking around the room as if her perfect argument was just waiting to be discovered hiding in a corner. "What are you going to say to her parents? They'll be angry you didn't tell them you knew what was going on with their daughter."

"Lord, she's an adult, Patty, not a child." Lillian shook her head. "It's her choice if she tells her parents, not mine. I'd hope her father and mother would understand that."

"From everything I've ever heard her say about her parents, they'd understand it was her choice. She says they would blame her, not me," said Stephen.

"Well, look at you—able to answer all these questions for her. You certainly know a lot," Patty snarled. "When have you two talked?"

"Obviously, when you weren't around," he said with his lip curled.

"What did I tell you? Stop fighting." Lillian pushed the Wedgewood plate further onto the table and folded her arms in its place. She stared at Stephen. "Do you have plans to see her?"

He met her gaze and was forthright. "We talked about seeing each other tomorrow."

"Patty has raised the prospect of legal issues. Are you violating any nonfraternization rules?" Lillian asked.

Stephen shrugged. "No—as long as I'm not her direct supervisor. Believe me. I've read our office manual. It's conveniently vague."

"You're not her direct supervisor? You're the senator! It's your office. Really, Stephen. That doesn't pass the smell test." Lillian shook her head with disapproval.

"I think we're beyond the smell test, Mom," Megan said. "We're looking for the letter of the law in any public defense."

"Then I'd like to ask Phillip to take a look into the sexual harassment rules for Senate employees," Lillian said, referring to the family's private attorney.

"Go right ahead. I'm a lawyer. I'd appreciate an impartial review of the law," Stephen said.

"Impartial review?" Patty sniped. "A politician should care enough about his image not to endanger himself like that."

"Which brings us to the second issue of public perception," said Marco. "This is why I'm suggesting the family be around when Stephen and Anne get together. If it was ever to get out that Stephen and Anne had become friendly, it needs to appear to be a respectable relationship. It can't be unseemly."

"No blowjobs in the Oval Office?" Patty laughed.

"Patricia Caryn McEvoy, I appreciate your vigilance in protecting this family, but will you please stop it? I need you to be helpful here," Lillian said with a scowl.

Pursing her lips, Patty slumped in her chair in acquiescence. Only Lillian had ever been able to control her.

Lillian turned to Marco. "What are you proposing?"

"That Anne becomes a family friend. In order for things not to look like Stephen and Anne are sneaking around, he needs an alibi. If family members are always around, it looks better."

"Chaperoned by my family?" Stephen shook his head. "Please, not that. I'd rather—"

"Not that. I know," Marco said as he gave Stephen a man-to-man look. "It wouldn't need to be someone following you everywhere, just someone in the house when you're there together. That way, you have an alibi."

"Plausible deniability." Patty nodded, trying to get back into her mother's good graces. "It begs the question why she's there in the first place, but it does give it an air of respectability."

"Hmm. I don't think that's enough," Lillian murmured. "I will be asked whether I knew of Anne and what I think of all this." As she took another moment to smooth the tablecloth, Lillian was stone-faced. She raised her eyes to Stephen. "If you continue in your pursuit of Anne, I have three options. The first is to have you go about it alone without any family involvement. I believe you will surely lose your seat under that scenario. The second is for the four of you to work out some arrangement for you to see her. That would lessen the scandal, but only so much. I think it's still unlikely you could survive politically."

"And the third?" Stephen asked.

Lillian was well aware of her exalted status in the public eye. She'd been called "the Dowager Empress of Colorado," and on occasion, she used it to her advantage. "The third option is that I give this my blessing, and I take part in the alibi. You might survive a scandal if I help." She gave Stephen an icy side-eye. "*Might* survive."

"I think Mom's right," said Megan.

"Well, I'd like to see Anne again, and I don't want to wait a year and a half," Stephen declared.

Lillian checked her watch and announced, "Then bring her over here at two o'clock. I'll speak with both of you and decide then."

Stephen's eyes widened. "What? Mom . . ."

"Do you want my approval or not?" Lillian asked.

"Of course. But what are you going to say to her?"

"I don't know yet," Lillian lied.

"Okay. I suppose." Stephen straightened in his seat like a dutiful son. "I'll call her and ask her over."

"I think this is a good compromise, Lillian," Marco said with a nod. He turned to Patty. "But it's been my experience that treaties don't work if one side isn't invested in it."

Patty glanced at her mother, obviously looking to make a good impression. "I've been overruled. I accept it. I'm happy to chaperone or whatever else we have to do to make things between them at least *appear* platonic. I'll be damned if we lose this campaign simply because my brother has an uncontrollable crush on an intern."

"We're going to control it. That's the idea." Megan smiled.

A few minutes later, Stephen went into a spare bedroom and called Anne on his mother's landline.

"Hello?" It was clear she was hesitant answering a call from an unknown number.

"Hi. It's Stephen. How are you?" he asked.

"Great. I'm happy you called." The warmth in her voice confirmed it was true.

"Well, I was wondering if you were also free around two this afternoon."

"Um . . . sure. What are you thinking?"

"My mother would like to have you over." Not wanting to pressure Anne any more than he had, he decided to play down the meeting. He chuckled. "I understand you two met recently. You've been holding out on me."

"Er . . . yes . . . we haven't had much time to talk since you got back. I'm sorry I didn't tell you."

"Well, it's my fault we haven't been able to talk. I'm the one who should apologize." His smile grew bigger. "But you might've pulled me aside to let me know. I practically choked on my eggs when my mom told me."

"Sorry about that." She paused, and the apology left her voice. "Wait. Did you just say I'm supposed to pull you aside in the middle of your office? You want me, the intern, to tug on the senator's arm as he walks by so I can whisper in his ear? Are you crazy?"

"Okay, so maybe that's not a good idea. But could you've talked with Megan?"

"No. I wouldn't have been comfortable doing that. I don't know what you've told her about us."

"I understand. I just was in shock when Mom announced it to my entire family."

"Oh my God. Patty and Megan were there, too?"

"Oh yeah. And Marco."

"I'm so sorry. You must've been completely caught off guard."

"Don't worry about it. It was rough in the beginning, but it helps that my mom likes you." His mother had said something to that effect earlier, so he wasn't lying. "She'd like to see you again."

"Okay . . ." Her deep breath was audible across the phone line. "What's her address?"

§§§§

Anne pressed "end" on the phone and stared at it as she let the conversation sink in. *Oh my God. I have a date with Stephen to meet his mother again.* She shook her head as if the movement would make the idea absorb into her consciousness. Dread and excitement grew inside of her, until reality set in with the inevitable question—*What should I wear?*

§§§§

At two o'clock sharp, the doorman called Lillian and announced Anne's arrival. Before Stephen even brought it up, she told him to answer the door. She understood they might want a few words together before they all sat down. The meeting would be awkward enough as it was.

When the two walked into the living room, Lillian was just placing her mother's china tea set on the coffee table. She looked up and saw Stephen with his hand proudly on Anne's shoulder. *Oh dear*, Lillian thought. *He really likes her.*

Perfectly dressed for an afternoon with a suitor's mother, Anne was smiling. Lillian returned the smile. "Good afternoon, Anne. It's a pleasure to see you again."

"Thank you for inviting me over, Mrs. McEvoy," she answered.

"Please, call me Lillian. Still to this day, when I hear 'Mrs. McEvoy' I think of my mother-in-law."

Stephen crossed his arms. "Hey, Mom. Why don't you tell her about Grandma, and how you and Dad got together? That's a good story."

Only Lillian detected the smug tone in Stephen's voice. She raised her eyebrows. "I think that might bore Anne. Besides, she's probably already knows that ancient history. It's certainly been told in the media again and again."

Anne looked uncertain, as if she didn't know if she should admit she'd heard it before. "Only a little."

"Come on, Mom," said Stephen. "You'll give her a better version."

Lillian flashed her son a look to tell him she knew what he was up to. After a second of rumination, she decided the conversation might break the ice. "Oh, all right. I suppose it is amusing." She gestured to the sofa. "Please sit. Anne, can I get you tea or coffee?"

"Thank you. I'll take some tea."

As Stephen and Anne took their seats, Lillian poured tea and handed out cookies. She launched into her story. "Patrick was my second husband. My first marriage ended in divorce, but it was the best thing that ever happened to me. My first husband was my escort when I was a debutante. It was always expected Henry and I would marry, and we did—right after I graduated from Sarah Lawrence."

"Were you too young?" Anne asked.

Lillian smiled at what she thought was an excellent question, showing a cautionary outlook on life. Given what the two were embarking on, Lillian thought it smart Anne considered such things. She took her tea and sat down. "No. I wouldn't say that, though I understand why you ask. I have friends who married at the same age who remain happy with their husbands. We were never really happy, even in the beginning. That was our problem."

"That's too bad. When did you divorce?" asked Anne.

"I was twenty-five. It was rather scandalous. Neither of our families was the divorcing kind. Our parents only accepted it because we didn't have children." She rolled her eyes and smiled. "Of course, *I* was blamed for that, but you've seen my children. *Obviously* the problem wasn't with me, but we didn't know it at the time."

"Obviously not." Stephen chuckled. "Tell her what you did next."

"Ah, to the great dismay of my family, I moved to Paris and became a governess to a French government official's family. He wanted his children to speak fluent English. I'd majored in French in college and lived in Paris for a semester, so I knew the country well." She laughed. "I thought if I was going to be a barren old maid, I might as well do it in Paris."

"So did you meet your husband there?" Anne asked.

"No. In Colorado, six years later. At the time, Patrick was a junior member of Congress, and his father was senator. The family I worked for was vacationing in the West, and we'd stopped in Rocky Mountain National Park. Patrick was there for an event. He heard me speaking French to the children and came over to talk."

"And the rest is history?" Anne smiled.

"Almost. He didn't know I was an American, and he started speaking in terrible French. I told him if he wanted to impress me, he needed to speak in English."

"It caught Dad's attention," Stephen said with a nod. "Normally, women didn't talk to him that way."

"That's great." Anne laughed. "I guess he impressed you, then."

"He did. We fell in love, almost overnight. I quit my job to stay in Denver with my family." She shook her head. "Unfortunately, his mother didn't like me. Even though he had been quite the ladies' man, she didn't think he should settle down with a Protestant, over-thirty divorcee."

"But you still married. What happened?" Anne asked.

"It was very romantic." Mrs. McEvoy sighed happily. "A year after we met, we eloped."

"That does sound special, especially given the circumstances."

"It was. Patty was born the following year. Then Megan came along a few years later. And finally, Stephen." She smirked. "My ex-husband has *still* never acknowledged the birth of any of my children."

"I bet he never will," said Anne with a smile.

Lillian nodded. "Would you like another cup of tea?"

"Yes, please," Anne answered.

As Lillian poured Anne's second cup, she used the mundane activity as a segue to the real subject of the day. "So that was my scandal." She gave Stephen a sharp glance before passing the cup to Anne. Meeting Anne eye to eye, she asked, "What do we have going on here?"

With a chiding tone, Stephen jumped in. "Mom, we talked about this already."

"We did. Now I want to hear from Anne."

Anne's eyes shifted to Stephen and then back to Lillian's. She shook her head. "I don't know yet. I'd only say we're proceeding cautiously."

"And so you're aware of the risk—of everything?" Lillian said as she cocked her head in skepticism.

"Of course," Anne answered, her brow furrowed. She obviously didn't like the friendly conversation turning into an interrogation.

Stephen leaned forward in his seat and said, "Mom—"

Anne briefly placed her hand on his arm and showed her good manners, despite being put in an awkward situation. "It's okay. I don't mind. It's a reasonable question."

"But not appropriate," Stephen countered.

"I think this entire situation is well past appropriate, Stephen." Lillian leaned back in her chair and crossed her arms. "I only want what's best for you, but since you're an adult, you have to decide that."

She turned to Anne. "It's not that I don't like you. Actually, I do. I just want to make sure the two of you have thought this through completely before you proceed any further. Stephen says he has. Have you?"

Anne nodded, but looked at her askance. "With all due respect, some might say I have more at risk, personally, than anyone here. You know what kind of family I come from—what's expected of me, what my life should look like. Of course I've thought this through."

Lillian studied Anne for a moment, admiring her candor. *She's lovely, and if it weren't for the election, I'd be more than happy he found her.* Turning to Stephen, she saw he wore a frown until he looked at Anne and they shared a smile. Lillian sighed to herself as she saw what was in motion before her—for better or for worse, Stephen was falling in love. She resigned herself to the fact she was powerless to stop it and her job was to steer her son the best she could.

To the shock of everyone in the room, Lillian leaned over, clasped Anne's hand, and smiled. "I'm very reassured to hear that. Thank you for answering me so honestly."

She turned to Stephen, who smiled warily. She gave him a confirming nod and issued her decision. "I have bridge at three today, so I need to leave shortly. I hope you two have a nice time together tomorrow." She rose from her seat and smiled at Anne. "And I'd love to have you over for brunch soon."

Chapter 11

On Sunday, Anne perched herself at the window of her basement apartment, on the lookout for Megan's car. When it pulled up, she bounded out the door, climbed in, and received a warm welcome from Megan and her husband. Anne thought Marco devastatingly handsome, charming, and proud of his humble roots. It made her question everything she'd ever thought of the McEvoys—maybe they weren't as snobby as she'd assumed.

As they arrived at the McEvoy family home, she changed her mind again, though. The stately building was ominous with gray stone and a grand glass and iron awning over the front steps. A twenty-foot high, decorative iron fence separated the house from the rest of humanity.

When Stephen opened the door to the house and welcomed everyone in, she gave him a quick once-over. She'd feared his idea of casual was a button-down and khakis, as he'd worn yesterday with his mother. Instead, he wore a T-shirt which clung to his body, accentuating every muscle normally hidden by his daily dress shirts. She'd never seen so much of his skin bare, and she thought he might as well be naked. His accompanying jeans were faded blue and slung low on his hips. He'd passed her test with flying colors, and she grinned.

After he took her hand and they all said hello, the foursome walked inside the palatial foyer of the home. Anne surveyed the entry, noticing every fancy cornice while Megan and Stephen spoke about dinner. When they reached the end of the hallway, Marco ushered his wife out of the foyer.

"So, come by the kitchen around six," Marco called over his shoulder. "We'll have dinner started."

"We'll be downstairs either in the gym or watching football, if you want to find us," said Megan.

As they walked away, Anne heard Megan whisper to Marco, "Shouldn't we check on them from time to time?"

"*Absolutely* not," muttered Marco.

Anne felt a rush of nervous delight when she realized she would be truly alone with Stephen for the entire afternoon. She looked up at him with smile. Unsure of what to say, she remarked, "This is quite a house."

"My grandfather built it when he was a congressman back in the twenties." He shrugged and smiled. "It's a little over the top. I'd rather not live here, but I lost that battle." He motioned toward a door. "Come on. Let me show you the library. I think you'll really like it. It's my favorite room in the house."

Through a sunny, yellow sitting room and two pocket doors, they entered a library, the likes of which she'd only seen in movies. Cherrywood bookcases ran floor to ceiling with sliding ladders that would allow even her to reach a book at the top. A few comfy chairs for solo reading resided in corners and by the windows, and a leather couch sat in front of a fireplace with a giant bearskin hanging above the mantle.

"Wow. This is amazing," she said as she took her hand away from his. She wanted to explore the beautiful room by herself. As she admired the books and furnishings, the enormity of the McEvoy wealth hit her for the first time, and it made her chuckle.

"You know, stereotypes are reversed here." She smirked. "I'm from the Republican family, but we're middle class. You're all wealthy Democrats. Go figure."

"Middle class? Doesn't your family have a ranch?"

"Okay. Upper-middle class, but still middle class. And yes, we've got some land, but it's been in the family for generations. It's nothing like *your* family's ranch—I'm sure of that." She playfully swatted his arm. "I don't want to make you uncomfortable. I just think the role reversal is kind of funny."

"I guess it is." He smiled and glanced around the room. "As I said, I wouldn't have chosen to live here."

"Why not? It's a beautiful home."

"Yeah, but I live here alone. I kind of rattle around the place. It's nice when the whole family comes for dinner or to watch a game, and everybody is always here when there's a snowstorm. That's fun. Usually, though, I feel pretty isolated."

"I can see that, but what did you mean when you said you lost a battle? Why do you have to live here?"

"My mother thought it would be more senatorial if I lived here."

"She's right," Anne said with an apologetic shrug. "Though I understand wanting a place of your own."

He moved his hand to her face and gently stroked her cheek. She wondered what might happen next, but he quickly pulled his hand away. His brow furrowed as he briefly touched her nose. "You're cold. I guess it is chilly in here. Let me light a fire."

"Thanks," she said, feeling a little awkward. "That would be nice."

As he took some of the neatly stacked wood beside the fireplace and positioned it in the hearth, she sat down on the floor nearby. Pointing to the bearskin, she asked, "So how did that big guy give up his life?"

"You'd have to ask Senator York. He gave it to my dad as a gift years ago."

"Interesting gift." She glanced up and down the shelves. "Some of these books look old."

"Yeah, a lot of them are hard to find now." As he built the fire, they talked about his father's collection of rare books. At one point, he glanced over his shoulder and regarded her for a moment. "How is it you've read so many books?"

"I told you I grew up in the middle of nowhere. I like to read."

"You must. You're making me feel inferior."

"Yeah. Right. As if, *Senator* McEvoy." She rolled her eyes.

The comment caused him to turn around again, and he smiled. "Has anyone ever told you you're quite a smartass?"

"Not in so many words." She laughed.

"I don't believe it," he said, turning back to stoke the fire.

"Okay. Maybe my brother. He hates it."

"He's your brother. Brothers are obligated to be annoyed by their sisters."

"You speak from experience."

"I do, but Megan and I get on each other's nerves and we're still friends."

"What about Patty?"

"Well, I can't say Patty and I are friends, but we've got an eldest sister/ little brother thing going on. We're each other's greatest defenders."

With the fire established, he leaned his back against the sofa and sprawled his legs across the antique rug. "But you're friends with your brother, right?"

"We're pretty close."

"What would he think of me?" he asked hesitantly.

"Honestly? He'd be suspicious."

He raised his eyebrows and nodded. "As my family was of you."

"It's understandable."

"They're less suspicious now, though." He smiled.

"So I got a seal of approval yesterday? Is that how we're here together?" she asked warily.

"Come here and I'll tell you." He patted the space next to him and took her hand again as she scooted closer. "I'm actually happy how things went down. It smoothed some things over."

"How so?"

"Ah . . . well, let's just say it was good my mom had already met you."

"So she didn't think I was like Monica Lewinsky? A trampy intern?"

"Something like that." He smiled. "It also made it easier when I had to tell my family how I felt about you."

Silence took over the room, as Anne couldn't respond quickly to something so heartfelt. She swallowed hard and quietly asked, "And? What did you tell them?"

The smile didn't leave his face, but his voice was serious. "I told them I care enough to take a risk, and I *think* you feel the same way."

"I do," she said under her breath.

His smile was so sweet she had to look away for a moment. She glanced down at their entwined hands and impulsively grazed her fingertips over his dark arm hair. When their eyes met again, neither said anything. They were alone, they were touching, and it was quiet; she was certain he would kiss her next.

She was surprised when he spoke instead.

"I'd really like to kiss you right now, but I don't want you to think I got you alone just to touch you."

"I don't think that at all." She laughed, but quickly grew more serious. "I'd like to kiss you, too, but I don't want you to think I'm just here because of who you are."

"And I don't think that either."

His eyes lowered as he inched toward her, and she met him halfway and tenderly kissed him three times. Each kiss was open and wanting, and afterward, he smiled. "I think we should do that again."

"More." She smiled mischievously.

"Definitely more," he replied as he reached his hand behind the nape of her neck and kissed her again.

Weeks of sexual tension were finally released. She couldn't get enough of him, and he responded to her physical cues with a quick maneuver so they lay on the rug. As they rolled around, their hands and mouths roamed each other's bodies. She lost all sense outside the moment. Arching her body toward his, he found the button of her jeans, just as she wanted. When he abruptly stopped, she was disappointed.

"I'm sorry . . . I didn't mean . . ." He stumbled over his words as he pulled away.

"Um . . . yeah." She looked down, confused by the sudden end.

"Let me explain. It's not that I don't want to touch you. I promise I do." He moved onto his side and stroked her hair. "You're so beautiful and special. It's just that I told myself I wasn't going to maul you first thing when we're alone, and look what I do."

"I think I was the one doing most of the mauling." She rolled onto her side and smiled shyly.

"Maybe so." He smiled and leaned on his elbow. With the back of his hand, he gently touched her cheek. "Given the situation, I can't see how it would be any different."

"Why do you say that?"

"I think we have a certain amount of . . . chemistry between us, otherwise we wouldn't be going to these lengths, right?"

"I think you're right." She chuckled. "And when you add in the fact we're a little frustrated by it all . . ."

"Exactly." He laughed and nuzzled into her neck. "Hard as it was to stop, I'd rather not have our first time happen when I have to send you home at the end of the day."

"That's sweet of you, but how are we ever going to spend the night together?"

"I don't know, but I'll figure something out." He ran his hand over her hip. "I can't keep my hands off you for too long."

"Obviously I've got a similar problem," she said with a coy smile.

"Which only makes you more tempting." He sat up and smiled. "It's a little hot in here. I can't handle both you and this fire anymore. How about we go out back and get some fresh air?"

"That sounds nice and . . . necessary." She giggled.

After he poked out the fire, he fetched their jackets from the closet and led her through the formal living area. The walls and furniture were discreetly decorated in understated beige and brown, with more colorful pillows and curtains. A bank of windows showed off the expansive grounds.

Wandering through french doors, the two made their way onto a large patio dominated by a pool and hot tub covered for winter. Beyond, the yard spread into a giant L-shape around the house. Anne could only see a portion of it, but it was large enough that she was in awe of its size. The huge, mature trees and unkempt shrubs and plants made the land unique compared to the manicured lawns of most of Washington.

"You'd never know from the front of the house you have so much space back here. I love how it's grown wild."

"I like it wild, too. It's big because my grandfather bought some additional lots and let things take their own shape. He didn't like being in a city much. He missed Colorado. I didn't really know him, but we have that in common."

"It's wonderful . . . very special."

He tucked her closer to his side and kissed her hair. "I knew you'd like it."

As they strolled through the grounds, she pointed to a small basketball court with a ball in the middle of it. "Who plays basketball?"

"I do. With Patty mostly, occasionally Marco, but usually it's just me at night trying to hit some baskets when I'm stressed."

"So you're out here at midnight playing basketball by yourself?"

"Yeah, sometimes." He chuckled. "Kind of pathetic, isn't it?" The same soulful look of regret crossed his face again. She wished she could make him feel better.

Shaking her head, she attempted empathy with lightheartedness. "Not pathetic. Just sorta sad." She tugged on his hand. "C'mon. Let's play."

"You play basketball?" he asked as she pulled him toward the court.

"Badly. I played with my family growing up."

"Okay, then. We'll see how you do."

When they got to the court, she tossed her jacket to the ground, picked up the ball, and started a slow dribble. "Let's play Horse."

"Not Pig?" he asked and went onto the court.

She rolled her eyes and smiled. Standing up on her toes, she replied, "I'm not *that* bad," and gave him a quick kiss.

When she pulled away, he grabbed her right back into a longer kiss, which made her drop the basketball. After a minute, he murmured, "Not bad at all, actually."

"You're not too shabby yourself." She chuckled.

"Wait 'til you see me play basketball," he said and picked up the ball. With a grin, he passed it to her. "Horse it is then."

Talking politics and working up a sweat, they had a great time. Anne turned out to be no better on the court than she'd professed. It didn't help that she wore boots rather than sneakers, but she was so good-natured, Stephen didn't give her too much grief.

When she stopped for a moment to catch her breath, Stephen studied her. The way she held the basketball perched on her hip drew attention to her curves, already made prominent by the tight jeans and clinging sweater. She was a woman—a politically astute woman—but the ponytail and damp wisps around her face highlighted her freckles and made her look young and fun. He could picture her playing basketball while debating her parents and teasing her brother.

She had a family who loved her—and would hate him.

It pained Stephen to think anyone would assume he'd taken advantage of her, but it hit him even harder when he considered someone who loved her would think that of him.

She furrowed her brow and looked behind her. "What? What are you looking at?"

"You."

"Why?"

"No reason." Taking a few steps closer, he shook his head. "I was just thinking about what you said about your brother."

"What's that?"

"That he'd be suspicious of me."

"Yeah . . ."

"It's not true," he said as he approached her.

"Um . . . yes . . . actually it is." She cringed. "Sorry."

"No, he'd be more than suspicious. He'd think the worst and want to kill me."

"Oh . . . *that*. Maybe initially, but I could talk him out of it."

"I still hate the idea that he'd question my intentions with you."

"And what *are* your intentions?" she asked with a smile and an arched eyebrow.

He took the basketball and tossed it on the ground. Wrapping his arms around her, he smiled. "Well, they're good, I assure you, but I can't say they're pure."

"Yeah?" She wore a giddy smile.

"In fact," he said as he kissed her neck, "they haven't been pure for a long time."

"That's good, because mine aren't pure either." She ran her fingers through his hair and kissed his forehead.

"Mine *are* good, though. I promise," he said, placing his forehead on hers.

"I believe you."

"I'm glad." He sighed and pulled away. "Because I haven't told you about something that happened back in Denver. I had a run-in with Dan Langford."

"What happened?"

"Let's go sit down."

After finding a bench under an old oak, they sat and talked. He relayed the entire scene with Langford and finished with a simple question. "So what do you think?"

"I think it sounds like him." She shook her head. "Boy, can he be childish when he gets pissed, or what?"

"Really? That's the way he is?"

"That's what my dad says. Langford was probably surprised by how friendly you were. Maybe he felt foolish, so he got petulant and mean, and I was just a convenient topic to taunt you with. I'm sorry."

"Don't be sorry. Patty didn't want me talking to him at all, other than to say hello."

"Well, it's nice you did, but I can see why she thought you should say hi and move on."

"Because he's going to needle me now whenever he can?"

"Yeah. There aren't too many upsides to talking with him or his staff. My dad knows his campaign manager, Trey Johnson. He's got a *really* hardball reputation."

"I'll let Patty worry about him." He chuckled.

"But doesn't it worry you at all that my name came up?" She frowned. "It's not a good sign."

He stared at her for a moment, debating whether or not to tell her Patty came to the same conclusion. He decided not to worry her, and instead repeated his mother's optimistic plan. "He doesn't know about us, and we'll make sure it stays that way."

"But . . ."

He smiled and pulled her onto his lap so he could look into her eyes. "If we're going to give this a try, we can't second-guess ourselves all the time. We need to be confident, and besides, I told you I've decided you're worth the risk."

Quiet for a moment, a smile spread across her face. "See. You say something like that, and I just want to throw myself at you."

"I should keep talking, then," he murmured, going in for a kiss.

They spent more time outside before heading indoors to watch a movie in his large office. The comfort of being in each other's arms was more enjoyable than the film, and they soon fell asleep on the sofa. They only woke when they heard a knock on the door.

Marco's voice came from the other side of the door. "We've started dinner if you want to join us for a glass of wine."

"Okay," Stephen answered groggily. "We'll be there."

The conversation was effortless among the foursome at dinner, with Megan and Stephen trading sibling barbs while Anne asked Marco everything about his work. She was interested in a climate change treaty he was working on.

After a long and lovely meal, Stephen squeezed Anne's hand as they walked to the car. He didn't want her to leave, and he racked his brain looking for a way to get her alone again the coming week. Unfortunately, he worried that he couldn't hide his feelings for her when they were in the office together.

Anne was the first to speak. "I had a great time. Thanks for having me."

"No, *I* had great time. Thanks for coming over." His smile turned into a frown. He didn't want to say the next piece, but he thought it was prudent. He liked her too much. "About tomorrow . . . I was thinking it's probably better if we didn't talk as much in the office."

"Probably a good idea." She sighed.

He left her at the car door with a soft kiss. "Good-bye. I'll see you tomorrow—even if I can't talk to you."

Chapter 12

The following Saturday morning, Anne expected Lillian McEvoy to answer the door, so her heart fluttered when Stephen let her in. All week, they'd exchanged knowing glances and smiles, but no words.

"Hey." He smiled and welcomed her in.

"Hi." She wanted to say something more, but she was once more distracted by his appearance. He was again unshaven and in faded jeans. A starched, white button-down was the only nod to a formal lunch with his mother. She returned his smile. "I like it when you don't shave."

"Really? Why is that?" he asked as he set her bag on a nearby table.

"I don't know. It's sort of a manly-man thing."

Stephen's smile turned from warm to wicked, and he pulled her into his arms for a long kiss.

When she pressed her body against his, she suddenly stiffened. "I'm forgetting where we are."

"Can't you hear her banging around the kitchen? It's okay." He chuckled and kissed behind her ear. "My mom has a bridge game every Saturday. She'll be at a friend's on another floor most of the afternoon. We can be alone."

"Great."

"Did you bring a book?" he asked, motioning toward her bag. "The apartment has some terraces—very private. It's nice; we could sit outside."

His mother's voice carried from the kitchen. "Stephen, can you please get the soup tureen from the buffet?"

"Sure, Mom." He smiled. "That's my mom's way of telling me she wants to see you. Come on."

Anne admired the elegant décor as he led her to the kitchen.

When they walked in, Lillian McEvoy turned from the stove. "Anne, welcome. Thank you for coming today. I'm so happy to have you."

"I'm happy to be here. Thank you for inviting me." She motioned toward the stove. "Is there something I can help you with here?"

Lillian peeked into her pot. "Well, thank you. How about you stir the soup while I plate the meat?" She smiled. "And we can talk."

Lillian monopolized the conversation with Anne throughout their lunch, asking her about her family, horses, and school. Each time Stephen attempted to break in, his mother shut him down. He grumbled in irritation, while Anne smiled at her sulking senator.

Stephen tried again to change the topic to one where he could also engage. "Mom, have you seen Grayson lately?"

"No, I haven't," she said dismissively and turned back to the center of her attention. "Now, Anne, tell me about your holiday plans."

"I'm staying here for Thanksgiving, and I'll go home for Christmas."

"That will be nice." Lillian smiled. "I was going to say if you were flying to Colorado for Thanksgiving you should go with us, but please do at Christmas instead. We have plenty of room on the plane."

"Mom, are you sure about that?" Stephen asked. "I don't know if . . ."

Anne's eyes widened slightly, but she remained silent. Flying in a private plane with the McEvoys was hard to imagine.

"Why not?" Lillian asked as she looked at their surprised faces. "Greg flies with us, and Anne is my friend. He could even drive her to Silverthorne."

"Um. Mom. There are appearances. And more importantly, I never planned on telling Greg about Anne and me."

"That would be a mistake." Her lips pursed in disapproval.

"Why? What are you thinking? I didn't want him to get caught up in any scandal if something were to come out. What's your take?"

"He can protect you. He'll hear things in the office you and Megan won't. You benefit far more from Greg knowing than not."

"Excuse me, Lillian. Greg knows my family," Anne said hesitantly. "I'm not sure it's such a good idea in case my family hears—"

"You don't need to worry about that," Stephen placed his hand on Anne's shoulder. "Greg would never do anything to hurt me. I think my mom is right."

"Then you and Megan should tell him on Monday," Lillian declared, smiling at her own astuteness. "Now, let's have some sorbet."

After lunch, they cleared the table, and Lillian checked her watch. "Oh my. I have to go. My bridge game starts in five minutes. Please leave everything in the kitchen, and I'll take care of it when I get home . . . around five or so . . . not earlier, though. "

Anne objected to leaving the dishes for Lillian, so while she went off to play bridge, Stephen and Anne cleaned up. As Anne washed the crystal, he moved behind her.

"She gave us fair warning for when she'd be back." He kissed her neck.

"We can have some privacy; that means she really likes you."

"That's nice of her." She leaned her neck to the side so he had better access.

He gave her another kiss. "Let's get these dishes done so we can do more of this."

When they finished cleaning the kitchen, they took their respective reading onto an expansive terrace off the living room. Large planters with flowers framed the patio, and outdoor furniture with plump pillows made it an exterior living room. He led her to a large double-size lounger, big enough for the two of them.

After they sat down, he peered over her textbook. "I'd rather be reading yours," he muttered.

She eyed the briefing memo on his lap. The title included the words "Federal Trade Commission." She wrinkled her nose. "I'm not trading."

"You're smart not to." He sighed, but continued reading.

She looked at him—stretched out in his jeans like a model. "You know, you don't look very senatorial right now."

"That's good." With a sly smile, he took off his sunglasses and inched closer. "I'd prefer you didn't think of me as a senator, and I certainly don't want to think of you as an employee."

"What do you think of me as?"

"Someone very special."

Something about what he said struck her core because it didn't make sense. "Special? Look at all the women you've been with. Like that actress, Jennifer Hamilton. She's gorgeous." She shook her head in doubt. "It doesn't make sense."

"Come here." He pulled her close and looked straight into her eyes. "I think you're absolutely beautiful. Each and every one of your freckles is adorable, and you have the most beautiful eyes." He stroked her arm and said in a seductive voice, "And I can't *wait* to see the rest of you."

When she looked down, embarrassed and delighted by his words, he lifted her chin. "One day I hope we can go riding, because if it's possible, I bet you're even prettier on a horse. And you make me laugh and think, and you're so damn cute when you tease me, I just want to kiss you. I will never be bored with you."

Her heart swelled with his words, and her whole body felt warm and fuzzy. She gave him a sweet kiss. "Well, I'm certainly never bored with you."

He smiled, but his brow soon creased. "I know my past is going to come up again, but for now can we put it behind us? Because that's where it belongs."

"Okay. I can do that."

"Thank you," he said and gave her a kiss. After a moment, he pulled away and tugged her bulky fisherman's sweater. Furrowing his brow, he had a playful pout. "This sweater is offensive. I can't see your body. If I can't touch it, at least let me see it."

Examining her sweater, she recalled what she wore underneath. Not thinking it a big deal, she smiled and swiftly pulled the sweater over her head to reveal a tight, long-sleeved T-shirt.

"Ah. Much better," he said with an exaggerated sigh of relief.

"You're silly."

"And you look gorgeous." His ran his hand down her side, barely grazing her breast.

"I'm not exactly well-endowed." She hunched her shoulders slightly.

"Darling, you're perfectly endowed." He repeated the sweep of his hand down her other side.

Giddy again, she kissed him quickly. The kiss spurred him on, and he pulled her on top of him so that his hands could reach under her skirt and gently stroke her legs. With only sheer tights between his hands and her thighs, she felt almost naked under his touch, and she pressed into him. Then his hands abruptly stopped.

"You're not wearing anything underneath these?" he asked.

"Um. No. I hate how everything gets bunched up when you wear stockings and panties."

"My God. You're killing me." He put his arm over his eyes in feigned distress.

"I didn't expect to be making out with you at your mother's." She giggled.

"We're never coming here again." He smiled and stroked her cheek. "A night alone with you, that's all I ask."

"Only one night?" She raised an eyebrow.

"At this point, I'll take what I can get."

With a glance up and down, she admired his long, lean body. She nodded. "I'd take one night, too."

His smile turned into a devilish grin, and he pulled her snug in his arms. "I'm glad we've come to an agreement." After a deep kiss, he murmured, "Until then, I'm just going to kiss you."

"Don't you have to read about the FTC?" She chuckled.

"Fuck the FTC," he said and kissed her again.

§§§§

The following Monday morning, Trey Johnson decided to try to reach Walter Smith one last time. For weeks, he'd wanted to talk with the Godfather-like figure about Langford's campaign. When the receptionist said Walter would actually take his call, Trey's eyes lit up.

After a minute, Walter came on the line. "Trey, so good to talk to you. I've been in Chile for the last month. The fly fishing is amazing there. You wouldn't believe . . ."

Trey rolled his eyes as Walter gave an extemporaneous speech about

South American fish. Talking to the idle rich about anything other than politics was the least favorite part of his job.

"It sounds like you had a great time. On behalf of Dan Langford, I wanted to thank you for your generous contribution and the other donations you've raised for the campaign. We appreciate your support."

"Happy to help. You know how much I want us to win, but now that I've got you on the phone I want to give you my opinion."

"That's the reason why I called. Your opinion is the most important." Trey didn't care if he was ingratiating; he needed Walter's help.

"Thank you," Walter replied, not sounding particularly impressed with the compliment. "Well, I do think Dan Langford is a natural born winner."

"I'm so glad to hear you say that. He sure is."

"But I worry he's not ready."

"What do you mean?" Trey's voice was calm, but he was alarmed to hear Walter say anything remotely negative about Langford. Walter was the most influential and shrewd funder of conservative political causes in the country. Trey needed him excited about his candidate.

"I'm not sure he's ready to take it to the next level. I'm not sure he's senatorial material."

Trey's mouth twitched. There was a caste system in politics from the local to state to federal levels. While upward mobility naturally occurred in the castes, some politicians lacked the polish and skill to lift themselves up. Walter obviously thought Langford was too provincial. Trey knew it was a weakness of Langford's, but it could also be a positive.

"I can see why you might say that. He's so 'down-home,' so to speak, but it works in Colorado."

"Maybe, though he's a stark contrast to Stephen McEvoy."

"I assure you Dan's brand of tough conservatism will do great against a pretty boy like McEvoy who was born with a silver spoon in his mouth."

"If Langford was only running against Stephen McEvoy alone, I might agree with you. In reality, he's up against the whole McEvoy clan. They're the Kennedys of the West, and since his dad's death, his mother's become the patron saint of Colorado. And frankly, McEvoy has done well for himself since he's been in the Senate. He's been pretty moderate."

"But nobody's perfect—not even Stephen McEvoy," Trey said, trying to salvage the call. "He has weaknesses. There has to be something that could be found on him. After all, the guy does have a reputation. He hates it when you mention it."

"Hmm . . . that's something to think about. Well, it *is* shaping up to be a good year for Republicans; maybe Langford will ride the wave. It would be nice to take that seat away from the Democrats and away from the McEvoy family."

"Yes, it would."

"Maybe I could do a little more," Walter mused.

"That would be wonderful. We'd really appreciate it." Trey brightened at the news, but he didn't want to get his hopes too high. "What are you thinking of?"

"Maybe we'll do some digging for you. Find you some more information on the guy, and then get it out into the open." Walter chuckled. "I think I'll call it the Colorado Research Project."

Chapter 13

Only a minute later, Langford picked up Trey's call. "What's up?"

"Life has just gotten much better," Trey said with some pride. "I finally got a hold of Walter. He's setting up an independent expenditure campaign called the Colorado Research Project."

"He's going after McEvoy? That's incredible."

"It's unbelievable." Trey smiled as he put his feet up on his desk. "We just need to tell him anything we know or hear. Then he'll dig deeper."

"Wait a second," Langford said warily. "There's no 'we' to this. You know the campaign needs to stay out of it. We can't coordinate with an independent expenditure campaign."

"Of course. *I'd* be the one talking to them." Trey nodded. "I just need you and the rest of the campaign to feed me information."

"I understand. Maybe we can work something out. If I hear something, I'll tell you, but that's all. I don't want to be nabbed by the feds."

"Come on. Nothing will happen to you. And so what if it did? There'd be a fine on the campaign or something."

"Or something—like my reputation," Langford answered, his tone gruff and dismissive.

"I understand, but let's not worry about that now. I need to start them with some information. Maybe there's an incident in McEvoy's past we can uncover." Trey paused a moment as he dreamt of a political gift from the Gods. "Wouldn't it be great if McEvoy paid off some girl to get an abortion?"

"What? You don't really wish an abortion happened, do you?" The horror in Langford's voice couldn't be missed.

"I guess not," Trey muttered unconvincingly. He felt stupid for bringing up such an emotional topic for Langford. "Well, maybe there's something else. Maybe when he was younger he got in trouble with the law and Daddy McEvoy had it swept under the rug."

"I'm sure that happened, but the guy was a prosecutor. McEvoy survived a background check. Whatever criminal activity he's done, it's not a big deal."

"Well, they could've missed something. Let's start with his weakness—women."

"I believe he's been with that actress, Jennifer Hamilton, and I've also seen a photo of him recently with Congresswoman Schultz from Massachusetts."

"Forget that. Only good press there. He doesn't stick with anyone for too long, though, and there could still be something in his past with other women. Maybe we should start with his family," Trey said as his mind ticked through options. "Maybe old Patrick McEvoy did something we can tie to Stephen."

"We have to watch out if we go there. Lillian McEvoy's incredibly popular. She's the grieving widow, and she'll come out to protect the family name."

"Oh, they'll do that regardless. He's the candidate, though—she's not. She can only help so much."

"That's true," Langford admitted in a hopeful voice. "Listen. I don't want to be negative. I think it's great Walter's taken notice of the campaign. I'm sure you can dig up some dirt on McEvoy, or better yet, McEvoy will do something dumb. Then Walter can run with it."

"Yeah. Something will bubble up." Trey grinned at the prospect. "It always does, and Walter's here to help."

§§§§

Every time she thought of her last date with Stephen, Anne covered her mouth to hide her goofy grin. But her smiles ended on Monday morning when Stephen gave her only a blank glance as he strode past her accompanied by two other senators. Though she hadn't looked at him with any recognition either, she still felt hurt. She'd hoped for at least a smile or nod. The week before, those little gestures got her through their drought of communication. She became worried.

He's never going to acknowledge me unless we're alone? What kind of relationship is that?

Shortly after five that evening, Stephen observed her leaving for the day. She'd taken off her heels for the commute home and wore her green Converse. The contrast between her black skirt and stockings with the green low-tops made him smile; it was *so* her. He had a sudden urge to call to her, but thinking of the consequences, he stopped himself.

For the first time since he'd taken office, he hated his job. Before he met her, he'd experience bouts of regret followed by acceptance of the choice he'd made. Now, he wished for a normal life. *If only I could meet her for a beer after work, have dinner, take her home . . . but I can't.* He shook his head in grim resignation and went to his office for his five o'clock meeting.

The next day, he planned on catching her eye as he walked by her cubicle, simply for some connection. When he saw her, though, she furtively glanced at him and looked away. He stared at her, hoping she'd raise her head again, but she didn't. Something was wrong, he thought, and it was his fault.

§§§§

Later that afternoon, Anne's stomach did flips as she followed Megan to her office. She hadn't expected Stephen to talk to her again, and she worried an impromptu meeting wasn't a good sign. When Megan closed the door, leaving her alone with Stephen, she smiled anxiously. "Hey."

He took her hands and returned the smile. "Hi. You look pretty today."

"Thanks." She touched the knot of his tie. "You always look good."

"So do you." He kissed the top of her forehead. "But you look better when I actually get to talk to you."

"Yeah. Um. Why *are* we talking? I thought we weren't going to do that here."

"Come on. Let's sit," he said as he led her to the sofa. When they sat down, he pulled her close. "I was tired of not seeing you."

"Yeah. It sucks," she said with a scowl.

"Tell me about it. I've been thinking it's only going to get worse. I'm going to Colorado later this week, and then there's Thanksgiving. We're going to have a lot of time apart with no way to communicate. And I know it sounds conspiratorial . . . but I think cell phones are risky."

"I understand . . . but if one of us is away, it makes more sense that we can't communicate. I don't like being here and not talking. I get anxious." She shook her head. "It's a very odd situation to be in."

"What do you mean?" he asked as he stroked her hair.

"It's strange because it's two different worlds. When we're together, like right now, we're so close, but it has this clandestine feel about it. Then out there in the office, we don't even acknowledge one another, and I can't talk to you after work either." She hung her head. "I don't know . . . I wonder if this is how a mistress feels."

"A mistress?" His eyes widened. "You feel like a mistress? That's the last thing I want you feeling."

"Well, obviously not exactly like a mistress." She gave him an awkward smile. "I mean . . . we're pretty chaste."

"True." He laughed, before his expression soured. "You know you're not a mistress, right?"

"Of course. That was the wrong word."

"I'd hope you feel like my girlfriend." He smirked as if he knew he'd sprung something on her.

"Ah." Her breath caught in surprise. She hadn't expected such a declaration that afternoon, and she grinned. "And I do, when we're together."

"Good." His smile soon turned into a frown. "I'm a lousy boyfriend, though."

"What do you mean? I have a great time with you."

"Where should I begin? I can't pick you up. I can't take you home. I can't go out in public with you. Hell, I can't even talk with you in public. I trap you inside. My family is always around, and I can't touch you the way I want."

"Stephen, it's all right," she said gently as she smoothed his hair. "It won't be like this forever."

"But you feel isolated, and I don't like that. I want you to be happy." He smiled. "Because you make me so happy."

"Of course I'm happy with you. It simply would be nice if we talked during the week."

"Let me figure something out." He leaned in for a kiss. After a sweet embrace, he murmured, "Mmm. You made my day much better."

"And you, mine."

"Today's a big day." He raised his eyebrows.

"Why's that?"

"Today's the day I tell Greg about us."

"Yikes." She chuckled nervously. "Let me know how that goes."

"Oh, you'll hear soon enough." He smirked. "He'll come talk to you."

§§§§

Just as Stephen predicted, Greg asked to speak with her. She smiled, knowing the topic, but he kept a stern face and suggested some fresh air. Once outside the Hart Building, he led her across the lawn to the Taft Memorial and Carillon, on the farthest part of the Capitol grounds.

Surveying the area, Anne saw they were alone except for the cars whizzing past them on the street. "You didn't drag me all the way out here just to show me this ugly memorial, did you?"

Greg laughed for a moment, but his expression softened into one of a concerned elder brother. "I just need to know one thing. Are you okay with what's going on with you and Stephen? Is this what you want? Do you want to see him romantically while you work in his office?"

"Yes." She nodded stoically.

"Are you sure?"

"Of course," she replied, laughing at his earnestness. "I've gone into this with eyes wide open. We both have."

"Eyes wide open? You know if this turns into a mess, you'll be humiliated? You'll be the joke of your law school class or even Jay Leno, for that matter."

"I know." She winced at the thought. "I don't like thinking about it, but I know it's a possibility."

"But have you thought about your family?"

"Of course. I've considered everything. This didn't happen overnight. I want to be with him."

"Okay . . ." He exhaled and clasped his hands together in obvious relief. "That's what I needed to hear. I'll do everything I can to make sure this stays quiet. I want things to work out for you two."

"I really appreciate it." She smiled and touched his arm. "You're the best."

"I'm only doing my job as your friend and your boss," he said with a warm grin. "You know he's crazy about you. I've never seen him like this before."

"I'm pretty crazy about him, too." She shrugged nonchalantly, but her beaming smile gave her away.

He shook his head as they started back to the office. "But damn, this is going to be hard to conceal. Stephen and I talked at length about it. You've got a good plan. I just wish I could get you off staff—have you go work for someone else in the Senate. But at this point, I'm not sure it would help."

"No. Not really. Then the question would be *why* did I leave?"

"Yeah, it might even draw more attention. At the moment, there's no good answer." He smiled. "Well, I'm an optimist. We'll work it out. It's gonna be crazy, though."

§§§§

At the end of the day, Megan asked Anne again to come to her office. Anne was surprised when Stephen wasn't in the room. "Is everything okay?" she asked.

"Sure." Megan smiled and handed her a cell phone.

"Why are you giving me this?"

"You are now me, and after this evening, Stephen will be Marco. We're giving you our cell phones. Marco thought it up this morning."

"Oh my gosh, thank you," she exclaimed and stared at the phone. "This is really kind of you."

"I unlocked it, so you should program in a new password. As long as you only dial the numbers I've already got in it, no one will be the wiser as to who owns the phone. I've got another for work, so the numbers are all friends and family anyway."

"This is so sweet of you. It's been hard not talking to Stephen—this afternoon, I wanted to tell him about my conversation with Greg, but I couldn't."

"And now you can." She smiled. "Two things, though. The first is you shouldn't text. That's still dangerous if anyone were to hack into the phone.

And the second is the number for my hair salon is in there. The name of it is *Finis*, and Joey is my guy. He's amazing. His number is a bigger gift than this phone."

"Thanks." She laughed. "And no texting makes a lot of sense."

"I bet Stephen will call you tonight. It may be late because he and Marco are having dinner," Megan said with a wink.

§§§§

Burma Star, Marco's restaurant of choice, was nearly empty when Stephen arrived later that evening. The only other party was a large Burmese family sitting at a giant, round table at the front of the restaurant. Stephen spied Marco at a table in the far back; he spoke with a gentleman in an apron who looked to be the owner or the chef. As the man walked away, Marco rose to greet Stephen with a hearty handshake and backslap.

"Thanks for meeting me here."

"Thanks for setting it up. It's good to see you."

After they ordered dinner and were served their beers, Marco relaxed in his chair. "I'm not going to beat around the bush. I want to see if there's anything I can do to help you and Anne. I feel for you."

"Thanks. I appreciate it. It's a dicey situation I've gotten us into, but . . . I'm happier when I'm around her. I can't deny that."

"It's obvious you're really happy, but it's got to be hard."

"It is. We're trying not to talk at all in the office. You know, so we don't slip up. But it's tough because we don't see each other much."

"I thought that could be a problem for you two." With a smile, Marco reached into his pocket and produced a cell phone. He presented it as Megan had given hers to Anne, minus the hair stylist.

Stephen was overwhelmed by gratitude. "This is really thoughtful. You've outdone yourself as a brother-in-law. Thanks very much."

"Happy to oblige. No texting about sex, okay?"

"No texting at all. Don't worry about that. Sex or no sex." Stephen chuckled.

"So any other problems?"

"Well . . . now that you've brought it up . . . can I ask a favor of you?"

"That's why I'm here. Shoot."

"Could you and Megan spend the night at the house some time?" He grimaced. "I hate to ask, but I don't really have any other options. I can't ask Patty or my mother."

A waiter arrived with their appetizers, so Marco didn't answer immediately. When the waiter left, he smiled. "I understand. We can come over."

"Thanks—but I think you need to check with Megan. She won't approve, and I'd rather not have to persuade her."

"I'll deal with Megan. I love my wife, but she's not thinking clearly here." Marco shook his head. "It's not like her—must be because this is so personal."

"I suppose."

"She should know this situation is all about perception. If you are found out, it doesn't matter what you have or haven't done. You're cooked either way. Everyone's going to believe you *were* doing it."

"You're right about that." He snickered.

"In my mind, that means you might as well do what you want. There's nothing to lose. With all this secrecy you've got going on, you two should at least be enjoying yourselves." Marco raised his glass to toast the sentiment.

"Sounds *damn* good to me." Stephen laughed and raised his glass.

"When you're ready, we should plan a weekend at the cabin in West Virginia. It can just be the four of us. In the meantime, I'm happy to help you out whenever. I'll work on my wife." Marco chuckled. "And I'll deal with Patty, too."

§§§§

Late that night, Anne sat in bed reading when an unfamiliar ring came from her bag. *Oh my God. It's Megan's phone.* She scrambled off the bed to get it and saw the name 'Marco' on the screen. She answered it with an anxious, "Hello."

"Well, hello, *Megan*," Stephen greeted her.

"Hi, *Marco*." She grinned. "I wasn't sure if I'd hear from you tonight."

"I couldn't resist."

"I'm glad."

Their first phone conversation was wonderfully mundane and normal as they caught up on their respective days and the coming week. As the conversation edged away from routine, he was curious about the portion of her life he was excluded from. He first inquired about her apartment.

As she described her bedroom, she mentioned the patio in the back. He asked for more specifics. "It sounds like an easy entry into your house." His voice was full of mischief.

"Um. What are you? A burglar? No, you're a senator. How do you explain if you get caught sneaking around the back of my house?"

"Not sure. But it would be fun to try. So what are you wearing?"

"Excuse me?" She giggled. "I'm not sure Megan would approve of me talking about that on her phone."

"There was nothing improper about my question," he replied with a sexy chuckle. "You could be wearing a snowsuit."

"But I'm not." She was coy.

"Then what are you wearing?"

"A tank top and boy shorts."

"Like boxers?"

"Tighter. Like boxer briefs."

"Tighter? Nice." His voice oozed approval. "Hopefully I'll get to see them soon."

"How's that going to happen? Are you going to scale a wall?"

"No, little Miss Smartass." He laughed. "Marco suggested he and Megan go with us for a weekend together at my family's cabin in West Virginia."

"Really? Wow. That sounds fun."

"I think it would be. You'd really like it. It's beautiful out there. Old sleepy mountains."

"It sounds lovely." She grinned at the thought.

"Or, if we can't make our schedules work, he offered to spend the night at the house occasionally."

"Seriously?" Her eyes widened. She never expected they'd spend the night together.

"Yeah. How do you feel about that?"

"It feels a little like we're getting set up for a conjugal visit, but—"

"I know. I'm sorry this is so awkward."

"You didn't let me finish." Her admonishing tone turned into a sweet one. "I was going to say it sounds wonderful."

"Oh, good. I was worried you hated the idea."

"Are you kidding?" She smiled and sighed. "I'd love to spend the night with you, I'd love to wake up beside you, and I'm sure I'd love everything in between."

"I can't wait," he said under his breath.

"Me neither."

"All right, sweetheart, it's late. We should both go to sleep. I'll see you tomorrow and call you tomorrow night."

She grinned at the thought of another phone call. "Great. Night, sweetheart."

§§§§

The next morning the Senate had early votes scheduled on a Defense Department appropriations bill. Pentagon spending always garnered bipartisan support. Standing in the well of the Senate chamber, Stephen talked with senators about various amendments. The lawmakers spoke in hushed tones, cajoling and even trading votes, though none would admit the latter.

Not far away, Senator Helen Sanders chatted with a few of her Republican colleagues, but her focus was exclusively on Stephen. His smile shone brighter than usual; she wondered why he was so chipper. As she admired his handsome profile, she realized how much she missed their times together. *I bet he misses me, too.* She bit her lip, remembering their round on his mother's dining room table.

When Stephen finished his conversation, she sauntered over and motioned for him to listen. He lowered his head without a word, and she said in a husky whisper, "I've been thinking about you. Maybe we should get together again."

"I'm just not going to be with you on that one, Helen." His blank expression told her nothing, and he spoke loud enough for those around them to hear. His response was one that could have been in reference to any of the votes they cast that day. With a polite smile, he pointed toward the door. "I need to get to a meeting."

As he walked away, she laughed to herself. *He's playing hard to get.* She called out across the chamber, "I'm not giving up, Stephen."

Chapter 14

The following Sunday, Anne caught a cab on Eighteenth Street and gave the driver Stephen's address. She held her breath as the driver nodded in recognition of the neighborhood and exhaled in relief when he turned up the volume of the Redskins game. He ignored her until he asked for the fare in Stephen's driveway.

She stopped herself from laughing as she stepped out of the cab. In gardening togs and a big hat, Lillian McEvoy crouched on her hands and knees in a flowerbed.

"Hello, Anne. Isn't it a lovely day? I hope it will be just as nice when these tulips appear next spring."

"Hi. It is nice today. What color are you planting?"

"Oh, lots. These are my favorite." She held up a brown bulb in her grubby glove. "They're black. Patrick always thought they were macabre, but I think they're fascinating."

"I bet they look great against all the other colors." As she finished her sentence, the giant driveway gate automatically closed.

Lillian pointed her trowel at the door. "Please, go on in. Stephen is waiting for you."

"Okay. I'll see you later."

As she pushed open the heavy door, it sprung more easily than expected, and she realized it opened from within.

"Hey, sweetheart." Stephen stood in front of her grinning.

She smiled and gave him a peck. "Hey."

"It's good to see you. Let me take your things."

After he hung her jacket and bag in the closet, he led her into the living room. "My mom promised to stay out of our hair. She says she has two hundred bulbs to plant in the front."

She noticed a few brown specks on his hoodie and picked one off. "Leaves? Have you also been gardening?"

"She had me out back raking leaves."

"You don't have a gardener?" She snickered. "Or peasants or serfs?"

"Very funny." He smirked. "We do have *a* gardener. His name is Hal. I'm pitching in because my mom says the leaves accumulate too quickly, and they'll ruin her flowerbeds." He chuckled and nodded toward the yard. "I've got some big piles out there."

"Do you need to finish?"

"Later." He pulled her closer and leaned down for a kiss. "You're here now."

It was a kiss more appropriate for the bedroom than the living room, and to make up for the location, he picked her up at the hips and placed her atop the back of a sofa. They continued to kiss until he moved his mouth down her neck. Tilting her head, he took his kisses down along the neckline of her tank top. He chuckled into her cleavage. "I'm glad you're as happy to see me as I am you."

"Yes," she said a little breathless. "I'd say so."

Seconds later, the creak of the front door opening stopped everything.

"Stephen? Are you in here?" called Lillian. "I'm just getting some water."

An irritated Stephen shook his head and called out, "We're heading downstairs." He turned to Anne. "Sorry about that. This isn't the most private part of the house. Let's go watch football or something."

As he led her through the maze of rooms in the lower portion of the house, she glanced in the open doors. The downstairs was partially below ground, with a game room and gym. She pointed at a closed door. "What's in there?"

"Wine cellar."

"Naturally," she said as her mouth twitched in a smile.

"I know, I know." He chuckled.

"I'm only teasing you."

"And you're going to pay for it later," he answered as he squeezed her hand.

They reached the so-called theater, which was more of a giant living room; it held a large screen television and a bar with an additional sitting area. Anne sank into the cushy sofa and hummed. "I'm going to have to stop teasing you about your family's money. This is really comfortable."

"Nah. Don't stop giving me shit. We deserve it. My ancestors certainly didn't come by it honorably," he said as he opened a couple of beers.

"Not any less honorably than any other railroad baron family."

"That's not saying much," he mumbled. He nabbed a bag of pretzels and sat beside her. After he handed her a beer, he took a swig of his. "My great-great-grandfather kicked innocent people off the land they'd lived on for hundreds of years."

"And pillaged our natural resources to line his own pockets." She giggled.

"Ill-gotten gains. I admit it."

Her face softened, and she stroked his cheek. "And because you understand it and now you want to help people . . . well . . . that's part of what makes you such a good person."

"I don't know about that . . ." He shrugged.

"I do," she said and gave him a kiss.

He reached over and pulled her in tighter. Closing the distance between them, she grabbed his bulky sweatshirt. The lumpy material between them made her laugh.

"What did you say about my sweater last weekend? I think you said it was offensive because you couldn't see me."

"That's right. So what?" He chuckled. "You think my sweatshirt is offensive?"

"Definitely."

Without further comment, he leaned forward and yanked the hoodie over his head, as only men do. He was left in a white undershirt, which she eyed with approval.

"Better," she said and reached up to kiss him again. Her hands roamed freely across his torso.

As her hands lingered on his lower abdomen, he sucked in a breath. "Anne . . ." His voice was low and full of warning.

"What?" she asked with mock innocence, not waiting or caring for an answer. She was enjoying the moment too much. The room felt tucked away in the house, and the privacy added to her confidence. Since they started talking all the time on their borrowed cell phones, she knew him better, and now there was an opportunity to know him even more. She wanted to explore and enjoy him—and to please him.

When she lifted his shirt and dragged her fingers along the taut muscles of his stomach, he reacted instantly. "What are you doing?"

"Exploring . . . I guess."

She found the tempting stretch of hair from below his belly button and stroked it up and down. "Should I stop?"

"Uh . . ." He stared at her hands which toyed with him. "Fuck, no."

He found her mouth again in a hungry kiss. Simultaneously, he reclined in a silent plea. She tentatively moved her hand lower and found his erection trapped at an awkward angle in his jeans. She unzipped them, freed him from his confines, and lowered her head; it took no time before he was moaning his approval. By the end, he was quiet as he panted, catching his breath.

When he didn't open his eyes for a moment, she chuckled. "I mauled you. Sorry about that."

"Don't be," he said, opening his eyes. He leaned to give her a kiss, which grew from one of appreciation to one of want. He murmured, "Can I take you up to my room? I swear my mom won't go anywhere near it."

"As much as I'd like that, not today—not with her around." She decided while it would be horrible to have a mother walk in while you gave her son head, it would be even worse to have her walk in while you were naked with his head between your thighs.

"I understand. It seems unfair to both of us, though." His voice was husky. "I'd really like to touch you."

He kissed her again, and her hands roamed his bare skin. He groaned and caught her wrists in his. "If things are ending here, you need to stop touching me."

"Oops."

"No, it's not a bad thing." He kissed her forehead. "You're just too tempting."

"I could say the same thing." She smiled. "Maybe we should get some fresh air?"

"If you want to keep your clothes on while my mom is around, that's a good idea," he said with a smile.

They made their way into the backyard again, and as they strolled around the grounds, he told her about growing up in between D.C. and Colorado. After a while, Anne spied a small, weathered gazebo hidden among the brambles in the far corner of the property.

When she asked about it, he smiled. "It's my mother's. My dad built it for her."

"Wow. That's very sweet."

"He was a good carpenter. Let me show it to you."

He led her inside the structure, where she admired the ornate woodwork. "It's really lovely."

"You should see it in the springtime. It's covered in roses."

The setting was so stereotypically romantic, she unwittingly made a snarky comment. "Do you bring all of your lady friends here, Senator McEvoy?"

"No." Glancing around the gazebo, his brow creased like he didn't understand why she asked. "Actually, I've never brought anyone here." He smiled and his voice softened as he declared, "Until now . . . until you."

"Oh." Her breath hitched at the emotion she saw on his face. He looked genuinely troubled by her flippancy. A rush of embarrassment and confusion hit her. She thought of apologizing, but her rational mind overruled her. "But how can that be?"

"What do you mean?"

"Well, you've had girlfriends before—serious ones, I'm sure."

"Yeah, but . . . you're different," he said as he picked a stray leaf out of her mussed ponytail.

"How can I possibly be different? You've had your pick of women. You must have had some interesting girlfriends in the past. They couldn't all be bimbos."

"Bimbos? Are you referring to Jennifer?" He smirked and shook his head.

"Are you sure you want to have this conversation right now? I mean . . . we can. Of course, that means I get to hear about all your boyfriends."

She shrugged and sat on the gazebo's circular bench. "I'm curious."

"Okay." He chuckled and took the seat beside her.

Ghosts of boyfriends and girlfriends past were discussed. Anne revealed her childhood best friend who had become her first longtime boyfriend, only to later turn into a royal asshole. Stephen lumped together a series of girlfriends from high school and college, and she ticked off a list of run-of-the-mill college flings. Finally, Stephen's most serious girlfriend came up.

"We met in law school. Rebecca Pierce. It was serious."

"What's she like?"

"Brilliant. She's a partner at a big firm in New York."

Anne didn't appreciate the sound of that, especially as she guessed Rebecca was probably also gorgeous. She hoped it was a short relationship. "How long were you together?"

"Two and a half years. The serious marriage pressure started right after two years."

"You didn't want to get married?"

"I didn't want to marry *her*. Something was off. She was really upper crust East Coast. She fit into a lot of my life, but there was something which didn't quite match between us. I loved her, but there was no passion."

"And after her?"

"I swore off women after her."

"Huh?"

"Okay. That's not quite right. I swore off relationships. Too much trouble."

Anne nodded silently. If he thought relationships were too much trouble, why in the world was he in one with her?

"So, here we are," she said, breaking the silence. "In a troublesome relationship, but it's even worse. I'm the problem. I'm trouble."

"I don't think the relationship is troublesome at all, but you are trouble. There's no doubt about that," he said with a smile which diminished as he gazed into her eyes. "You're also the prettiest, most interesting woman I know, and you're more than worth the trouble."

"You sure?" she asked hesitantly, hoping to hell he meant it.

"Yes." He leaned in for a kiss and said three words which permanently changed things between them. "Because you're everything."

She intended to give him a quick kiss and say how she felt, but he would have none of it. Instead, he caught her in a full embrace and determined kiss. If he meant for his words and kisses to make her feel special, it worked.

After the kiss, she ran her fingertips along his brow. "I'm here for as long as you'll have me."

"That's going to be a mighty long time," he replied and kissed her again.

After a lovely afternoon together and dinner with Lillian, they stood in the foyer and waited for her cab. Stephen cradled her in his arms as they intermittently talked and kissed.

"I don't want you to leave," he said regretfully.

"I don't want to leave," she answered with a kiss behind his ear.

"We may not see each other—alone—until after Thanksgiving."

"You're going back to Colorado this week, right?"

"Yes, and I've got the state dinner."

"A state dinner is a big deal, though. Not many members of Congress are invited. Is Patty excited?"

"Very. She's been talking up her dress for the last month." He frowned. "I wish you could be my date. You'd look gorgeous. And you could charm Grayson some more and meet his wife."

"Well, I have nothing to wear, so it doesn't matter." She smiled. "In the meantime, we'll talk."

"And plan a trip to the cabin the first weekend I'm back."

She nuzzled into his neck and summed up everything. "Nice."

§§§§

Later that week, at the state dinner's cocktail reception, Stephen accepted a glass of water from a waiter when he noticed Patty. A determined political consultant had her cornered. He'd pursued her the entire year, and while he said he wanted a polling contract with the campaign, it was obvious he really wanted her.

Standing a good eight inches taller than the guy, she looked over him and silently mouthed to Stephen, "Save me!"

Stephen chuckled and shook his head.

"What's so funny?"

He turned to the woman's voice he recognized instantly. "Nothing, really. Good evening, Helen."

"You look dashing in that tux." She lightly touched his dinner jacket sleeve. It was a minor gesture, but considering they were in the middle of the White House and her fiancé was in the room, it was quite forward.

In response, he took a step away. "And you look striking, as always. Where's Smythe? I understand congratulations are in order."

"Yes. Thank you. Matt's over there." She smiled impishly and pointed to Congressman Matt Smythe as he spoke to a lobbyist. "I'm only engaged; I haven't taken any vows yet," she declared in a velvety voice.

"Not yet, but you will."

"Oh, not for a while. In the meantime, you and I are going to be working some late nights in December on the energy bill."

"Yes. It's a busy time of year." He searched for Patty. He was the one who needed saving now, but he couldn't catch her eye.

"Well, I thought we could discuss some of the issues . . . like we used to . . . over your desk." She grinned wickedly. "We both used to get a lot out of those discussions."

Knowing he needed to handle his reply delicately, he smiled as he let her down. "Yes, but I think that time is over."

Taken aback by his answer, her brow furrowed. "Why? I haven't seen you around with Diane anymore." When he didn't reply, she surveyed the room and pointed to Patty. "You're here with your sister."

"I take my family members with me to events all the time." He was annoyed as hell, but he remembered he had to keep things light. Helen was a conniving woman, so he forced a smile. "They make the best dates for functions like this."

"That's probably true," she said as his smile worked wonders on her. "Family members don't require any commitment—that's good when you want some . . . variety in your life."

"Yes, something like that," he muttered, looking away. Variety was the last thing he wanted in his life.

"Well, it's only a matter of time. I won't give up." As she turned to leave, she raised her eyebrows. "And you *know* we always work well together."

He closed his eyes for a moment and exhaled. When he opened them, Senator Grayson York approached him.

"Evening, Stephen."

"Hello, Grayson."

"You don't sound very happy tonight," he said, his hands clasped in front of him on his cane.

"I just had an unpleasant conversation."

Grayson nodded. "So, the chickens are coming home to roost?"

"I suppose. Helen was not one of my wisest choices."

"You don't say?"

The two men laughed at Stephen's questionable judgment.

"How are things for you?" Grayson asked. "We haven't talked anything but work since the fundraiser."

Stephen tilted his head, and when their eyes locked, he knew Grayson was asking about Anne. He scratched his forehead for a few seconds, wondering what to say. "Things are good," he answered with caution. "Great, in fact. This probably isn't the best place to talk, though."

Grayson looked around them. "Why the hell not? There aren't people for twenty feet, and we're in the White House, for God's sake. No bugs here." He shrugged. "But you don't have to talk if you don't want to."

"That's not it at all. I consider you my second father. I have no worries talking with you."

"Well, you're like a son. I want to know what's going on with you." He raised his eyebrows. "I gather you're no longer seeing Diane."

"Over and done with, and we're on good terms. She's dating a federal judge in Massachusetts—a much better fit."

"Yet, Helen persists."

"Unfortunately, she has returned." Stephen was grim.

"She must be looking for one last hurrah before she marries that dolt, Smythe. Don't worry about her. I'm pretty sure she's got a couple of other irons in the fire."

"You think so?" It never entered his mind Helen was seeing other men while they were together.

"Absolutely. I'm good at spotting those sorts of things. Comes with age."

"Who do you think she's with these days?"

"Well, definitely Anderson. I bet there are others."

Stephen mulled over the Republican senator. Anderson was divorced, with a reputation for sleeping around. Stephen also thought he was a royal asshole.

"They deserve each other, but I worry she's still going to be a problem for me."

"Because?"

"Because she pointed out I'm not seeing anyone else." He smiled and raised his eyebrows. "But actually I am."

Grayson nodded his understanding. He returned the smile and tapped his cane once for emphasis. "And I assume you're happy."

"I am." Stephen chuckled. "She's a friend of the family, you know."

"Is she, now? Lillian knows of you two?"

"Yes. My mother likes her a lot."

Grayson scanned the room as he jingled the change in his left pocket. "Really? So you're serious about her."

"Yes."

"Serious enough to damn the consequences?"

"Yes." Stephen sighed, thinking of all the potential repercussions, yet he stood firm in his decision. "I hope my dad would've understood."

"He would've." He patted Stephen on the back. "Well, Laura and I would be delighted to have you two for dinner. This friend of your mother's can also be a friend of ours."

"I don't think you want to be involved in this, Grayson. I appreciate the offer. It's very kind, but you know—"

The warning made Grayson laugh heartily. "You've got to remember, I can do whatever I want, and the people of Georgia will still reelect me. I've been in office since before most of them were born, and Atlantans drive on the Grayson P. York Highway every day. I've brought home so much federal money to our state I could be caught with an intern and I'd still win by twenty points."

Stephen laughed, but he kept thinking of Grayson's generous invitation. The elderly statesman offered a cloak of respectability to his relationship with Anne. "It's incredibly kind of you to invite us."

"Well, I'd like to get to know her, as would Laura. After all, it's not every day I get to spend time with a woman who can hold your eye."

Chapter 15

Thanksgiving week was hard on Stephen and Anne. For Stephen, Thanksgiving Day was his only time off, spent at their traditional family dinner and watching football with Marco. The remainder of the week, he was in full campaign mode, with meetings and events. Throughout the days, his thoughts turned to Anne, and rote campaign events were especially hard.

As he waited his turn to speak at an event for the state firefighters' organization, he tuned out and wondered what it would be like if Anne were at his side. His gut reaction made him smile—everything would be better. They could joke and endure the painfully slow events together, and she'd be supportive in a less-than-welcoming crowd.

Surveying the largely male audience before him, he was sure she could work the room. The firefighters were all chronically disaffected Reagan Democrats-turned-Obama Republicans. Down-to-earth and pretty, Anne also understood how a more conservative mind worked; they would eat her up.

Yet she had another side, and she moved easily in well-heeled circles. Thinking of the fancy fundraiser he attended the previous night, he was sure she'd also have done well there. He sighed to himself. If she weren't so young—if she weren't an intern—she'd be a perfect political partner. He wished she were there with him.

While Stephen was in Colorado, Anne missed him terribly, but she became even more troubled on Thanksgiving when she spoke with her parents. The initial lies she told her family at the start of their relationship seemed innocuous. She told herself they weren't really lies, but rather omissions. Yet, the more time she spent with Stephen, the harder it became to simply leave out important details of her life; omissions turned into white lies followed by outright lies. Thanksgiving Day proved to be the worst conversation of all.

"So, this Keith . . . you're having Thanksgiving together. Are you dating?" her mother, Mary Beth, asked.

"No. He has a girlfriend. We're just friends, and lots of people will be at the dinner." Anne cringed. She worried she sounded defensive.

"Well, are you dating anyone?"

"Sure. Sometimes." Anne closed her eyes. *Lie number one.*

"Well, that's okay to casually date. At this point in your life, you don't want to be tied down with a serious relationship."

"Right," Anne mumbled. *Lie number two.*

"Oh, I wanted to ask if I should buy your plane ticket for Christmas. When do you think you'll be coming in?"

She held the phone away and grimaced, thinking about Lillian McEvoy's offer to fly in their plane home for the holidays. She wanted to go with Stephen, but it meant the lies were stacking up. She punted the decision. "It's okay, Mom. I'll buy my own ticket. I'm not sure when I'm leaving."

"Are you not sure because of school or the internship?"

"Both." If only she could get off the phone and run away from the deception, but it was too soon to end the call. She changed the subject. "So what are you bringing to the Walkers for Thanksgiving?"

As her mother detailed her oyster dressing and cranberry stuffing, Anne closed her eyes in sadness. She hated deceiving her family. Yet how could she ever explain Stephen to them?

§§§§

The following weekend, while Megan kept the car running, Stephen unlocked the gate to the McEvoys' West Virginia property. It was a western cattle gate attached to a traditional barbed-wire fence, encircling blackness. The deep night, dark forest, and heavy snow gave an inaccessible feeling to the location, and the mile-long drive down a bumpy, dirt road clinched its remoteness.

Arriving in separate cars, Marco and Anne pulled up to the cabin behind them. Anne smiled and gave him a sideways glance. "Stephen said the cabin was private and rustic. He didn't mention it was gigantic."

Marco snickered. "The McEvoys have a different notion of size compared to us commoners."

"I'm learning that."

When Anne opened her door, Stephen stood there ready to help her out of the car. "Hey, how was the drive? I missed you."

"Marco's great company, but I missed you, too." She gave him a peck on the cheek. Her lips brushed the snow on his face, and it reminded her of the temperature. "Brr. It's cold out here."

"Go on inside with Megan. Marco and I will get the bags."

Adirondack chairs dotted the house's large wraparound porch. Anne guessed somewhere in the pitch black there was a nice view from those seats. As she followed Megan inside, she looked all around and smiled at the dark wood and homey décor. "It really *is* rustic."

"Of course." Megan chuckled. "We're in the middle of nowhere, West Virginia."

"I like it."

"I'd like it a whole lot more if it were warmer." Megan pointed to a bench. "Let's take off our boots here, and then we can turn on the heat. Don't take off your coat yet."

Stephen and Marco soon came inside, suitcases and bags in tow. Megan took the provisions to the kitchen en route to the thermostat.

"Are you freezing?" Stephen asked Anne as he untied his boots.

"I wouldn't say freezing." She smiled as she stood in her coat with snow crystals melting in her hair. "But I would say it's about forty degrees in here."

"There's only one way to deal with this place when it gets this cold," said Marco, setting his boots off to the side.

"What's that?" asked Anne.

"Get the woodstove going in your bedroom and get under the covers," he answered with a mischievous grin. "Works every time."

Anne chuckled, but looked down as she felt a nervous pang. It would be the first time she and Stephen slept together, in both senses of the term.

Megan sped by them, rubbing her arms in an attempt to create heat. "Food's in the fridge, and the heat's on. Night."

Stephen touched Anne's arm and smiled. "Come on. I'll take you to our room."

"Night, you two," Marco called out. "I'll have coffee ready in the morning, though I can't promise when."

"Thanks. We'll see you tomorrow," Stephen said. He pointed Anne to a short set of stairs off to the right. "We go down here." After eight creaky stairs, he opened a door to a large room and turned on the lights. "This is it."

As he placed the bags on a chair, Anne looked around the room, which could be described as refined country. A hope chest sat at the foot of a giant sleigh bed, which was covered by a floral duvet and a mound of puffy pillows. It looked comfortable, and the extra quilts folded along the bottom only made it more inviting. The old black iron stove sat near a sitting area and french doors to the outside. Another door, slightly ajar, led to the bathroom.

She turned to him and smiled. "It's lovely."

"It's the guest bedroom. I thought it would be more private." Wrapping his arms around her waist, he nuzzled her hair, still damp from the snow. "I hope it's comfortable, too."

"I'm sure it will be." She kissed him; it began as sweet but slowly turned passionate. She was surprised when he pulled away and placed his forehead against hers.

"Can I admit to some performance anxiety?"

"*You?*" She lifted her head to look him in the eye. She thought of the handful of guys she'd been with compared to what had to be a multitude of women for him. "*I'm* the one with performance anxiety."

"You have no reason to be anxious." He shook his head with a shy smile. "But I've got it on two counts."

"Two? How so?"

"First of all, and to be expected, I've wanted to be with you for so long." He stroked her hair. "I'm a little nervous now that the time has arrived."

"I'm familiar with that feeling," she said with a chuckle, but it was a mask. She was deeply touched he'd admit something like that to her.

"Plus, I've got another problem." He smiled and nodded to a spot across the room. "I'm not good at lighting that stove."

"Come on." She pushed his arm.

"I'm serious. I've got two issues. I'm worried at being too slow and too fast."

"So you're worried you'll light the stove too quickly?" She smirked.

"Yeah, right . . ." He rolled his eyes.

"I'm joking." She smiled. Using his coat as leverage, she pulled him closer and stood on her toes to kiss him.

His lips were hungry for hers, and the spark between them flared once again. This time, though, there were no boundaries. She felt free in his arms, and her nervousness soon disappeared, leaving only unmet desire.

He hummed and murmured, "This is too good. Please don't make me light that fire first."

"I won't." She stepped away, and staring him down, she slowly pulled her turtleneck over her head. She tossed it aside and shook her hair out, but when she tried to look him in the eye again, his sights were set a bit lower. His attention was elsewhere. A hungry smile appeared on his face as he stared at her chest.

Her bra did nothing to enhance the size of her breasts, but the thin lacy material showed them off perfectly. She'd chosen it for a reason.

He ran a finger across the edge of the lace. "You're so beautiful, but you've got to be cold," he whispered.

"I'm okay." She reached behind her back, undid her bra, and tossed it aside.

Lowering his head, he fixated on her breasts, and she ran her hands through his hair. Her body was the center of his attention, giving her a rush like no other.

"I need to touch you," he said in a raspy voice.

"I want you to."

§§§§

Sometime long after the sun rose, Anne stepped out of the bathroom into the warm room and saw Stephen with his eyes closed again. She smiled. "I'm glad you're getting some rest, but don't you need to at least check in with someone? What if North Korea bombs us or something?"

He opened one eye and smiled. "Megan will tell me. She and Greg know only to bother me about work if there's a nuclear attack." He patted the pillow next to him. "Come back to bed."

"Okay," she said and sprang to his side in glee.

After making love, talking, and sleeping a little more, his stomach growled. She kissed the spray of black hair on his chest. "You're hungry, babe. You should eat."

"Maybe. What about you?" he asked. He was more focused on playing with her hair as it shone in the sunlight.

"I could eat something. We should take a shower first though. We probably reek of sex."

He raised his eyebrows and gave her chest a combination of sniffs and kisses. "Yes, you do," he said, and kissed her lips. "In the best possible way."

She giggled and touched his face. "Well, you do, too, and you smell of me, I might add."

"And I like it."

With a grin, she kissed him. "I *really* liked it."

"Hmm," he said after the kiss. "Let's get cleaned up, eat, and then come back here. What do you think?"

"Sounds good. Are we going to get grief from Megan and Marco for being antisocial?"

"Doubt it. I bet they haven't spent much time outside their bedroom either. According to Marco, they're working on getting pregnant."

"Really? That's so sweet."

"Yeah, it'll fun to be an uncle, and my mom will be over the moon when she's a grandmother." As he finished his sentence his belly rumbled again.

She rubbed his stomach. "Time to eat. Do you want to take a shower first?"

"I think we should take one together. Maybe we can kill two birds with one stone," he answered, waggling his eyebrows.

"Sounds good, but where *is* the shower? I only saw a big bathtub down here."

"Oh, that's right. Showers are upstairs." He smiled and skimmed his hand over her hip. "Wanna take a bath?"

§§§§

The next day and a half was spent just as that morning, with only a few hours out of their bed. Bodies, hearts, and minds were explored, and as the magical weekend dwindled away, they spoke less and touched more. With only minutes left together, Stephen curled up next to Anne, his cheek against her breast as he looked outside the windows.

"I don't want this to end," he said softly.

She played with the short black spikes of his hair. "I don't either."

"No, I mean I really don't." He maneuvered so he could look her in the eye. "I don't want to go back to the way things were. I want to see you, and I want to talk with you—in person—during the week. I've thought about it a lot. I'm happier with you than when I'm without you."

She could see the intensity in his eyes, and she swallowed hard as her own feelings welled up in her. Too emotionally raw, her response was awkward. "Yeah . . . we do the all-the-time-together thing really well."

"I'd say we do." He reached for her hand and kissed it. "So, let's figure out how we can spend more time together during the week. There has to be a way."

"There are ways, but they pose more risk. You know that." She brought his hand to her lips.

"I'm willing to assume the risk." He smiled and shook his head. "I'm not going back to life without you—that's for sure."

There were many interpretations to what he said, and Anne wasn't sure which one he meant, but every potential meaning made her giddy. It was a feeling of silly, happy love and connection—and something she'd only ever felt with him. She gave him a sweet kiss and declared, "Good. I'm not going back either."

Chapter 16

Later that week, the Yorks invited Stephen, Anne, and Lillian to dinner at their brownstone on East Capitol Street. When it was time for dessert, Grayson announced he needed a "snort" following such a wonderful meal. While the women prepared dessert, he led Stephen to the sitting room where he poured some of his favorite bourbon. Stephen settled on the sofa, avoiding Grayson's large, leather chair, which dominated the room like a throne.

Grayson handed him a snifter. "Cheers," he said, as he eased into his seat.

"Cheers." Stephen took a drink, the sweet alcohol causing him to purse his lips.

He nodded at the dining room, as if Anne remained there. "So . . . what do you think?"

"What do I think? Haven't Laura and I shown you what we think? We think she's charming." Grayson raised his eyebrows. "And astute. That's a good thing."

Stephen hesitated for a moment. "And what do you think my father would say about—"

"Please, Stephen." He reclined in his chair. "Stop worrying. He'd think the same damn thing as the rest of us."

"That's good to hear." Stephen smiled and sighed.

"Want to know what else I think?"

"What?"

"Stick a fork in you. You're done."

"Huh?"

"It's obvious you're completely taken with this young lady. There's not another who'll catch your eye."

Stephen nodded slowly as he considered what he'd said. It was an objective observation by someone he trusted implicitly as a friend and as an advisor. The statement caused the same reaction to the one he'd had when he heard his father died. He needed to question it in order to believe it, even though he knew it to be true. "You think so?" he asked hesitantly. "You think she's the one?"

Grayson frowned in disbelief. "Don't you?"

"Maybe . . . I haven't thought about it like that yet. I only know how she makes me feel." Grayson looked at him like he was crazy, and Stephen felt stupid for being so unaware of himself. He tried to express his heart. "She means so much to me."

"Well, if you don't mind me saying, you need to start thinking about it. You need to decide how you feel about her . . . what you want to do."

"What do you mean?" he asked warily.

"Let's not kid ourselves. This is going to come out, one way or another."

"And?"

"And that Langford character is going to spend millions of dollars trying to define you in the media. You need to know where you stand, what your intentions are. A wishy-washy response isn't acceptable, and if that's what you plan to give, you should stop seeing her right now."

Stephen remained silent. Everything Grayson said was true, yet the calculations were different than a normal political analysis. He was uncertain how to respond as it required answers from his heart.

Tapping his cane on the floor twice, Grayson laughed. "Now, wipe that worried look off your face. This doesn't require much thought, and you're always overthinking things. She's a good woman, good company, and a pretty little thing. Just get on with it."

"You think it's that simple?" Stephen chuckled.

"Most things in life are that simple, son," Grayson answered and took another drink.

§§§§

The next morning, Anne felt a tap on her shoulder as she stood at the copier making extra maps of the Capitol. She turned to see Stephen at her side.

"Come to Megan's office in five minutes." He winked and left.

Timing it just right, she walked to Megan's office. Megan stood in the hall speaking on her phone. After Megan gave her a nod, Anne slid past and closed the door.

A grinning Stephen pulled her into a long embrace. She chuckled afterward. "You brought me in here just for this?"

"Hey, what do you mean 'just for this'? I thought it was a pretty good kiss," he said with a pout.

"It was good." She smoothed his tie and smiled. "This is the thing we try to avoid, though, right?"

"Right, but I'm in a good mood." He grinned.

"Why? You have another long night."

"Not with the forecast. That's why I brought you in here. Lillian McEvoy thinks it would be terrible for her friend, Anne Norwood, to be alone during the coming snowstorm. She's extended an invitation to join her for the duration." He raised his eyebrows suggestively. "What do you think?"

She grinned wickedly at the possibility of spending what could be days with him. "At your house? I like it."

"Good. Come by as soon as you can after work."

"Okay." She cocked her head as she considered what the sleepover would entail. "Not to be presumptuous, but I'm wondering what the sleeping arrangements will be. Will your mother expect us to be in separate beds?"

"God, no. She's not that way at all. We're adults." He laughed and swatted her butt. "I'm looking forward to being an adult with you."

"Are you sure you're an adult?" She smirked and poked him in the arm.

"Such a smartass," he whispered, as he smiled adoringly.

"You're easy to tease."

His response was on the tip of his tongue, yet he caught himself. His gut response was to tell her, "And you're easy to love." The realization that he wanted to use the loaded word *love* made him stop and think.

He stared at the woman he found compelling in every way, and his thought process took the emotion one step further. *I do love her. I do.* He grinned at the realization. The three words almost burst out of his mouth, but he kept them contained. Of all the places he might tell her he loved her, it certainly wouldn't be at his job.

§§§§

Anne's cab driver told her she was his last fare of the night and she was lucky to get the ride. As she looked at the thick, wet snow dumping on the empty streets, she agreed.

Lillian let her in the house, saying, "Aren't you glad you're going home with us next week? They say the airports are going to be shut down for a few days. Your flight would never have left anyway."

"I am glad. Thank you. And if I ever have to explain why I went with you, I can also use the weather as an excuse." She smiled anxiously. "I do wonder why Greg isn't more concerned about me flying with all of you. It still makes me kind of nervous."

Wrapping her arm around her, Lillian led her through the foyer. "Anne, you haven't grasped something yet," she said. Her voice was equally sweet and sinister. "I'm Lillian McEvoy. I can get away with most anything." She grinned and squeezed her. "Isn't that fun?"

"It must be very liberating," Anne replied with an uneasy chuckle. "Aren't you worried about Stephen, though?"

"Certainly, I worry about my son, but I try to be constructive. I think of ways to avoid problems." Lillian nodded. "And in the meantime, I'm glad you're here spending what's going to turn into a long weekend with us."

"Thanks. I'm happy to be here."

§§§§

The next morning, Anne rolled over in bed to find Stephen staring at her from his pillow.

"Morning, sweetheart," he said without raising his head.

"Morning. Why are you smiling?"

"I was thinking about how happy I am having you here all the time."

She snuggled into the curve of his body. "I like it, too."

As Stephen pulled her in for a kiss, she felt his morning erection, and she responded at once. The kiss escalated into lovemaking to start the day. Something was different, though, as if an extra bit of electricity flowed between them.

It wasn't simply that the room was lit from the first sun in a few days. Nor was it the need to be quiet, which made their faces hold the expression of every touch and emotion. Everything physical was emotional, and everything emotional was physical.

Afterward, Anne lay in his arms and stroked his chest, thinking of how safe and comfortable she felt with him. At ease in body, mind, and soul, she sighed in enjoyment. Since the weekend at the cabin, her feelings for Stephen had solidified. She was in love; she was sure of it.

She thought he felt the same way. Of course, she wasn't certain, but she sensed something had changed between them. She kept hoping he'd acknowledge it because she wasn't going to say it first. *No way in hell am I doing that.* It was one thing to tell her high school boyfriend she loved him. They were childhood friends-turned-lovers; everything had flowed easily between them.

With Stephen, though, she was in a predicament. Their relationship was out of balance in age and power, and she needed him to say it first. If she put her heart out there before he did, she put herself at emotional risk.

Gazing at him, she smiled, with the intention of reminding him how good things were. "This is nice."

"Really nice." His lips curled into a small smile, and he touched her cheek. She opened her mouth in anticipation, hoping he might add something. With an adoring gaze, he said, "I love you, Anne."

She gasped and joyfully declared, "I love you."

As his smile grew, she giggled, and he pressed his lips to hers. The kiss was one of a familiar discovery, as if they had happily found something they'd thought lost, but actually was within them all along.

§§§§

The following week, there was another late evening in the Senate. Long hours of energy bill negotiations kept senators working far into the night as they awaited potential votes on the matter. Some senators even slept in their offices rather than heading home.

Senator Helen Sanders thought it the perfect night to reunite with Stephen. When she walked into his office reception area, the place was dead quiet; the average person walking in would scurry right back out. Only those who belonged would cross the threshold. Of course, Senator Helen Sanders wasn't the average person, nor did she pay heed to unspoken boundaries. She strode right to the door of the main office and walked inside.

Marching through the empty office quickly, she passed both his chief of staff and sister without saying hello. When she entered Stephen's office, she expected to see him at his desk, but instead, she found him sitting on the sofa laughing and talking with a young woman. They were so engrossed in one another, neither noticed her.

She sized up the cozy scene at once. The girl sat comfortably, her pumps on the floor and her stocking-clad feet tucked underneath her. It was obvious she was completely at ease sitting alone with Stephen, and his body language was that of a man engrossed in the conversation. He was turned toward the girl, with one ankle resting on his knee in the most casual of positions. His other arm was stretched across the sofa, and he could easily touch the girl's face if he wanted.

Anyone who walked into the room would agree on one thing—the two people sitting on the sofa not only enjoyed each other's company, but were familiar, as well. Whether or not they were romantically involved was open to debate, although a savvy person would assume it. Helen waited a second before speaking, as she considered the situation. *So Stephen likes this young thing.*

"Hey Anne," said a voice from behind Helen. She turned to see Stephen's chief of staff barging into the room. He sounded out of breath. "I just got off the phone with my dad. He says he saw your father today. He said to tell you hi."

"Oh, Senator Sanders," he said in surprise. "I apologize for not seeing you. Good evening."

Stephen sprang from the sofa and didn't even give the girl a backward glance as he lavished attention on Helen. He came to her side and grinned. "Helen, what brings you here so late?"

Helen naturally assumed the girl's look of grave concern was one of rejection. To Helen, it was the look of a woman dropped from a man's radar screen as soon as someone better showed up.

Helen smiled coyly at Stephen. "I'm just here to talk things over. We should return to some ideas we kicked around in the past . . . get things started again."

"Why? I don't think our positions have changed." His smile didn't falter, and his voice became firm.

"Well, let's talk privately. I've got some new thoughts on the matter."

"Hello, Senator Sanders."

Helen turned to Megan and acknowledged her with a nod.

"Stephen, I think there's going to be a vote," Megan announced.

Only a second passed before the blaring ring, which notified senators of a vote, came through the speaker by the senate clock on the office wall.

"Shall we walk together, Helen?" Stephen gestured to the door.

"Certainly."

"I'm going to follow you two, in case there's some press outside the cloakroom," Megan called out.

Helen didn't like the idea, but she didn't object. As they walked to the senate floor, she glanced over her shoulder at Megan. Deciding she was far enough away, Helen turned to Stephen. "So who's the pretty young thing in your office? Greg seems to know her well."

Stephen shrugged. "That's Anne Norwood. Her father is a local D.A. from where Greg grew up. My father knew her dad." His voice hardened. "She's a family friend."

"Well, you two seem to be friendly." She raised her eyebrows. "Is she a *friend* of yours?"

"She's a *friend* of my *mother's*." He rolled his eyes.

Her mouth twitched in thought. *Plausible. He's a man. He's going to flirt with someone like her.* She abruptly switched topics. "Have you thought of my proposal? And don't say you don't know what I'm talking about."

"Helen, I don't see married women . . . ever." Despite the firm letdown, he spoke softly and with a smile.

She wrinkled her nose in dismay. "But I'm not married."

"You're engaged to be married—to a congressman, I might add."

"You're no fun," she answered petulantly. The image of him talking with Anne crept into her mind. She pushed him again. "But what if I wasn't engaged? This wouldn't be because of someone else, would it?"

Megan's voice rose from behind. "Stephen, I just got an e-mail—I need to talk to you now about that *Rocky Mountain News* article."

Stephen turned to his sister. "Walk with us. What's the paper asking about?"

"Humph," Helen huffed. As Megan caught up, Helen muttered, "I'll see you later, Stephen," and walked on.

Chapter 17

A few days later, Anne walked down a hallway of the Hart Building, completely engrossed in a Government Accountability Office report on safe drinking water standards. She didn't look as she turned a corner and ran straight into a hard body. When she looked up to apologize profusely to the stranger, she saw it was Senator Haddow's handsome legislative director. "I'm so sorry! Excuse me."

"No problem." He smiled and extended a hand, while he spoke in a smooth voice. "I'm Stacy Jones. We haven't met, have we?"

As Anne struck up a friendly conversation with Stacy, the vulture eyes of Senator Helen Sanders easily spotted them on the second level. From the floor of the Hart Building atrium, she spied them as she walked with Stephen from the senate chamber.

Helen's conversation with Stephen was frustrating. She'd tried to change the topic from the front page of *The New York Times* to a more prurient one, but he wouldn't budge. She chuckled to herself at an opportunity to taunt him. "Isn't that your little friend up there? Is that her boyfriend?"

Stephen's eyes flew above the massive Calder sculpture in front of them and landed on Stacy and Anne, casually talking and laughing on the second floor. His mouth set into a hard expression. "I have no idea."

Though they continued to walk, Helen noticed that his attention never strayed from the pair. "They make a very striking couple," she slyly remarked.

"Yes, they do."

She nodded at his emotionless reply, which confirmed her suspicions. She was certain something was going on, but she wasn't sure what. Stephen was too smart to be involved with an intern. Yet he glared at the girl, looking as if he wanted to scale the wall.

He turned to Helen with what looked to be a forced smile. "I need to run to a meeting. It's quicker if I take the stairs."

"Of course. We can talk later," she said, suppressing a giggle.

As he sped up the stairs, she preened, proud of her intuition. *So Stephen likes that girl, but he can't do anything about it.* Amused by his predicament, she chuckled to herself; she was confident he'd be back in her bed soon enough.

On the second floor, Anne was telling Stacy she had a boyfriend when Stephen walked up.

"Good morning, Stacy . . . Anne."

"Good morning, Senator McEvoy." Stacy smiled at Anne. "I should be going. Nice meeting you. I hope to see you around."

"Yeah, nice meeting you."

As Stacy left them, Anne looked around furtively. Stephen had created the worst of all situations—they were alone for the entire world to see. She spoke at once in a hushed voice. "I was just going to get a Coke."

"Oh, yes. Go right ahead. And have a good Christmas if I don't see you again." He ended with a wink.

She smiled, shaking her head. "Merry Christmas, *Senator* McEvoy."

§§§§

Later that night, Stephen greeted his mother as she arrived at the house. She said she only popped in to pick up a few Christmas presents, so he left her alone and returned to chip away at his pile of work. Half an hour later, his head was down as he read the day's press clippings when Lillian walked into his office.

He looked up just as she placed on his desk a small piece of antique luggage made of crocodile leather and decorated with brass hardware. He eyed her warily. "What's that?"

"Grandma McEvoy's jewelry case—the one she traveled with. Before she became bedridden, she went through all of her jewelry and put everything she thought worth keeping inside this case."

"So?"

"When she died, she gave the case and its contents to your father."

He shrugged and stated what he thought was obvious. "And now it's yours."

"Ha! You know she always hated me. I'm the last person in this family my mother-in-law would want her jewelry to go to. I've never worn a single piece of it."

"Are there things in there for Patty and Megan? They'd probably want something from it as a Christmas present."

"I'm not sure." A mischievous smile brightened her face. "Have you found Anne a gift yet?"

He smiled and shook his head. "Thanks, Mom, but no. We're not making a big deal of it. We made a pact we wouldn't spend more than ten dollars on our gifts. I'm giving her a photo I took."

"Nothing in this case will cost you anything."

"True." He wanted to give Anne something more—something special—though he doubted the jewelry case held the right gift. "But given Grandma McEvoy's tastes, I can't imagine there's anything in there that's right for Anne."

"Oh, I bet there is. She had a lot of jewelry—including some fine art deco pieces that were very simple, if I remember correctly." Her eyes lit up with excitement. "Let's take a look."

While his mom had piqued his interest about the box's contents, he didn't want to investigate it with her. He downplayed his interest and shut the box. "I will later. I need to get a little more work in."

"Oh, all right." She sighed. "Promise me you'll look through it, though. I'm going home now. Don't stay up too late. You need your sleep."

"Sure. Night, Mom."

As she said good night and left the room, he went back to his reading until he heard the front door shut. He set his papers aside, moved the case closer, and opened it. The top velvety tray was filled with flashy baubles Anne wouldn't like. Hoping his mother was right, he removed it to search for simpler pieces. He looked at the second tray and immediately spied what his mother intended him to find; after all, she never acted without a reason. A small ring box covered in frayed, black silk sat nestled amid pearl brooches and ruby earrings. Knowing what was inside the box, his gut reaction was swift. *No . . . not yet.*

§§§§

In the wee hours of the morning a few days before Christmas, Trey Johnson sat in the only open donut shop off Interstate 70 in Colorado. He didn't have much family, and Langford had invited him to spend the holidays with his, but Trey declined. He wanted a week in Hawaii instead. Eating breakfast before his 5:00 a.m. flight, he picked at an apple fritter and drank mediocre coffee while he read the previous day's paper.

When a black Mercedes pulled up in front of the shop, he was curious, but his eyes widened when Stephen McEvoy's chief of staff, Greg Miller, and a young woman got out of the car together. He'd met the man once at a candidate forum in Denver. He didn't have a clue who the blonde was, and he wondered why she was with Greg, given the hour and location. Trey smiled, deciding he might need to taunt Greg—if just to see how his opposition would react.

When the two walked in, Trey focused on reading his e-mail to give them enough time to get their coffee and food. After they paid and moved to a station of cream and sugar, Trey cleared his throat. "Greg, isn't it?" Trey stood and extended his hand. "I'm Trey Johnson. We met back in the summer. I work for Dan Langford."

"Oh, hi," Greg answered slowly, as if struggling to place him. He placed a plastic lid on his coffee and shook his hand. "Yes, I'm Greg Miller. I work for Senator McEvoy. Good to see you again."

Trey looked at the woman for a moment and smiled at Greg as a hint he hadn't introduced them. Greg immediately said, "Uh, Trey, this is Anne Norwood. Anne, Trey Johnson."

"Hi. It's nice to meet you." Anne smiled as she switched her coffee to her left hand and offered her right for a handshake.

"Nice to meet you." Trey pumped her hand a few seconds longer than necessary, trying to place the girl. He'd never met her before, but her name sounded familiar, and it was somehow connected with McEvoy.

"We should hit the road," Greg said, nodding at the door.

"Yeah, it's late," said Anne, as she readjusted her bag.

"Late for you and early for me." Trey chuckled and stared at them. They didn't seem like a couple—more like coworkers or friends. He wondered if Anne worked for McEvoy. Looking out the window, Trey commented, "Nice ride. Who says government work doesn't pay?"

Greg shrugged. "I promise, it doesn't." His face soured after he spoke.

Greg's response amused Trey, so he needled him again. "Must be nice to have a boss who lends you his car, especially a car like that."

Shaking his head, Greg ignored the dig. "Hope you have a Merry Christmas."

"You, too." Trey chuckled and looked at Anne, hoping to learn more about her. "And Merry Christmas to you. Maybe I'll see you again during the election."

"Maybe," she said. Her lips pursed, and she gave him the briefest of smiles. "Merry Christmas."

"Merry Christmas," Trey said, and returned to his seat.

While Trey began reading again, Anne and Greg left the shop. As the door closed behind them, Anne quietly asked, "Are you worried about him seeing us together? With one of their cars?"

Greg raised his hands up and shrugged like he was estimating their odds. "I don't know. Is it helpful? No. Do we have a reasonable explanation for everything? Yes. But I'll tell Stephen and Patty anyway. Don't worry about it."

"Okay . . ." she replied. Despite his rational explanation, she wasn't convinced, and it wasn't just her female intuition. If she were Trey, she'd be suspicious, too.

§§§§

A week later, high in the Rocky Mountains, Anne snuggled into her nook at Stephen's side. After hours alone together, it was almost a primal intimacy. His scent had become a mixture of hers and his, and she felt safe from the outside world. Light snow drifted past the windows of the tiny cabin, and if the air hadn't been so dry, the single room would've felt like the tropics. As they lay with the covers kicked to the bottom of the bed, she chuckled. "So this is a stove you know how to light."

"Very funny," he smirked and kissed her hair. "I've spent my whole life coming to this place. My dad and I would use it as a base camp."

"Well, it's a nice place to have in the backcountry. I guess I shouldn't ask how long your family has owned this inholding."

"I can tell you it was long before national forests." He ran his fingers down her bare thigh.

"Speaking of your family. We're alone. Aren't we violating the rule that your family be around . . . somewhere?"

"They're around." He chuckled. "Somewhere."

She didn't laugh because she was worried. Instead, she asked hesitantly, "You don't care?"

"No, I do." His brow furrowed. "A lot . . . but it's because I care about you so much."

"What do you mean?" Confused, she wrapped the sheet tighter around her as she sat up to look him in the eye.

He shook his head in dismay. "This isn't coming out right."

"What is it?"

He sighed and smiled. "I love you," he said as he brushed her hair off her face. "I don't want to hurt you, or for you to get hurt by others."

"I don't want that for you either." She smiled at his sweetness. "I love you, too."

He waited a moment, and with his hand on her cheek, he said, "I'd like to meet your family."

"Huh?"

"You heard me. I want to meet your parents and your brother."

"Why?" She was dismayed and couldn't help her immediate reaction. "Are you *insane*?"

"It sounds crazy, but listen," he said as he took her hand. "I want your family to know about us. I want them to understand. That way if things come out, they won't be blindsided. They'll know we're serious, and not . . . well, not whatever the media makes us out to be."

She took her hand away from his and pressed her temples as she debated all the ramifications. "Okay," she said, dragging out the last syllable. "You're right."

Her hands froze as she considered what it would actually be like to tell her family, and words flew out in a state of panic. "You're right, but oh my God, I can't do that!"

"It's okay. It's okay." He placed his hands on her shoulders. "I'll be there, too. It'll be fine."

Silent for a moment, she breathed deeply and placed a hand on her heart as she became resolute. "No. I'll tell them first, by myself. These have been my choices . . . my actions. I owe it to them. You can come over afterward."

"That's fine. I understand."

"What do *you* want to say to them?" she asked warily.

"Well, I suppose I'll start by telling them I'm in love with you."

Anne imagined her family's reactions to those words: her brother's usual sneer when he found something corny, her mother's raised eyebrows when she heard good gossip, and her father's crushing glare when he became angry. She cringed at the thought. "Maybe you shouldn't lead with that."

He rolled his eyes. "Of course, it's not going to be the *first* thing I say."

"Oh, good."

"But I want to tell them something in particular," he said more seriously.

"What's that?"

"Well, I should tell you first." He took her hand in his again and gazed into her eyes. "I love you, and that's not going to change."

"That's nice to hear," she said softly.

He chuckled nervously. "Don't you understand? I don't ever want to be with anyone else."

"You've said that before."

"It's not just that." He grimaced in frustration. "I never want to be *without* you."

His roundabout explanation finally made sense; she knew exactly what he meant. He felt the same sense of forever that she did. Her heart swelled, and she threw her arms around him. "And I don't want to be without you. I love you."

He kissed her briefly before becoming solemn again. "I don't expect an answer or even a response to what I'm about to say. I'm not going to push you."

"Push me? What do you mean?"

He took a deep breath and declared, "I want to marry you, Anne. I want to be your husband and you to be my wife. I want everything that entails—a life together forever."

Her mouth dropped open as if to speak, but his words had taken every one of hers away. Marriage was the farthest thing from her mind.

Though she was quiet, he gently put two fingers to her lips to silence her. "Please," he said and lowered his hand. "I can guess what you're thinking, and it's all very rational. We've only known each other a few months, and we've been together for even less. And you're too young. Our futures are too uncertain—well, at least mine is. Yours is on track. Regardless, neither of us knows what city the other will be living in next December. I understand all the uncertainties, and I don't want to pressure you. So I'm not asking you to marry me."

His last words threw her for another loop, and her brow knitted together in confusion. A devilish grin appeared on his face. "At least, I'm not asking today. One day, I will. I promise."

She smiled and shook her head in a combined feeling of joy and relief. "I love you, but why are you telling me this now?"

He kissed her hand. "I wanted you to know how I feel about you—how important you are to me—because I want to tell your family. It's trite, but I want to let your father know my intentions."

"Are you *sure?*" she joked.

Stephen laughed and pushed her hair behind her ear. "I'm so ready to marry you. If I thought you were ready, I'd ask you right now to elope with me tonight."

It was all too much. Prior to that moment, she wouldn't have believed anyone who told her that at the age of twenty-two she'd be talking with a man about marriage—let alone talking elopement with Stephen McEvoy. Her mouth gaped again, though this time she uttered a playful gasp. "You're crazy."

He smirked and raised an eyebrow. "May I remind you that's what everyone's going to say about *both* of us?"

"We deserve it." She giggled.

"Yes, we do," he said as he pulled her into his arms.

Chapter 18

The next day, Anne stared at the bedroom alarm clock. Two forty—the time of reckoning. She needed to talk to her family before Stephen arrived at three. She looked around her room; with each passing year since she'd left for college, it seemed less like hers.

Though she'd redecorated over time, removing any reminders of high school and adding new things from college, her attachment to the place had waned. It was no longer her home because it wasn't where she really *lived*. That thought made the task ahead of her seem a little easier.

She went downstairs and to the den, where her father and brother were entranced by the University of Colorado football game on the large television. Beside her dad, her mother sat in a matching leather recliner and searched for a new trifle recipe on her laptop.

None of them acknowledged her presence; it was simply expected she'd sit down and laze away the day with them. She took a seat on the other end of the sofa from Mark and waited a moment before taking a deep breath. In a controlled voice, she asked, "Can you turn off the TV? I need to tell you something."

Her brother gave her an annoyed sideways glance. "No way, it's the fourth quarter, and the game is tied."

"You need to turn it off. This is important."

He grumbled, and her mother chided him. "Mark, mute the game."

Elton turned to his daughter, seeming more curious than concerned. "What's so important?"

Her parents stared, their faces full of questions, and Anne realized she was about to tell them the truth for the first time since she'd started seeing Stephen. With a frown, she admitted her failings as a daughter. "I need to apologize. I'm really sorry, but I've been keeping something from you for a while now. I felt I had to do it because I didn't know what I was going to do. I'm so sorry to have lied to you."

At once, Mark's attention turned away from the game and toward her. He gasped in alarm. "Oh my God, you're pregnant."

Anne rolled her eyes. While it was a reasonable guess on his part, she was annoyed he'd thought it. "*No*, of course not."

Her mother placed her hand on her heart and exhaled. "Thank God."

"Well, then, what is it?" Elton's eyes narrowed.

"I need to tell you about someone I'm seeing."

"I knew you were dating that Keith," her mother said with a smile.

Anne looked down, ashamed by her mother's warmth. It was time to lay her cards on the table. While she'd been dishonest with her family, everything else about her relationship with Stephen felt right—like it was supposed to have happened just as it had. She raised her head, and an unconscious smile spread across her face as she spoke. "It's not Keith. It's someone else, and despite all the problems around us being together, I've never been happier."

"So who the hell is he?" her brother asked.

"It's Stephen McEvoy." She said his name with confidence and happiness, and a huge feeling of relief came over her.

The reactions around the room differed. Mary Beth's mouth gaped, Elton's brow slowly morphed into deep furrows, and Mark's lip curled.

He leaned forward and asked, "You're kidding, right?"

"Not kidding." She shook her head, still smiling. "It's been about two months."

Mary Beth stole a brief glance at her husband. Anne knew the action well. It was the parental check-in they always did to confirm they were on the same page about any news or delicate topic. After twenty-seven years of marriage, they could confer simply with their eyes.

Mary Beth announced their joint opinion in the form of a question; she was incredulous and whispered their disappointment. "Oh, Anne, what have you done?"

Elton's concerned expression turned into one of suspicion, and Mark chimed in with his own words. "What in the hell? You're an intern in his office! Are you crazy?"

"I know what you're thinking. I've thought the same things, and I understand your concerns." Anne sat up straighter, showing her resolve. "Believe me; it took a long time before we got together. And I swear my relationship with Stephen isn't like that. We're serious."

"Oh, I'll bet he's serious about you . . . about as serious as he is with any intern."

"It's not like that," she repeated. She stared, hoping her brother would understand. They'd always taken up each other's causes with their parents.

Yet this time she couldn't convince him. He shook his head. "I wish you'd talked to me."

Her mother's expression soon changed from shock to anger. She pointed at Anne and snapped, "We did not raise you to be this kind of person and to be with a man like him. He's your boss, and he has a horrible reputation. It's beyond me how you could do this—"

"Mom, that's not true. You raised me to be independent, to make careful decisions. I've done that—Stephen is different than you think." She evaluated the stunned, angry faces around her and decided to show them just how different he was. "He's coming over at three to meet you."

"He's coming here?" Mary Beth exclaimed. Her eyes flew to the antique clock on the mantle, which kept only semiaccurate time. "In eleven minutes?"

"More like eight," Elton muttered, pointing to the time on the cable box. Anne looked at him and waited for some sort of reaction to the news, but he remained quiet.

"Great. He's coming to visit." Mark huffed. "What the fuck? I can't believe you've done this to yourself; I can't believe you've done it to this family."

Her mother closed her eyes as if trying to find some calm in the storm. When she opened them, she gazed at her daughter and gave her a short, motherly lecture. "Anne, this is not going to end well, especially for you."

"Mom, I know the risks. I went into this with my eyes open. It's not like I got swept off my feet or taken advantage of."

After she spoke, Elton finally reacted with a slow shake of his head, his mouth set in a hard line. "I've been listening, and it's hard to believe any of what you just said."

"What do you mean?" she demanded. A disappointed look from her father usually made her question herself. For the first time in her life, it didn't. She was sure of what she felt for Stephen, and given those feelings, she was confident she'd acted appropriately.

When Elton didn't answer immediately, Mark jumped in. "He means you're being foolish. You're twenty-two, still in college, and you're having an affair with a United States Senator—one you work for and who, not to mention, is a *Democrat*." He practically spat out the last word.

"Since when do you care about politics?" She was annoyed her lifelong comrade had let her down. "And I'm not having an affair. Neither of us is married."

Mark raised an eyebrow. "A minor point."

"No. A major point. It's not sleazy." She pursed her lips and gave one of her best defenses. "His entire family knows we're together, including his mother. She's very supportive."

"Lillian McEvoy knows about you?" her mother asked in alarmed surprise.

Anne realized her mother might be a lost cause for a while, so she turned to her dad, who'd assumed his skeptical expression again. "Dad, please listen. You think I've been dumb and I was taken advantage of, but it's not true. Doesn't the fact that his mother supports us—and he's coming to meet you—say something about our relationship . . . about him?"

"Frankly, it could say a lot of things, both positive and negative," her father replied in a stern voice.

The chime of the doorbell rang through the house. Anne looked at her watch. *Thank God, he's early. He must have guessed this wasn't going to go well.* She announced with a forced smile. "That's him."

"So soon?" Mark glowered before turning his attention to the football game. She looked at her parents. Her mother muttered to herself as she put away her laptop, while her father moved his recliner upright and took a drink of his cold coffee. Neither of them spoke, so she left the room.

When she opened the door, Stephen stood on the edge of the porch and kicked snow off his boots. In jeans and a ski jacket, he looked decidedly un-senatorial. Seeing him as she loved him most, she smiled. "Hey. Come on in."

"Hi," he said as he looked up from his boots. He entered the house and gave her a quick kiss. "How's it going?"

"Okay." A twitch of her mouth revealed the truth.

"That well?" He grinned and whispered, "Don't worry. I'll handle it."

When they entered the living room, Elton stood at once. Anne knew the action was ingrained in him from his military days—he always saluted the rank, even if he didn't respect the man. Her mother and brother also rose, and Elton was the first to speak. He extended his hand to Stephen without a smile or formal greeting. "Senator McEvoy."

"It's nice to meet you, Mr. Norwood." Stephen shook his hand. "Please, call me Stephen."

Elton only nodded in response and turned to his wife. "This is my wife, Mary Beth."

"Good afternoon, Mrs. Norwood." Stephen smiled, eagerly shaking her hand.

His charm appeared to work. She smiled as her eyes darted between Anne and him. "Thank you for stopping by."

Stephen reached out for Mark's hand. "You must be Mark. Anne talks about you a lot."

"Yeah. I bet." He smirked as he gave Stephen a halfhearted handshake.

Once everyone was comfortably seated, Elton stared at Stephen. "So what's going on here?" The phrase was casual, but the delivery was one from a career prosecutor—cold and direct.

Anne watched as Stephen's body language changed. As if he was having a heart-to-heart with disgruntled constituents, he casually leaned forward with his elbows on his knees and hands clasped. He was confident and engaged in his response.

"Mr. Norwood, I suppose Anne has told you the basics, and I can understand why you'd be unhappy with our relationship. No parent would wish for this. And I know we've put you in a hard spot, politically. I'm sorry. I also wish I had met Anne under different circumstances. But despite the problematic situation we're in, I don't regret anything that's happened between us."

"Humph." Mark shook his head, as if he was listening to sheer stupidity. "The regret comes later, in case you didn't know."

Stephen was undeterred; he sat upright and smiled at Anne as he took her hand. Meeting Elton's stubborn glare, he spoke determinedly. "I don't regret anything because I love her. And if she agrees, one day I hope to make her my wife. I understand I'll have to earn your blessing."

"You two want to get married?" Mary Beth screeched.

"Someday," Anne replied in short, not wanting to dwell on the marriage issue.

"Oh my God," Mark mumbled, as he rubbed his eyes.

"Will you knock it off? I don't want to hear it from you," Anne snapped. "You're twenty-five years old, and the most serious relationship you've ever had was a summer fling in high school with Tammy Brewer, and all you did was sneak off to the barn every day."

Anne's jab at Mark had a collateral effect besides shutting him up—Mary Beth had someone new to be angry with. She scowled at Mark, obviously furious her son had messed around with the pastor's daughter in their barn.

Elton quieted the room as he asked a critical question for everyone involved. "Who knows about you two?"

"My immediate family—my mother, sisters, and my brother-in-law. They're very supportive of Anne and me, especially my mother. Anne's become a friend of the family, and most of the time we spend together my family is around."

Anne examined her parents' reactions. Her mother nodded, as if she found some comfort in the respectability his family's presence brought to their relationship. Her father's expression remained impassive.

"Greg knows, too," Stephen said with a nod.

"So that's why he dropped you off," her mother said. "I wondered why."

"Greg's been very helpful. My mother thought it would be wise to tell him." Stephen eased into the sofa and squeezed Anne's hand. "Also, my family's closest friend—who is like a father to me. He knows of us."

"Who's that?" asked Elton, as he tapped the arm of his recliner.

"Senator Grayson York . . . and his wife, Laura. A few weeks ago, they hosted my mother, Anne and me for dinner. Grayson was my father's best friend. He's my sister's godfather and my closest colleague in the senate. He would never hurt us."

"I've always liked him," Mary Beth admitted with a small smile. She glanced at Elton and shrugged. "He's funny . . . and a moderate."

"Yes, Grayson is a wonderful person. He likes Anne a lot." Stephen looked at Elton and said in a more sober voice, "Our family attorney is also aware of the situation."

Elton's expression instantly changed. His eyes skewered Stephen, and

Stephen answered his glare at once. "I think you'd understand it was wise to inform him. You shouldn't take it as a sign of anything else. In order to protect everyone involved, including Anne, it's better he not be caught flat-footed."

Elton took a deep breath. "At least you understand this is bound to come out. Politicians in your situation usually have so much hubris they delude themselves into thinking nothing will happen."

"Dad, haven't you been listening?" Anne said, irritated by her father's attitude. "This isn't like that."

Stephen gave Anne a brief look, as if to warn her against fighting with her family. He turned to Elton. "Obviously, it's better for everyone involved, including you and your family, if our relationship is kept quiet until after my reelection. That's the desired outcome, but we're taking precautions in case something does become public."

Quiet for a moment, Elton crossed his arms over his chest and reclined in his chair. "So your story is Anne became a friend of yours and your family. You two became involved, but you kept things private for obvious reasons."

"It's not a story," Anne muttered. "Those are facts."

"They *are* facts," Stephen agreed. "And because it's my personal life, I haven't commented on it."

"We both know the personal is political here. You'll have to comment." Elton's tone changed from conversation to interrogation. "What will you do when it comes out?"

Without flinching, Stephen met Elton's stare and spoke politician to politician. "I'll address it publicly with my family and—hopefully—Anne at my side, though that's her choice. I'm also certain Grayson would make a statement of support to corroborate the truth of things."

Anne imagined the scene, which in the past she'd envisioned with dread. Despite the terror of it, she knew she'd want to be there with him. She nodded. "I'd be there."

"And you'll be the butt of a million jokes," Mark said, this time with concern rather than sarcasm. "Your career will be over. Think about it."

"I told you I'm willing to take the risk." She shook her head. "The negative publicity won't last forever. It never does."

While he was the least political person in the family, Mark was the first to address what had been left unsaid. His voice saddened in disappointment with his sister. "And it could hurt Dad."

"Dad, you know I'm sorry, don't you?" asked Anne with some sadness.

Elton glanced at his wife and was silent for a moment. He sighed, in deep thought. "Politically, this is more of an annoyance than any harm to my career. I've been around too long. That said, it's going to be a problem for some of my relationships within the party." He looked at the heavens as he thought of how it might play out. "I'm going to hear about it."

"What will you say? What will you do?" asked Anne, scared to hear the answer.

"I'll say I love and support my daughter, but she's an adult who makes her own decisions. This was a decision I don't agree with." He looked at his wife to confirm his statement. "That will be the only thing said publicly by the family."

"I understand, and I appreciate it," Stephen said with sincerity. "Given the situation, I wouldn't expect any more from you."

"And none of you will tell anyone, regardless of what happens, right?" Anne looked at each member of her family to confirm their answers.

"That's right," Mary Beth said with a grim smile. "It's best for everyone involved."

As Mary Beth finished speaking, the phone at Mark's side rang. He picked it up and curtly answered, "Norwood residence." Seconds later, he sputtered in surprise, "Oh. Hello . . . Mrs. McEvoy. No, this isn't Elton. I'm Mark Norwood, Anne's brother."

Elton and Mary Beth looked at one another in astonishment. Anne smiled at Stephen and whispered close to his ear. "Did you know she'd call?"

"Not at all. I only told her this morning I'd be here today." He smiled. "She's much smarter than I am."

Another moment passed and Mark said into the phone, "It would be nice to meet you, also." He glanced up at Mary Beth and pointed to the receiver. "Let me get my mother for you."

Mary Beth took the call and answered in a chipper voice, while still acknowledging the social stature of the woman on the other line. "Hello, Mrs. McEvoy. Thank you so much for calling. I truly appreciate it." She listened for a moment and said, "Well, thank you, Lillian. You're really very kind to call." As the two women spoke, Mary Beth left in search of a private room.

Elton's expression and demeanor finally changed. The concern and anger vanished for a moment as he chuckled at his wife talking with Lillian McEvoy. He smiled at his daughter. "Oh, Anne . . ."

§§§§

It was midmorning the following day when Anne joined the extended McEvoy family at their mansion off Cheeseman Park in Denver. The visit was initially social, but when Greg arrived it turned into a campaign meeting.

The entire family sat around the giant dining room table. Lillian had made tea and coffee for everyone, with shortbread cookies to tide them over until lunch. She called the meeting to order. "Well, the news is out now. Dan Langford has raised over a million dollars in the last quarter. That's a significant amount of money for someone like him. Before things get hairy, I want a family consensus on financing the campaign with family money. Personally, I'd rather not, but I suggest we do if it becomes necessary. Patty agrees."

Patty was firm. "I think it's best, though we need to handle it carefully."

"We don't want to appear to be 'buying' a Senate seat to keep it in the McEvoy name," remarked Megan. "Langford would have a field day with that in the media."

"And I don't want it to appear that we don't have supporters for the campaign, because we do. At the moment, fundraising isn't an issue," said Stephen.

"But these days people expect wealthy candidates to contribute to their own campaign," Anne said with a shrug. She didn't understand why they were worried about appearances. Everyone knew the McEvoys were rich.

"It's the amount that's the issue . . . and timing." Greg shook his head. "I would wait until the last possible minute and contribute the minimum amount."

Patty concluded the discussion. "Mom, I think we're all in agreement."

"If it's settled, then let's talk about how we message this—" Megan's ringing phone stopped her train of thought, and after she read the caller's name, she frowned. "*Washington Post.* I need to take it. I'll be right back. They're probably already looking for a quote on Dan's numbers."

Megan was out of the room for only a few minutes. When she returned, her face was grim. "Walter Smith has set up an independent expenditure campaign to defeat Stephen. What do you want to say?"

Stephen collected his thoughts. Walter Smith was public enemy number one for Democrats. Any comment from Stephen about Walter needed to be pitch perfect.

Patty jumped in. "No. I'm the campaign manager. This is entirely political. I'm the appropriate messenger here, not Stephen."

Stephen nodded. "She's right." He chuckled in admiration of his fearless sister as she scribbled on a notepad. "Let's see what Patty has to say."

Handing a piece of paper to Megan, Patty said, "Here. Read it to him."

Megan took the call off hold and said, "Stu. Hi. This is from Patty McEvoy, Senator McEvoy's campaign manager."

She paused a moment before relaying Patty's statement. "Quote: 'Bring it on. The McEvoy family has never been afraid of a fight.' End quote." Waiting a few seconds, she asked, "You got that?"

§§§§

Late in January, Stephen turned off the flashlight to darken the tent as Anne laughed inside their joined sleeping bags. She stripped down to her underwear and stowed her clothes at the bottom of the bag to keep them warm during the cold West Virginia night.

"Okay," she said, snuggling down into the bag. "You promised to keep me warm if I went on this ridiculous expedition with you. We could be comfortably in your bed back at the cabin."

"Just give me a second, and I'll warm you up. I want to get out of my clothes, too."

The pitch black rendered Anne blind, but she heard him lower the zipper so he could join her. As he stashed his clothes at the bag's foot, she reached out and touched his long underwear.

"One good thing about the middle of nowhere is we don't have to worry about being too loud." She giggled.

"If you keep teasing me, I promise I'll be very, very loud." He kissed his way behind her ear, leaving a trail of tickles she felt everywhere.

"Really?" She smiled into the darkness and slipped her hand into his fly.

§§§§

The next morning at dawn, Worthington Clements and his dog were out for their morning constitutional, snowshoeing around his property. The snow did little to muffle the sounds of enthusiastic sex coming from the red tent a hundred yards away. Initially, the elderly gentleman rolled his eyes in disgust, but he caught himself quickly. He thought of his younger days and smiled. "Aw, hell. You're just jealous," he mumbled aloud.

When he came closer, his booming accent, born of the hollows of West Virginia, overrode the laughter coming from the tent. "I can hear you're enjoying yourselves in there, but I'd like to inform you that unless your name is Clements or McEvoy, you're trespassing. Now, I know it's not Clements because I have no living relatives and no heirs. And I seriously doubt you're a McEvoy."

Inside the tent, Anne's wide eyes stared in shock at Stephen, who lay on top of her. Not two minutes before, he had yelled her name in orgasm. Closing his eyes, Stephen smiled. When he opened them, his voice was loud. "Actually, Judge Clements, it is a McEvoy."

"Judge? A local judge?" she whispered in panic.

"Federal," he murmured.

She closed her eyes and threw an arm over her face.

"Stevie? Is that you? What are you doing out here?" the judge asked.

Stephen donned his shirt, propped himself on his elbows, and zipped open the door of the tent enough so he could peer outside. Judge Clements, a dear family friend, poked his head into the tent's rain-fly; the man's blatant curiosity brought a smile to Stephen's face.

"Morning, Judge. I'm sorry. I must've crossed over onto your property."

Judge Clements laughed. "Well, it's good to see you, son. Are you here alone?"

Stephen caught the hint. The judge knew full well he wasn't alone, but as a southern gentleman, he asked for the lady's benefit. Stephen grinned.

"No. I have a friend with me." He turned to Anne, who'd raised her arm only enough to glower in complete disbelief. "Anne, I'd like to introduce you to Judge Worthington Clements."

Glaring at him, she grabbed her own shirt. Once clothed, she rested on her elbows as Stephen further unzipped the tent. "Judge Clements, please meet Anne Norwood. She's a very good friend of mine and my family."

"It's a pleasure to meet you, Ms. Norwood." The judge grinned as she shyly peeked out and waved.

"Good morning, Judge Clements." The judge's dog pushed his nose in between his owner's legs and Anne smiled. "I see you're not alone either. Your dog is pretty."

"This is Buster. He's a mutt just like me." He played with the dog's ears. "Why don't you two strike your camp and head over to the house? I'll make you breakfast."

"Oh, Judge, that's very kind," said Stephen with a glance at Anne. "But —"

"Please," the judge pressed. "Breakfast is the one thing I know how to cook well."

Well-mannered Anne nodded to Stephen, and he smiled. "Then we'd be honored, Judge. We'll be there in about twenty minutes or so."

When the judge went on his way, Stephen zipped the tent door. He turned back to Anne, though she wasn't to be seen. Her body was hidden in the bag as her voice filled the tent. "I. Am. Mortified."

After they arrived at the judge's cozy lodge, Anne straightaway took him up on the offer of his guest bed and bath. Given her nervousness, Stephen guessed she was as interested in the opportunity to escape from further embarrassment as she was in the hot shower.

While he assembled the makings of steak and eggs, the judge struck up a conversation. "So, Stevie, I haven't seen you up here for a while now. Is the busy life of a senator keeping you away?"

Stephen leaned back in his chair at the kitchen table. "In part."

Judge Clements nodded silently as he seasoned the steaks. "And Anne? Who is she?" he asked, his attention remaining focused on the food.

"She's special." Stephen smiled, but his tone had a serious edge.

The judge met Stephen's eyes and returned the smile. "Well, that's obvious."

Worried Judge Clements was jumping to all the wrong conclusions about Anne, Stephen rallied behind her. "No, it's not what you're thinking, Judge. Anne is different. She—"

"Of course, she's different, Stevie. All evidence points to that." He threw two steaks in a cast-iron skillet and turned to Stephen. "I've never seen you hike out here with anyone besides your father—let alone go camping with a woman. I'm a confirmed bachelor with eighty-six years to prove it. I was pretty certain you'd be a lifelong bachelor as well. I know if you're bringing a woman into a part of your life which has always been solitary, she's very special to you."

"You're right." He smiled.

"She's lovely, and she's got to be smart to hold your interest." The judge turned his attention again to the steaks. "She's a little young, though.

Correct?"

"Correct." Stephen took a drink of strong coffee before he elaborated. "And I should tell you, our relationship isn't public."

"Why not?"

"Because she's an intern in my office at the moment." He said it matter-of-factly and trusted the judge to keep quiet until he told him otherwise.

Judge Clements raised his eyebrows to the point of crinkling every bit of wrinkled skin on his forehead. "But you said she's a friend of the family. I'm guessing Lillian knows? What does she think of all this?"

"I'd say she's cautiously accepting—more so every day." Stephen nodded. "It hasn't been long, but Anne has become part of our family."

Without skipping a beat, the judge smiled again. "Well, if that's so, I also approve."

Pleased with the warm acceptance in the judge's voice, Stephen quieted for a moment while his mind sped ahead. "I'm glad to hear it. In fact, I wonder if you'd be willing to do a favor for me one day."

Chapter 19

The energy debate raged on in the Senate through February, which forced Stephen once again to keep long hours, and after the previous close call with Helen, Anne rarely stayed late at work. The office was particularly quiet at night since Megan cut back her hours. Her pregnancy had brought joy to the whole family as well as exhaustion and morning sickness for her.

One evening, Greg watched as Helen again strode through the office as if it were her own; he was alone as he chased after her. "Senator Sanders! Senator, can I help you?"

She made it to Stephen's office door, turned, and smiled. "No. I need to talk to Stephen."

"But—"

"I'm sorry. It's an urgent Intelligence Committee matter; it's classified. You understand." She slipped into the office and shut the door in Greg's face.

When he saw Helen open the door, Stephen quickly told Anne he'd call her back. He put on his suit coat as if it were a flak jacket and mentally prepared himself for whatever Helen might be up to. "Good evening, Helen. I'm in a hurry. I was just about to get a Coke with Greg. Do you want to join us?"

"Not really." She smiled as she slowly took off her own suit jacket and threw it on a chair.

"I'm very sorry," he said with a smile, hoping to charm his way out of the situation. "I don't have time. I need to return a call." He pointed to his phone on the desk.

"Oh, you have time." She unbuttoned her blouse.

"I really don't." He soon realized what she was doing and panicked at the thought of being alone with her. "Helen, stop. You shouldn't do this."

"Maybe I shouldn't, but you know you want it." She let the blouse drop off her shoulders, exposing a black lace bra which barely covered her nipples.

Stupefied into silence, his mind reeled at the scene playing out before him; it was one he had seen before—but not recently. More than once in the past, Helen had pranced into his office and shed all her clothes, while he'd drawn the curtains and unbuckled his belt for their usual office quickie. This time, he closed his eyes and exhaled his words in a punctuated cadence. "Helen, please put your clothes on. This isn't happening."

"Why not?"

He opened his eyes to see Helen standing with one hand on her hip and the other dangling her bra as if she were in a burlesque show. Objectively, she was a titillating sight. She was a beautiful woman wearing a form-fitting—if conservative—skirt with sheer stockings and high heels, and she was naked from the waist up. Only months earlier, Stephen would have eagerly explored her body, bringing them both pleasure. That night, though, he found nothing appealing about her. He only wanted her to leave.

Yet Stephen knew better. She was a dangerous woman who'd made herself vulnerable before him. While he'd like nothing better than to toss her out on her ear, he had to walk a delicate line. What he'd initially said wasn't helpful to his cause. He needed to backtrack and let her down gently —and believably, as if he were the Stephen of old.

"Baby, you know I want it, but I can't," he said in a smooth voice. "You're so fucking hot. But you're engaged, and I'm up this year. I can't have any scandal and neither can you."

"Oh, no one will ever know." She tossed her bra over the chair where her blouse and jacket rested, and came closer. "It's just like old times."

As she neared him, Stephen backed up and to the side. He decided he had no choice but to be firm. "It's not like old times, Helen. Things have changed. I asked you to put your clothes on."

Her demeanor stiffened immediately, and she took a step back. Arching an eyebrow, she put a hand to her hip. "Exactly how have things changed, Stephen?"

"There's too much at stake for both of us. It's more than just my election. You're engaged. You're exposed now, too. "

"But this is private." She gave him a brief smile and reminded him of their common predicament. "And more to the point, we've always had mutually assured destruction. Both of us lose if this gets out, so neither one of us will let it happen."

"Come on. That doesn't mean others aren't ready to pounce on anything they can get on me, even if you're collateral damage in the process."

"You're talking about Walter, aren't you?" She shook her head. "He wouldn't jeopardize my seat just to get Dan Langford elected. Besides, he's a friend of mine."

Stephen frowned at how she'd called Walter a "friend"; it sounded like they'd been more than friends. He covered up his concern with a quick retort. "That may be the case, but anyone could hurt us—not just Walter. I'm not going to risk it . . . for both of our sakes."

"Humph." Her eyes narrowed, and her voice became accusatory. "You say you're worried about things between us getting out, but I think there's something more. You're seeing someone else. I can tell. And that's the reason you won't touch me."

"Of course, I'm seeing someone else. I always am." His mouth twitched as he said it, betraying his assertion that nothing had changed for him. He worried he'd given something away, so he waved his hand in nonchalance. "So what?"

"No. This is different. If you were only screwing someone else, you'd at least touch me. I'm standing in front of you half naked, and you've done everything to keep looking me in the eye instead of my breasts. I know you —that's not normal."

"I told you—"

"I'm not buying it." She crossed her arms so her breasts rested on them. "Who are you seeing?"

"We've never asked that of one another. Why start now?" He felt like he was losing control of the conversation.

"Because I want to know about this woman," she said with determination. "You're acting differently. She must be special."

"I don't know . . ." He shrugged.

"Then why won't you tell me who she is?"

He grasped for a reason. "Maybe you could say I don't want to jinx it."

She gave him a cold stare. After a moment, she sneered and huffed. "Fine."

The look in Helen's eye left him unsettled. He couldn't trust her at all anymore, and he needed to salvage the situation. "Baby, I'm sorry," he said as he stroked her naked forearms while avoiding her breasts. "We had a good thing. Let's not wreck it right now." For good measure, he stepped back and gazed at her. Despite her singular self-confidence, she had always responded to a well-timed appeal to her vanity. "And you're still gorgeous."

She smiled and sighed as she reached to the chair for her bra. "Oh, all right. I'll leave you alone. For now . . ." Placing the bra over her breasts, she turned around. "Can you help me with the hooks?"

Facing her back, Stephen rolled his eyes undetected. "Sure," he crooned. Once her bra was hooked, he patted the closure, hoping to put the matter to rest for good.

"So you're really worried about keeping your seat?" she asked as she found her blouse.

"Of course. You've seen the polls. I was ahead but now we're dead even. Add that to the fact that it's a bad year for my party, and it doesn't look good." Lines of worry creased his brow.

"Well, if they ask . . . and they probably will, I won't go to Colorado and campaign for Langford. I'll sit this one out. It'll piss off the party, but I'll make an excuse."

"I appreciate that, Helen. I'd do the same for you." Stephen wasn't lying, but after he said it, he wondered if she was being truthful.

She tugged the ends of her jacket straight and stepped closer. With greed in her eyes, she placed her index finger on the center of his tie and grinned. "I know you would. And I expect *this*," she said, waving her finger between the two of them, "to resume the day after the election. Think about it."

She abruptly turned and strutted away without looking back. "I'm very curious about this woman. You know I'll find out who she is." As she placed her hand on the doorknob, she turned and smiled. "And she can't be as good as me."

"Well, you're right about that," he replied with a nervous snicker. As she closed the door behind her, he muttered, "She's better."

His feigned good humor instantly vanished as he sank into the nearest chair he could find. Pinching the bridge of his nose, he grappled the impending disaster. He stewed on the matter only a few seconds before yelling, "Fuck!"

Straightaway he furiously pressed numbers on his phone. He skipped all pleasantries when Patty greeted him on the other line. "I need to talk now."

"I'm getting ready for bed. Whatever it is can wait until the morning. I'll see you in the office early, if you want."

"No. It can't wait"

"Why not?"

He relayed a twenty-second, yet still graphic, synopsis of his encounter with Helen.

After hearing the words "Helen" and "tits," Patty responded, "Eww. Gross."

"Can we skip the commentary?"

"Hardly! Wait 'til everybody else hears. So, did you and she—"

"No! Of course not. I can't believe you'd even ask me. I'd never do that to Anne, nor do I have any desire to."

"Cut to the chase, then. Besides having to stare at her boobs, what happened?"

He relayed the entire tawdry tale, focusing on the fact Helen was determined to discover Anne.

As soon as he finished, Patty announced, "I'm calling Phillip. I want a private investigator put on her tomorrow."

"You want a P.I.? What? No. There's no reason for anything like that."

"Like hell I'm not. We can't be caught unprepared. Somehow, someway, she's going to put two and two together about you and Anne, and she'll leak it. I want some ammunition to keep her quiet. She's such a slut. I'm sure there's some nice dirt we can use against her. Let's keep up this game of— what do you two call it? Mutually assured destruction?"

"Well, I know one of the men she's been with lately," he said as he tugged at his tie in frustration. "It's Senator Anderson. I don't like him, but I'm not sure if even he deserves to be caught up in a mess with her."

"Anderson? Whatever. I couldn't care less about him. This is great because two Republican seats could be in trouble if this got out."

"Wait. This isn't the way *we* treat innocent people. I can't believe you. We're not like that. Dad would never have approved of this."

"Are you nuts?" Patty exclaimed. "You've got to be fucking kidding me. Dad would have stopped at nothing to protect us. Helen is out to get you. Do you think that for one second Helen would do anything differently if she was in your situation? Do you think the Republican Party would act any differently? Don't be naïve."

A few moments passed before Stephen responded, his voice full of regret. "Talk to Grayson. He probably knows something."

"Thank you," she said, her voice filled with self-satisfaction. She waited a moment and ventured, "So, are you going to tell Anne?"

"Of course," he grumbled as dread overcame him.

Chapter 20

The following night, Stephen was so grumpy Anne could tell something was wrong. His cranky behavior was like none she'd seen, and when he brought her into the library to be alone, she was worried.

"Anne, I have to tell you about a predicament we're in," he said as he reached for her hand.

"What's that?"

"I just want you to know it's entirely my fault due to my past mistakes."

"Okay . . ."

Stephen's expression was full of regret. "They're mistakes that are now haunting me. I'm sorry, but someone is suspicious about me—and about whom I'm seeing. This someone is very tenacious. We could be exposed."

Terrified of what might come next, she swallowed hard.

When she gave him an anxious glance, he pulled her into his arms and kissed her hair in reassurance. "But I need you to know it doesn't matter. I don't want anything to change between us. I love you. I want to spend the rest of my life with you. That's all that matters."

Nestling into her favorite crook between his arm and chest, she was still despondent. "I don't want to change anything either, but what's going on? Who is this 'someone?' What's happened?"

"It's Senator Sanders. Before you came along, Helen and I were together for a while and . . ."

She stared off as she listened to Stephen recount his history with Helen. Of course she knew Stephen had been with many women before her, and she hated it when the subject came up. Having to hear in depth about his time with Helen was particularly difficult. She listened, though, resigned to the facts as he laid them out.

It was only when Stephen told her about the prior evening that she ripped herself away and exclaimed, "She did what? And in your office? Who would do that?"

"She would." He winced. "It wasn't uncommon for us to . . . uh . . . meet in my office."

"Oh." The thought made her stomach turn. Anxious about what was coming next, she pursed her lips. "Okay. Move on. She's standing half-naked in front of you. And . . ." Before she finished sentence, her heart started beating double time; her speech became wobbly. "And what did you do? Did you . . . touch her?"

"No." He closed his eyes and shook his head. "I realize that I deserve to be asked that, but the answer is no. I mean it every time I say I don't want to be with anyone else."

"That's good to hear." It was an understatement. She was ecstatic to hear him say it again, and she gave him a kiss which reassured them both.

He smiled afterward and shrugged. "Let me tell you the rest."

As he gave her a blow-by-blow account of the remainder of his encounter with Helen, Anne cringed. She was angry and sad and without any means to respond. She wanted to claw Helen's eyes out and expose her to the world for what she truly was, yet even the simplest rebuke like a slap or a snide remark was out of the question. Anne was powerless as a senator pursued her boyfriend. It was a crushing feeling. And after hearing the whole story, she came to the same conclusion as Patty—they needed to protect themselves from Helen.

At the end of their discussion, he faced her and said emphatically, "I have to say it again—I'm sorry. I love you. I want you to be happy."

More than anything, Anne wanted Stephen to be happy as well. After such a difficult conversation, she needed to comfort him. "I'm okay," she said, even though she really wasn't. She wrinkled her nose with a grimace. "Though, I don't like that she stripped in front of you."

"Don't worry." He kissed her forehead. "I didn't like it either."

"Good."

He winked. "On the other hand, if you want to show up in my office one day and strip for me, that would be a total turn-on."

"Humph." She smirked and reached up for a kiss. "We'll see."

§§§§

Later, in the middle of the night, Anne woke in a panic. She sat up and looked around Stephen's dark room, trying to get her bearings.

Because he was a light sleeper, her stirring woke him. "What? What is it?"

Emotions she'd stuffed away earlier in the evening came bubbling through. She blurted out, "I'm ending my internship. Right now."

Stephen groaned into his pillow. "We've been through this. It doesn't help. We got together while you worked in my office. Who cares if it was one week or three months?"

She shook her head. "I don't care. And we should stop seeing each other . . . until the election is over."

Not speaking, he sat up and pulled her tightly to his chest. "That I will not let happen."

Adrenaline coursed through her. Anne wasn't ready for the conversation, but she knew they had to have it. She leaned into the warmth of his arms. "No, I think it's the only way. So far, we've managed to keep everything quiet. No one knows, and if anyone suspects, we have a good alibi. Let's quit while we're ahead."

He squinted, appearing confused and half-asleep. Despite her confidence in her proposal's logic, her voice became quieter and more hesitant as she continued. "We could just take a break. The election is only nine months away. That's not so long. We could still talk."

When he didn't respond immediately, the same panic hit her, as it had for some time. She worried that, though they loved each other, if he lost the election, things might change between them.

"And in November, maybe we could pick up where we left off." The fear bubbling inside her chest made it sound more like a hopeful question.

Stephen's expression slowly changed to one of full comprehension. He was incredulous. "What do you mean by 'maybe we could pick up where we left off?' I hate your idea about not seeing one another, but I'm more concerned by what you just said." He blinked rapidly. "Are you having doubts . . . about us? Is that why you're proposing this?"

"No. No. Not at all. I don't have any doubts." She was relieved he'd picked up on what she said, and it opened the floodgates of her pent-up emotions. She wrapped her arms around him. "It's just overwhelming. I feel guilty. And I worry what's going to happen between us if you lose."

He shook his head. "Anne, I love you. I want to marry you. I'd ask you at this very moment if I thought you'd say yes. What happens with this election has nothing to do with how I feel about you. I'll love you the same regardless of whether I win or lose."

"But if—"

"No. No buts. And please don't feel guilty. Listen to me. Say that we are exposed, and it's ugly, and I do lose the election. The truth is I'll be a happier man if I lose and we're together than if I win and we're apart."

His words soothed her, and she gave him a tender kiss. "I love you."

"And I love you." He responded with a more intense kiss, followed by a quiet embrace. "I can see why you feel the pressure. It's not just me; everyone in my family is obsessed with the election."

"Just a little." She smirked.

"Don't feel bad. It gets to me, too." He smiled and pressed his lips to her forehead. "But my family supports us—even Patty. Believe me, if she didn't, she'd let me know. And they all would much rather I be happy and with you than be the miserable, single bastard I was before we met."

For a brief moment, she thought of the photos in the gossip rags of him smiling with Jennifer Hamilton. "You weren't miserable." Her mouth twisted with sourness.

"Compared to how happy I am now, yes, I was miserable," he said with a sheepish smile.

She sighed and stared at him squarely. "But what if you lose?"

"I don't know . . . the White House would probably offer me an appointment of some kind." He played with her hair. "Or maybe I'd be like all the other defeated senators and get an ambassadorship somewhere good —like Australia. That would be fun for both of us, right?"

"Right. As an ambassador, you're going to take your girlfriend along with you—like the State Department would let you do that." She rolled her eyes.

"Maybe you wouldn't be my girlfriend." He squeezed her hand and grinned.

"Whatever." She chuckled, but her face soon became serious again. "Really, Stephen, how will you feel if you lose and it's because of me?"

He shook his head and smiled. "Do you remember the night in the car when we talked about *Master of the Senate*?"

"Yeah." Her brow furrowed because she wasn't following him.

"What did I say about it?"

She was silent for a moment as she recalled the conversation in the backseat of his car. She remembered what he said, and things fell into place. "You said . . . something like you didn't aspire to be master of the Senate."

"Exactly. I'll be okay. Life will be different than I envisioned it at one time, but it will be better because of you."

"But what would you do?"

"I don't know. For a while I'd probably spend time on the ranch . . . doing things up there. Then I'd live wherever you were—either here or in Colorado. I'd go into private practice or go back to being a prosecutor. Hell, if I wanted, I could be the U.S. Attorney for the state if the job opened up."

"You'd be easily confirmed by the Senate." She chuckled.

"Exactly." The hope was evident as he stared into her eyes. "And we could get a house together. It would be a nice life."

Holding his gaze, she saw his sincerity. As much as he enjoyed all the power and trappings of being a senator, he'd be equally happy with a quieter life. It was one of the reasons she loved him. She leaned in for a kiss. "I'd like that life." After a long kiss, she sighed. "Of course, I still have to get a job for the next year."

"Why don't you work on Grayson's committee staff? He'll hire you."

"The Senate? No friggin' way." She giggled. "I'm getting outta there. I want a lowly administrative job in a giant law firm where I can get lost in the mix."

He chuckled and tousled her hair. "Well, Grayson could get you one of those, too."

Chapter 21

One night in March, Stephen looked up from his laptop as Anne appeared at his office door. He rose immediately. "Is something wrong?"

"No," she said, locking the door behind her.

"Well, it's nice to see you, sweetheart, but what are you doing here so late?" He walked toward her. "And why are you locking my door? You know I don't do that."

"I'm in the office because I had to cover the front desk while that big meeting was going on. And as for the door, I'm taking extra precautions," she said as she met him halfway. "I asked Greg if he could do me a favor and stick around for another hour. I told him we needed to talk—in person."

"About what?" Her naughty smile told him it couldn't be bad.

"Well, Greg probably thinks we're having a fight, but that's the last thing I want to do."

"But you still want to talk?"

"Actually, I don't want to talk," she said as she wrapped her arms around him.

"What do you want to do?"

"Well, I've been thinking. My internship is going to end soon, and there's something that's been bothering me."

"What's—?"

"Let me finish," she said as she kissed his nose in mock reprimand. "I'm tired of thinking about Helen and God knows who else you've been with in here. I realized this afternoon that maybe I needed to lay claim to the place before my internship ends. Then, when you talk about your office, I'll think about us."

"Lay claim to my office? Like how? Erect a flag?" He snickered.

"Like this," she replied, and laid a giant kiss on him. The kiss, which started as a smolder, sparked into a fire. He didn't want to stop it, but he needed to take some precautions. She whined in disappointment when he pulled away.

"Give me a second." He went to the window and closed the curtains. "No one can see anyway, but it's better to be safe than sorry."

When he turned around, she was perched atop his desk with a sly smile. "Are you ready now?" she asked as she unbuttoned her blouse.

§§§§

A few minutes later, Helen began her walk to the condominium she kept only a block away from the Senate. The brisk air of early spring was invigorating, and she breathed in the chill of the night. As she always did when she passed her side of the Hart Building, she looked up at her office. It never ceased to cause a smile, as it reminded her of her rarefied place in the world. She was about to look away when something out of the ordinary caught her eye.

Just a few floors down from her office was Stephen McEvoy's. She stopped on the sidewalk and stared at the windows of his office. Something was different—the curtains were closed.

When they would meet in his office, there was one step in their routine he never skipped. He always closed the draperies before anything happened between them. Staring at the curtains, she sneered as Stephen's latest rejection cut at her pride. *So, Stephen's fucking someone in his office.* She wondered who it might be.

Something she'd seen only an hour earlier flashed in her mind—that girl sitting at his front desk. She thought back to all her conversations with him in the last few months, and as she gaped at his windows, it came to her. She was shocked by her own conclusion. She had no proof, no real reason to believe. Yet her intuition told her it was true.

He's with that girl.

Helen couldn't believe her discovery as she gawked at the shuttered draperies of Stephen's office. It took a moment to remember the girl's name; she barely remembered the names of her own junior staff, let alone an intern in another office. Yet Anne's name soon came to her, and the scene she had witnessed months ago came into focus. There was the cute intern curled up with Stephen on his office sofa. She imagined the two of them together again behind the curtains.

Looking behind her, she spied a large, concrete flower planter the Capitol groundskeepers kept in perpetual bloom. She perched herself on the planter so her coat avoided the tulips and her legs stretched comfortably before her. The houndstooth pattern of her suit pants caught her eye, as Stephen's words from months ago resurfaced.

She's a friend of my mother's.

She chuckled aloud as she thought to herself, *Oh, I bet she is.* It was a reflexive, sarcastic answer, but she realized it could very well be true.

She remembered her last encounter with Stephen when he spurned her. There was only one reason he'd reject her—he was seeing someone he cared for enough not to cheat. What she hadn't understood was why he wanted to keep the woman's identity a secret. She quickly put two and two together. Anne was special—special to his mother and special to him. In fact, she needed to be exceedingly special for him to risk everything.

He had the trifecta of wealth, fame, and good looks; ninety-nine percent of men with the trifecta slipped up when it came to women. But Stephen McEvoy should be the kind not to fail. He was too smart, disciplined, and carried too much family honor. For him to make such a colossal mistake—especially when he was up for reelection—meant he'd changed dramatically.

Helen closed her eyes and shook her head. The girl had probably thrown herself at him, and he fell for her.

She recalled Anne chatting with Senator Haddow's handsome legislative director. The memory of Stephen's jaw locking and his terse responses made her reconsider. Stephen had pursued the girl, not vice versa. Thus, she truly was special to Stephen. He was in love.

While jealous of Anne, Helen was taken in by the sweet, if improbable, story. But as a political animal, she understood the unlikely occurred all the time. In politics, anything could happen, and it often did. Elections could be lost and won in only a few days; that was how upsets occurred.

Sure in her assessment of the situation, Helen wondered what she should do with the information. Party loyalty aside, she harbored no ill will toward Stephen and didn't want to out him. She still liked him, even if she thought his political views were detrimental to the future of the American way of life.

Yet Helen believed she needed to keep her friends close and her enemies closer. It was handy to have leverage over someone. She might not wish Stephen ill, but she wanted to make sure he knew his secret wasn't safe. She rationalized that it was for his benefit, too. He should know his secret was out. She grinned. *Oh, I can't wait to tell him . . .*

§§§§

The next morning in the well of the Senate, Stephen caught a glimpse of Helen just as he was leaving. He nodded to acknowledge her, but quickened his step to avoid any conversation. He hadn't taken two strides when he heard her voice.

"Oh, Stephen! Do you have a moment?"

Keeping up his façade for her, he instantly transformed into his old self. "For you, Helen? Always."

As she angled them to a vacant corner of the room, he dreaded what she would say. They hadn't spoken since that night in his office, and he always hated it when she hit on him in the Senate chamber.

"Sorry I wasn't with you on your amendment," she said as she briefly touched his forearm.

"I never expected you would be," he replied with a smile. Unlike many legislators, he never took it personally if someone voted against him.

"You look tired. That was another late one last night, wasn't it? I'm exhausted."

He noticed she said it without appearing tired at all; instead, she seemed happy and alert. While he was weary from staying up late, his night had been great. He and Anne had made good use of his office, and she'd followed him home where they had slept soundly in his bed. He kept a straight face as he lied, "You're right. Last night was grueling."

"It was so late when I finally left, I decided to stay in my condo rather than go home to Arlington." She casually fiddled with her earring for a moment. "And as I was walking home last night I happened to notice something."

"What's that?"

"Your office drapes were closed." She wore a simpering smile.

Despite the jolt to his world, he didn't flinch. He acted as if she'd told him the sky was blue. "So?"

"So I know what was going on behind the curtains."

Fear came over him, but he simply shrugged.

She jumped on his silence. "And I know who you were with. I figured it out."

He blinked twice, betraying nothing of his internal panic. He decided his only recourse was to take the issue head-on and play it straight. Crossing his arms over his chest, he chuckled. "Really? Inquisitive, aren't you?"

"Inquisitive and intuitive. You know how women are."

"My mother is Lillian McEvoy, and I have two sisters. I know a little about women."

"I suppose so."

"And what exactly do you think you've discovered?"

"For starters, I know why you close your curtains." She raised her eyebrow in accusation.

"Now Helen . . ." He smiled because he took some joy in reminding her of their mutually assured destruction. "How would you explain why you think such an extraordinarily mundane act like closing some drapes means anything other than I closed my drapes?"

She laughed. "*That* is something I hope never to have to explain."

"Good. I'm glad we still have a deal," he said, hoping to have shut down the conversation.

"Oh yes. Don't worry. I won't break our nonaggression pact. But what about the girl?"

"The girl?" he asked, pretending to be confused rather than worried. "I'm sorry. I don't know what you're talking about."

"I think you once called her a family friend. She must be a very good friend of yours to be in your office so late."

Stephen could lie easily and effectively, but even he couldn't skirt the truth when there was factual evidence to the contrary. Anne had stayed late at work the night before, and there were witnesses. Rather than tell a ridiculous falsehood, he blunted the facts. "I believe you're referring to Anne Norwood. Yes, she's an intern and a family friend. And she was at work late yesterday. There's no secret there."

"No secrets?" She pursed her lips. "I'm willing to bet my next election that's not true."

"Are you suggesting I would risk my career with an intern?"

"Yes."

Her stare taunted him, but he gave her nothing other than a prompt, terse response. "Unlikely."

"But not out of the question."

He rolled his eyes playfully as he turned to walk away. "Always good talking with you, Helen. We'll have to do it again."

"Yes, we will!" she called cheerfully, and walked in the opposite direction.

As soon as he was safely back at his desk, he phoned Patty. "Helen knows about Anne."

"How?"

There wasn't a chance in hell he was going to tell Patty about his night with Anne in his office. Furthermore, he didn't think anyone—including Anne—would want to know the details of how Helen figured it out. "It really doesn't matter how she found out. What's important is that I've got things under control."

"Are you crazy? Under control?" Patty's sneer came through the phone loud and clear. "She's evil. I wouldn't trust her even if she were a Democrat."

"She agreed we still have a mutual nonaggression pact."

"For now . . ." Her voice was thick with rue.

"Yes, for now.

"Listen, I've got a busy day. Can you tell Megan and Mom? I don't think there's anything to do right now."

"Sure, I'll call them." She chuckled. "So Helen Sanders is the first to know. What a witch. I don't suppose you want to hear me say I told you so?"

"No, I don't." Without saying good-bye, he ended the call.

§§§§

Later that evening, Anne listened stoically as Stephen broke the bad news. It was one thing to be found out, it was another thing entirely for Helen Sanders to be the one to do it. Anne hated her. Stephen apologized profusely for causing the mess, but she was miffed. She was reaching her boiling point with his past constantly being thrown in her face. She asked only one question. "Based on your . . . experience with Helen, do you think you can keep her quiet?"

"Yes." He nodded, but then qualified his answer. "God willing."

Chapter 22

A few weeks later, Dan Langford was all smiles as he left a meeting at the Republican National Committee. As he and Trey exited the doors of the stately building, Langford placed his straw cowboy hat back atop his head. "You're going to tell Walter, aren't you?" he asked Trey.

"Absolutely." Trey smiled at his boss's joy. "The RNC dumping money into your race is huge. It's great we've been able to tighten those poll numbers in the last few months. You've been doing good work. Keep it up."

The grin on Trey's face slowly disappeared when he saw Anne Norwood emerge from the Capitol South Metro station across the street. The night at the donut shop came back to him, and he instantly became curious—who was the woman and why was she in D.C.? "Do you know that girl over there?" He pointed to Anne.

Langford looked to where Trey indicated. "Why, that's Anne Norwood. Elton's daughter. Remember I mentioned her to McEvoy that day at the TV station."

"Oh yeah . . ." Trey said as his voice trailed off in thought. "Who's Elton?"

"Elton Norwood. He's the Summit County district attorney."

"*Those* Norwoods? Her family are Republicans. What's she doing working for McEvoy?"

"Well, Elton is a moderate, and obviously he's done a poor job of controlling his children if his daughter is working for McEvoy."

"Huh," Trey said. He mulled over the situation as he assessed Anne from afar. He decided from her face to her figure she was attractive. "I wouldn't call her a child."

"It's still inexcusable she's working for *him,* of all people."

"You know, I saw her before Christmas around three in the morning at a donut shop by the Denver airport," Trey told him. "She was with McEvoy's guy, Greg, and I think they were driving one of McEvoy's cars."

"That's strange."

"That's what I thought," Trey answered, his mouth askew in thought.

Langford shook his head. "Well, I expect to see Elton this weekend at the state Republican convention. The last time I spoke with Anne, we ended on a bad note. I should go say hello. I might be able to find something out."

"Good idea."

Langford cut across First Street to meet her on the corner by the Cannon Building. He ignored the pesky Capitol police officer permanently stationed at the corner to bark at jaywalkers.

Anne waited patiently for her turn to cross the street, but her face fell upon seeing him. She soon forced a quick smile. "Good morning, Mr. Langford."

"Good morning, Anne," he said with a tip of his hat. "It's nice to see you again. What are you doing here?"

"I'm going to a hearing," she answered. When she heard her words, she decided it was unnecessarily curt, even if Langford had been rude the last time they talked. "It's a hearing of the Transportation and Infrastructure Committee's Subcommittee on Railroads, Pipelines, and Hazardous Materials. Exciting stuff."

"Sounds fascinating." He chuckled. "So, how you've been? I'll be seeing your father this weekend."

As Anne uneasily relayed only the most mundane details of her life, Trey studied the scene from a distance. He scanned the surroundings and caught a glimpse of Stephen McEvoy exiting the Cannon Building. Trey's whole attention turned to McEvoy as he bounded down the stairs headed for his waiting car. Trey's eyes widened when the senator abruptly stopped and stared at Langford and Anne.

Trey knew there were many reasons why McEvoy would take interest in a conversation between the two of them. Langford was his opponent, and she was an intern in his office; the two shouldn't be talking. Yet something else beyond suspicion radiated from McEvoy. He glared at Langford, his fists were clenched, and while he stood motionless, he looked like he might launch himself onto Langford at any moment. Only after Anne waved good-bye to Langford and hurried down the sidewalk did McEvoy cross the street to his car.

As Trey watched him climb in and drive off, he tried to make sense of what had just happened. It seemed odd for McEvoy to be so interested in Anne and Langford. Of course, he should be suspicious of her talking with Langford, but something was off. Why did he look upset? Why did he stick around until they stopped talking? He was a busy guy; he had staff to worry about things like this for him. Why did he care?

In a minute, Langford was back across the street and at his side. "I didn't find out much."

"What'd you talk about?"

"Her schoolwork. She wasn't very forthcoming. I left it telling her I'm scheduled to speak at the CU commencement. I might see her there."

"There will be fifty thousand people there." Trey shook his head. "How are you going to see her?"

"Maybe not then . . ."

"You know, McEvoy came out of the building as you two were talking. He stared at you the entire time."

"Really?" Langford said as he adjusted his hat in thought. "Why does he care if I talk to one of his interns?"

"I really don't know . . ."

§§§§

In early April, the Washington, D.C. forecast was finally warm enough for the starlet, Jennifer Hamilton, to fly in for a special event. At seven that morning, she stood stark naked on the back steps of the U.S. Capitol. Two miles down the National Mall at the Lincoln Memorial, the immense statue of President Abraham Lincoln had a fine view of her bare ass. Scattered around her on the steps, the camera and makeup crew checked the lighting and angles and tended to her tresses and face.

"I'm not sure what angle you're going to use. But someone needs to tell the PETA people they're probably going to have to do some airbrushing because I only got waxed yesterday. I'm a little red and bumpy." She playfully wiggled her bum in the direction of President Lincoln. "You know how that is."

More than one of the crew members around her averted their eyes so they could roll them—as did the PETA representatives.

The savvy PETA communications director hurried the crew along. "We've got to get this shot in before the cops arrive. And I need time to get you ready for the hearing. We should go over your testimony."

"But I wanna look good," whined Jennifer.

"You look great," said her publicist. "And we should do this quickly. You don't want to be arrested."

A PETA rep chuckled. "If there's a problem with the photo, we'll just slap the 'I'd rather go naked than wear fur' banner right over it."

In a few hours, everyone was happy. Jennifer's photos made a splash in the media, drawing attention to the animal rights cause and her naked assets, and PETA was pleased with her impassioned testimony before the Congressional Animal Protection Caucus.

Not everyone was pleased, though. Megan and Patty stormed into Stephen's office.

"We have to meet now," Megan demanded.

"I'm busy," Stephen said as he pointed to Greg on the sofa.

"This is important," Patty retorted. "Greg, go get Anne."

"Uh . . ." Greg's eyes shifted between Patty and Stephen. "Isn't it kind of obvious if I do that?"

"Oh, who cares at this point? It's her last day in the office, anyway," said Patty.

Stephen signaled to Greg to follow Patty's instructions. "Why does Anne need to be in here?"

"Because she should hear this. She *is* your girlfriend."

"What do you mean?" Stephen was wary.

"Oh, you'll see . . ."

A minute later, Anne was seated next to Stephen on his sofa with Patty, Megan, and Greg in chairs, and Lillian on the speakerphone.

"Jennifer Hamilton did a publicity stunt for PETA this morning, and she's said some things about Stephen," Megan announced. "We need to make a statement."

Lillian's voice blared out of the speakerphone. "Now, I don't like some of their tactics, but I'm in complete agreement with PETA. I got rid of all the family furs years ago. I hope everyone knows that."

"Nice to know, Mom. I'll make sure the press hears, too," Megan muttered.

"Cut to the chase, Megan. Just read the story," Patty said while she rubbed her eyes.

"Okay," said Megan. "This is from the AP story, but it's been picked up everywhere. It starts: 'Hollywood starlet Jennifer Hamilton lent her body and her name to the cause of animal rights today.'

"The story goes on from there, but here's our problem. Jennifer says, 'I'm going to ask my boyfriend, Stephen McEvoy, to pass a bill or something. He can do that, you know. He's a senator, and he would do that for me.' " Megan looked around the room with a raised eyebrow. "Thoughts?"

"Go get her to shut up," Patty demanded.

"I'll call Jennifer and tell her to knock it off," Stephen answered without hesitation. "Then I'm out of here for the rest of the day and can't be reached for comment. Tell the press I have no plans for introducing such a bill, and per usual, I don't comment on my personal life. You know what to say, Megan." He looked at Anne, who held his glance for only a second before looking away.

"Of course, I know what to say, but I've got enough on my plate right now. I'm sick of the questions about how we're putting family money into the campaign. Langford's new ads bashing us for it are getting a ton of coverage," said Megan, shaking her head. "The Republicans are now going to have a field day with this."

"Okay. Everybody leave. I'll call her," Stephen said as he loosened his tie.

"You want me to get her number from the receptionist?" Greg asked unwittingly.

"Nah, I still have it in my cell." As soon as the words left his mouth, he realized how horrible they sounded. He immediately turned to Anne whose expression had turned icy.

"Are you okay with this?" he asked softly. "I just have to leave her a message. Maybe there's a bright side . . . maybe we could spend the afternoon together?"

"No," she replied, chilling the entire room with her tone. "I have to work on my thesis." She rose at once and was the first one out the door.

§§§§

While the Jennifer fiasco blew over in the media that day, Stephen spent the afternoon in his home office, but he couldn't work. Guilt weighed on him. Once again, he'd put Anne in an awkward situation and himself in the doghouse. She hadn't returned any of his messages; something she'd never done before.

When his mother came to visit him, he was glad to have the distraction. "Hi, Mom."

"Stephen, you don't look very happy." She sighed.

"I'm not." He stared out the window, shaking his head. "And neither is Anne."

"Of course she's not happy. I can understand. If you don't mind, I think it's time we talked about you two."

Stephen slumped in his chair and turned it to her as she sat down. "What about us?"

"Well, you know I was opposed to your relationship from the very beginning, though I liked her."

"Yeah?"

"But I've been watching her over the months. I wanted to see how she would handle the stress of being with a politician. Would she have the necessary mettle?"

"And?"

"And I think she does. In fact, she's dealt with every situation very well. She's grounded and keeps a cool head." With more than a touch of reproach in her voice, she said, "And despite the difficult circumstances and unsavory . . . characters you've had to deal with—like Helen, for example—Anne has taken it all in stride. She's even agreed your responses have been politically necessary. Given her age, I'm rather impressed."

Stephen felt guilty for Jennifer's antics, but he also reasoned he couldn't be held responsible. "But what about today? She didn't like my response to the Jennifer problem."

Lillian pursed her lips disapprovingly. "Today? Well, everyone has their breaking point, dear. You treated her poorly. You didn't acknowledge that the situation was uncomfortable for her or that it was your fault." When he didn't immediately respond, she shook her head and continued her reprimand. "And your comment that you were sure you still had Jennifer's number was very inconsiderate."

He winced at his own words. "Okay. You're right."

"If your father had done that to me, I'd have given him the cold shoulder as well."

Throwing his hands up, Stephen justified the rest of his actions. "But what else was I supposed to do? You agree it was right to ignore Jennifer's comment? I never comment on my private life, and I certainly couldn't say the truth. 'No, I'm involved with someone else whom I love dearly.' "

"Oh, I agree. In fact, I think Jennifer saying you're her boyfriend is actually helpful to you. It's a deflection from you and Anne. But Stephen, it's time to come clean. You two need to out yourselves before someone else does."

He took a moment to comprehend what his mother said. "What? After all of this trouble to keep it under wraps? You want us to out ourselves in the middle of the campaign?"

"Yes. As soon as possible. I want you to publicly admit it. Admit all of it in an open forum and move on with the campaign. It's the only way— politically and for the health of your relationship with Anne."

Chapter 23

Stephen calculated all the possible outcomes if he were to go on the offensive and disclose his relationship with an intern. He grimaced at the thought, but his mother didn't allow him to speak.

"I'd counsel you," she said in the same tone she used for all of her political admonishments. "And as your mother, I'd prefer it if you disclosed your relationship by announcing your engagement. The public will be more forgiving of a relationship with an intern if you intend to marry her. They might even like the love story."

"Engagement?"

"Oh, I know," she said with a wave of her hand. "Normally I'm not so direct, but I feel I must be."

"Well, I . . ." He considered the frankness of their conversation and decided to tell her everything. "I'd be happy to ask Anne to marry me tonight . . . if I thought she'd say yes." A wry smile formed on his lips.

"Why wouldn't she say yes?" She laughed as if it were something easily dealt with. "It's obvious you're in love with each other."

"We've sort of talked around the issue. Maybe she'd say yes, with the condition we wait a few years." He shifted his weight in his chair. "I hate to say it, but I think that's a reasonable request—given her age and my past."

"Hmmm." She was quiet for a moment. "Well, your past has done you no favors. As for her age, I'd suggest you ask her after she graduates in May. Let her get one big rite of passage out of the way—that might help. And you don't have to get married for a while, but you'll at least be engaged. It's a nice compromise."

He cocked his head to the side as he focused on the urgency of her request. "But what's the hurry? I get your reasoning for getting it out there —so we can all move on—but why the engagement and why so soon?"

"Well, all mothers want to see their children happily married. I'm no exception. And believe me—getting you and Patty settled down with nice women has been something I've wanted for quite a while now."

"But what's the urgency? Why can't this wait? You just said we bought some time today with Jennifer's little stunt. I've got Helen under control. Why are you in such a hurry?"

"Oh dear," she replied with a roll of her eyes. "I suppose you're no different than any man. You don't think of these things."

"What do you mean?" He curled his lip, offended by her gender stereotype.

"Do I have to explain the facts of life?" She chuckled. "As soon as you two announce your engagement, everyone is going to think she's pregnant. The sooner we get it out there, the sooner it will become obvious she's not. If you announce your engagement by June, you've got five months before Election Day. People will see in just a few months she's not pregnant, and they're more likely to accept you as a real couple—not some shotgun relationship. If you wait too long, it won't be self-evident, and the question will hang over the election."

"Oh. I didn't even think about that."

"Now, I gave you Grandma McEvoy's jewelry case. We could—"

"Mom," he said with his hands in the air to stop her. "Give me some time."

"Oh, all right." She pouted.

"I'm sorry. It's just something I want to do myself." He snickered. "I know you're excited to marry off your wayward son."

"Maybe," she said, cracking a smile. "I'm allowed to be happy after all the grief you've put me through."

"That's true. So do you have any ideas on how I get out of the doghouse?"

"I suggest you grovel. It usually works." She rose and smoothed her skirt. "I feel much better after this little talk. Have a good night."

"Good night, Mom."

After his mother left the room, Stephen looked out his window, and his eyes settled on the scattered spots of pink, red, white, and peach peeping through the greenery. His mother's roses had begun their first bloom of the year. There was no conscious urge to act based on the symbolism of spring, but he jumped from his seat after seeing them. In his father's old credenza beside his desk, he found the jewelry case. He opened it and soon spotted the frayed silk box; his great-grandmother's diamond sat where she'd left it. He held the ring up to the light, shaking his head in distaste. *I hate it.*

He placed the ring back in its box, and after a few taps of his phone, he heard a low male voice say hello.

Tipping his chair back, he looked at the ring and smiled. "Hey Phillip. I've got a project for you."

§§§§

The following month, Anne held her mortarboard and diploma in her hands as she hugged her mother. Folsom Field was crammed with over fifty thousand people attending the University of Colorado commencement, and it had taken her some time to find her family.

Her brother was next to grab her up in a big hug. "Congratulations, sis."

"Thanks for coming," she said, giving him a squeeze. "I know how boring these things are."

"I wouldn't miss it." He smirked and rolled his eyes. "Even if I did have to listen to Dan Langford talk about family values—whatever the fuck that is."

"Are you turning into a Democrat?" she asked in feigned shock.

"Hell no." He chuckled. "But I might not vote for him if that's all he ever talks about. Dad was so bored he kept looking at his watch."

She laughed and turned to her father, patiently waiting for his hug. He wrapped his arms around her and lifted her off the ground.

"Congratulations, Annie. I'm so proud of you."

"Thanks, Dad." Tears pricked at the corners of her eyes. She wasn't prepared for the emotion overwhelming her. "I'm sorry to have been so much trouble lately," she whispered in his ear.

"No trouble," he said with a kiss on the cheek. "You're just being you, and we love you for it."

His accepting words made the tears multiply, causing her mascara to run down her cheeks. "I love you, Dad, but now I need to get myself cleaned up." She wiped away the wet blackness and smiled.

"Go do what you need to do." He pointed to an empty spot along a railing. "We'll be waiting over there."

Once she finished in the bathroom, Anne again searched for her family among the mass of bodies moving around the stadium. She found them right where her father had indicated, engrossed in conversation with another family. As she neared them, she felt a strong pull on her arm—a very familiar pull. She looked up to see Stephen.

He immediately took her into his arms inside a throng of screeching graduates and their families. Wearing a CU T-shirt and a Denver Rockies cap, he blended perfectly into the crowd.

Anne scolded him, albeit with a big smile. "What are you doing here?"

"I wanted to congratulate you, so I stopped by." He beamed and stole a quick kiss before he brushed her nose with his. "I'm only here for a minute. Trust me."

"How I do love you." She sighed, throwing her arms tightly around his neck.

"I love you, and I've missed you."

"I've missed you. And maybe this isn't the worst place for us. You're pretty incognito." She tipped his baseball hat farther down on his head.

"Did you listen to Langford?"

"No way." He grimaced.

"It was pretty bad. He only got to speak because his son was graduating from law school, but he went on and on about bringing morality back to government."

"So he made a campaign speech out of it? The guy has no class."

"Yeah, it was pretty pathetic." She laughed. "My dad kept looking at his watch."

"I'm glad I missed it."

"Well, I'm glad you came, sweetheart."

He glanced around him. "I should leave now, before . . . well, you know."

"I know." She nodded reluctantly, but then shook her head. "Wait. You're supposed to be in D.C."

"I am, but I'm here instead." He chuckled and leaned down to kiss her again. "Next weekend. We have a date at my ranch, right?"

"Yes, we do." After a few seconds of one last, sweet, stolen kiss, they pulled away simultaneously and parted ways.

A few minutes earlier, Trey hung in the back of the small mob around Dan Langford. It may have been his son's graduation, but Langford greeted everyone like it was a campaign stop. Trey was there for that reason—he refused to let Langford go to such an event without a staffer. Unfortunately, he was now bored to death.

When Langford was buttonholed by a state legislator, Trey used the opportunity to make a call. In a vain attempt to get a cell phone signal, he walked along the short, open wall of the stadium. He was annoyed at the world, but he stopped abruptly when he noticed a familiar face in the crowd.

Lifting his head to get a better look, he caught his breath at what he saw —Stephen McEvoy kissing Anne Norwood. Before Trey even blinked, the senator disappeared into the masses of graduation gowns.

Trey's heart raced as he confirmed to himself three things: he had in fact seen Stephen McEvoy, he'd witnessed McEvoy kissing Anne Norwood, and their kiss was anything but platonic.

Trey stared at the site of the incident. Only Anne's head could be seen bobbing away in the distance. He was confident he'd seen her kissing a man. *But was that really McEvoy? It seems too good to be true . . .*

He shook his head, remembering campaigns were very often won and lost on events which were too good to be true. He looked around to make sure he was alone and called Walter. The assistant tried to brush him off again, but he insisted the call was an emergency.

"Why can't this wait? What's so urgent?" Walter asked impatiently. "I'm going to see you at the RNC fundraiser soon."

Trey kept his voice low because the information was too precious. "I think Stephen McEvoy is having an affair with an intern . . . well, I suppose now she's a former intern, but still."

"Well, well, well." Walter chuckled, with the creak of his chair sounding into the phone. "It's always nice when something like this happens . . . except when it's with one of ours, of course. So give me the details. How do you know?"

Recounting all the suspicious events, Trey saved the best for last.

As he detailed the kiss, Walter was quiet until he finished. "And you're sure it was McEvoy?"

"I'm pretty certain. It looked like him, though he was in a baseball cap and a CU T-shirt."

"But there must twenty thousand guys there in baseball caps and University of Colorado T-shirts."

"I know it sounds shaky, but I think it was him. And it definitely was Anne—that I'd lay good money on."

"But wait a second here," Walter said slowly. "Didn't that actress, Jennifer Hamilton, say McEvoy was her boyfriend? He got in some hot water when she said he'd carry a bill for those animal rights freaks."

"She did call him her boyfriend, and we've had a great time in the press linking him to PETA." Trey became insistent. "But I'm pretty sure I saw him kiss Anne."

"So who is this Anne?"

"Anne Norwood. Her family are Republicans. Her dad is a county D.A. Langford knows him."

"Just a second, I want to Google them." The sound of taps at keyboard came across the line. After a moment of silence, Walter muttered, "We couldn't be so lucky that McEvoy would be with a little slut in his office."

"What do you mean?"

"Elton Norwood looks to be a respected man with a fine family." Walter sighed. "Well, too bad for them. Collateral damage."

"What are you going to do?" Trey asked excitedly.

"I'll look into it. We'll dig deep into McEvoy and get it all out. The media will love a storyline where McEvoy is a sleazebag who seduced an intern."

"That's so great," Trey said under his breath.

"Does Langford know?"

"No. Langford is the last person to know. He'll get distracted."

"Good thinking. Plus, we need to make sure he stays on message when it does come out." Walter was emphatic. "He can't get high and mighty. He needs to stand down. Let the media do his work for him."

"I swear I'll have Langford under control. He'll shut up. After all, he could win the election on this news alone."

"Yes, he could." Walter let out a throaty chuckle. "Indeed, he could."

§§§§

The following week, Anne pulled up to the McEvoys' ranch and smiled when she saw Stephen on the front porch. He sat on a weathered bench, stuffing a bottle of champagne in a saddlebag.

"Whatcha got in there, handsome?" she asked as she walked up the steps.

"Provisions," he said, tying the bag closed. He rose and took her into his arms. "Hey, sweetheart."

She reached up to give him a kiss. "I'm happy to see you."

After several kisses, made fonder by their weeklong absence from one another, they strolled to the barn where Stephen had saddled two horses. He gave her the reins of an elegant black horse, along with a carrot.

"This is Cinder. He's Patty's favorite."

"Does she know I'm going to ride him?" Anne asked, offering the carrot to Cinder.

"Sure. She suggested him for you." He swatted her butt. "Patty likes you."

"I like her." She shrugged. "I'm just a little afraid of her."

"Don't be. She's on your side now." He nodded to Cinder. "C'mon. Let's get on with our ride."

As they rode off into the rolling hills of the vast McEvoy ranch, they trotted along for a few miles until Stephen suggested they gallop to their destination.

"Where are we even going?" asked Anne, as she squeezed her legs, urging Cinder to pick up his pace.

"A creek. About half a mile ahead," he answered, and clicked his mouth to get his dappled horse moving faster. "There's another place I'd like to go, but it's too far. We'll still be alone here. I want some private time."

"Am I going to like this private time?" she asked coyly.

"I hope so," he answered, but his voice was serious rather than flirtatious.

Their picnic spot sat next to a small stream surrounded by columbine, shooting stars, and other flowers, all enjoying the mountain water. After a late lunch and an entire bottle of champagne, they lay talking and enjoying the sun. When the conversation dwindled, she nestled in beside him.

"Anne, I've been thinking about some things for a while now."

"Yeah? What's that?" she mumbled without opening her eyes.

"Well, remember when Jennifer pulled that stupid stunt?"

"How could I forget?"

"I know. It was bad, and I was wrong to have treated you so poorly. I made that clear, right?" His brow furrowed in contrition.

"You did." She sat up and placed her hand at the nape of his neck, caressing the short hair there. "Yes, you were sorry, and I accepted your apology." She chuckled. "I still don't like her, though."

"Understandable. I don't like her either." He took her left hand and gently stroked her fingers. "I just wish there was something I could point to . . . that you could point to . . . that showed how much I love you. Because I do. I love you with all my heart."

Anne was unsure what he meant and searched for something to say. "You have my heart."

Fumbling in his pocket, he looked away for a moment, and when he turned to her again, he clenched his hand and gazed into her eyes. He smiled shyly. "It doesn't have to happen next year. It can wait as long as you want, but Anne Norwood, will you marry me?"

She drew in a breath both in shock and in appreciation of the moment. The question reverberated in her mind, and she held his happy eyes as they searched for a response. Wisdom should've caused her to condition her response, just as it always did, but this time she felt no conditions on her love or what she wanted.

With a smile, she responded confidently, seriously, as she knew the answer in both her head and her heart. "Yes . . . yes, I will marry you." She threw her arms around his neck and asked herself aloud, "How could I not?"

"Oh, sweetheart, that's how I feel about you." They kissed, sharing more joy in that moment than either could've imagined. When he broke this kiss, he grinned. "I want to give this to you."

Her mouth fell open as he slipped the ring on her finger. She gasped at the beauty of it, but was also taken aback by its size.

"Oh my, Stephen. It's beautiful, but . . . but it's too much."

" 'Too much' how?" He smiled. "Too valuable? Too big?"

"Well, it's amazing." She admired her hand. "I've never had anything like it."

"But you should. It's yours now."

"Stephen . . ." The ring's size and brilliant luster dumbfounded her, as did the fact he'd chosen to give it to her.

Tipping her chin up to look into her eyes, he put her at ease. "I *want* you to have it."

"How on earth did you get it?" She shook her head, her eyes wide in disbelief. "*You* can't just walk into a store and buy an engagement ring." She glanced down at the modern, square-cut diamond, banked by emeralds. "Did Megan help you?"

"No, thank you very much," he said with a chuckle. He twisted the ring back and forth on her finger, making it sparkle. "I told my lawyer, Phillip, what I wanted, and he handled it for me, texting me photos of potential rings. It was fun."

"Well, it's amazing and perfect." She smiled. "I'm just going to have to get used to wearing something like it."

"Is it too visible?"

"No . . ." Her brow furrowed as the familiar hurt again built up in her heart. "Actually, I wish . . . I wish we *could* be more visible. I'm tired of hiding, and I hate that the world thinks you're dating Jennifer Hamilton." She thought she sounded whiny, so she tried to make light of it. "It kinda bums me out."

"It bums me out, too," he said with a snicker. Stroking her cheek, he quieted. "My mom thinks we should announce our relationship—come clean—just get the news out there and move on with our lives. She thinks it would be better for the campaign and for us. It would be tough for a while, but I think she has a point."

"What? Really?" Anne was shocked, but Lillian's reasoning had merit. "What does Patty say?"

"I don't know." He shrugged. "She usually follows Mom's lead."

Anne smirked, thinking of his crafty mother. Somewhere in the back of her mind, she recalled the time Lillian asked her over for tea and interrogated her. She'd also told the story about how she and Patrick had confronted their own problems with their relationship. It jogged another memory—a memory of Stephen telling her he'd elope if only she'd say yes.

But we can't do that . . . I can't do that. Yet despite the rules set for herself in life, she came to a decision which simultaneously made no sense at all and all the sense in the world. Her life wasn't turning out as she'd expected; it was better. Why should she hold back?

Leaning into him, her lips met his with a short, but deep kiss. She ended it with a quick peck and a smile.

"What?" he asked. "What are you thinking?"

She shrugged and made her own proposal. "Maybe we should just elope?"

Chapter 24

"Elope? You want to elope?" His eyes widened, stunned by the drastic change in Anne's attitude toward marriage.

"Well . . . you mentioned it once back in December," she said with hesitant smile. "Maybe it's not such a bad idea."

He gave no audible response. Instead, he crushed his mouth to hers with an intense, exuberant kiss. After a moment, he pulled away. "I think it's a great idea," he murmured.

She giggled and nuzzled his nose. "If you don't say so yourself."

"What made you think of it, though?"

"The whole idea of us coming out," she said as she pulled away. "If we were to out ourselves tomorrow, we'd be engaged, but there would still be whispers. They'd say it was an engagement of convenience, or people would think I'm pregnant. Even when it turns out I'm not pregnant, they could say we're only engaged for show and we'll break it off right after you get reelected. I think if we're married, we'll be taken more seriously."

"You're right." He chuckled, amazed her thought process was identical to his mother's. Then he remembered something his mother said. "But people are going to think you're pregnant, regardless of whether we're married or not."

"That's true . . ." She shrugged. "I guess we can't get around it, but when it's obvious I'm not knocked up, I'll still be your wife."

"Yes. I like the sound of that—you'll be my wife . . ." Finishing neither his sentence nor his thought, he kissed her again.

She laughed as he pressed his lips to hers. "I can tell you're smiling as you kiss me."

"I am. I couldn't be happier."

"But if we do this, isn't Patty going to go ballistic?"

"Maybe. Maybe not. I'm not asking her since we're supposed to be eloping."

"So, how do we elope?" she asked with a smile. "Should we go to a small town in another part of the state? We could drive somewhere remote like Ouray."

"Hmm. No." He skewed his mouth in thought for a moment. "I don't think we should. We should do this quickly but not rashly."

"Okay. I get it. We're eloping, but it needs to look respectable."

"Exactly." He paused and looked sideways at Anne. "Do you remember Judge Clements?"

"How could I forget him?" She rolled her eyes, but they soon flashed wide open. "No! I know what you're thinking. Absolutely not. I can't be married by someone who heard us having sex. That's too weird. I'd be so embarrassed."

"Anne . . . he doesn't care. Trust me. He doesn't think anything of it."

"Right. That is such BS—like he didn't think it was funny."

"Well, of course he thought it was funny. Who wouldn't? But he doesn't think any less of you. Quite the opposite. He knows how much you mean to me."

"He does?"

"Of course." Watching her waver, he pled his case. "Think about it. Judge Clements is the perfect choice. He's a family friend, and his reputation is impeccable. He'll help keep things quiet beforehand and stay on message afterward."

"Well, maybe. But are you sure he would do it? He seems pretty reclusive. This would give him a lot of negative attention."

"I sort of already asked him." He winced in apology for being presumptuous.

"What? When?"

"When we were at his house, I asked him if I ever needed a favor, would he do me the honor. We didn't talk specifics, but he knew what I meant. I doubt he's expecting an elopement, but he'll be fine with it."

"Oh, sweetheart." She shook her head. "What am I going to do with you?"

"Marry me?" he murmured and stroked her hair.

"Of course I'll marry you." They kissed again until she laughed. "I'm so happy, but this is also so crazy. If we go with Judge Clements, where do we get married? At your cabin?"

"Somewhere on the property. The wildflowers are nice this time of year."

"Don't we need a witness? I remember he had a dog, but I think we need a human."

"Oh . . . I've thought of that, too."

"How long have you had this planned?"

"I wouldn't say I've had it planned. I've just been thinking of contingencies depending on how things played out."

"You're incorrigible." She swatted his arm. "So who is our witness? Your mom?" Her expression changed, as she pursed her lips and shook her head. "I'm sorry, but I can't have her there. As much as I love your family, I can't get married with your family attending and not mine. I wouldn't like it, and my mother would kill me."

"No, no. Not my family. That's no fun." He winked. "It's not really an elopement if you tell your family you're doing it."

She smiled and climbed on top of him, straddling his chest. With her arms on either side of his shoulders, she kissed him and asked in a breathy voice, "Stephen McEvoy, can't you even get married without being naughty?"

"Eloping is sort of naughty, isn't it?"

"It's kind of respectable and naughty at the same time."

"Very fitting. That's the story of my life." He kissed her quickly and said in a husky voice, "I can't wait to get naughty with my wife."

"I don't know about that . . . can you be naughty with someone you're married to?"

"I certainly hope so. We'll have a license for it, after all."

"Very funny." She smirked while he pulled her body flush with his. After a minute of delightful distraction, she asked, "Aren't we planning our elopement?"

"Yes, I suppose so." He lifted her off and sat upright with crossed legs. "Now where were we before you sidetracked me?" he asked as he drew her into his lap.

"You said you had a witness."

"Oh, that's right. I'm sure I have two witnesses."

"Who?"

"Grayson and his wife, Laura."

"Are you sure? Do you really want to put him at risk?"

"Are you kidding? He'd do anything for our family. We're like his own kids. And frankly, he'd get a kick out of it. Any bad press he might get . . . well, he'd turn it into good press by making jokes."

"I can see how it would be fun for him." She nodded. "And having him and his wife there makes it more respectable. They're sort of like substitute parents and grandparents all rolled into one."

"Our parents may be a little more forgiving with them there."

"So . . . when, then? When do we do this? And how?" She gave his arm a playful squeeze.

"I think if you decide to elope, you do it as soon as possible, don't you?" He kissed her cheek and grinned.

"I think you're right." She laughed.

"Well, before we do anything, we should contact Phillip. We'll need help with logistics so we can keep this quiet."

"Isn't he your family lawyer? Won't he tell the rest of your family?"

"No. I'll make sure he knows he's only representing me. He helps all of us out individually from time to time."

"How can he help with logistics? He's here, isn't he?"

"He comes to D.C. occasionally when he has to. The first thing we need is a marriage license. West Virginia has a three-day waiting period."

She didn't comment on his preparedness this time, except to shake her head and smile.

"I told you back in December that I had done some research," he said with a smirk. "I should be less conspicuous in West Virginia than in Colorado, though we still need to get in and out of the courthouse separately, unseen, and unnoticed. I'll get Phillip working on that. Maybe the Judge can help with finding the least nosy county clerk."

"Do we have time? You're leaving tomorrow, and I'm not flying back until Monday."

"That's okay. We'll visit West Virginia on Tuesday, get home to D.C., wait our three days, and get married on Saturday." He smiled. "At least the three days gives me some time to get things planned and you to get your dress."

"I suppose I need to find a white dress." She looked down, but there was excitement in her eyes.

"Wear whatever you want. You'll be beautiful no matter what."

She gave him another quick kiss. "I'll make sure my dress is appropriate for something outside in the summer."

"What about wedding rings?"

She touched her new ring and smiled. "I think something simple is fine."

"Okay. I'll work with Phillip on getting the bands and anything else we need."

"This seems far beyond the average family attorney's role."

"It is, but he's used to it. Don't worry. He's well compensated and never complains. We trust him implicitly."

"So after the wedding, we'll stay the night at the cabin?"

He kissed her hair and wrapped his arms around her. "Out in the country . . . under the stars . . . I can't think of a better honeymoon."

"I can't either." She smiled and kissed his neck.

"Then in the morning . . . we'll drive back to D.C. to tell our families."

"Drive back in the same car?"

"Absolutely." He grinned. "We'll be husband and wife. Who cares?"

§§§§

On Tuesday morning, Anne walked into the Pocahontas County Clerk's Office in West Virginia. Looking like just another resident of the county, Stephen stood to the side, wearing a plaid shirt and jeans and reading the local paper. He lifted his eyes to Anne's and smiled. "My bride has arrived."

She scanned the room to see if anyone noticed them, but the other two people in the room paid them no attention. She walked the few steps to Stephen. "And here's my groom."

"How was the trip out here?"

"Fine." She kissed his cheek. "Actually," she whispered, "a little odd. Phillip had me take three different Metro lines just to get to Metro Center. I eventually met him inside the Marriott parking garage. It felt like a scene out of *All the President's Men*."

"I drove myself, but Phillip made me take a similar route to get to the rental car—minus the Metro, though."

"Yeah. You taking the Metro would be a sure sign you were up to no good."

A familiar West Virginia brogue made them turn their heads. Judge Clements held a door open. "Stevie, Anne, I see you're ready for Shirley now. She'll take care of you."

§§§§

The following evening Walter checked in with the private investigation firm, Zells and Dottham, to see how the work on Stephen McEvoy was coming along. "Anything new for me?" he asked as he multitasked and scanned the headlines of *The Washington Times*.

Mr. Zells was apologetic. "A little, but nothing concrete. We haven't been able to conclusively get Anne Norwood and McEvoy in the same place, but we have some circumstantial evidence."

"Okay," Walter muttered, unimpressed. "Start at the top."

"For starters, we know Jennifer Hamilton is out of the picture. We couldn't get anything out of her management, so we tracked her down—she was walking out of a bar in L.A. Our guy asked her if she was dating McEvoy. Apparently, she giggled a lot and said they were quote 'still good friends' end quote. Then she ran off with that guy from *Raptorman*."

"What else?"

"Well, we almost caught Anne Norwood going to his family's ranch."

"What do you mean almost?"

"Our guy followed her as far as he could down a county road, but she turned onto an ungraded road with a lot of rocks. He needed a four-wheel-drive truck with high clearance and he wasn't in one. She was in a jeep. Anyway, we know it's a back route to the McEvoy ranch."

Walter shook his head and rolled his eyes. "Plan ahead next time, okay?"

"Well, they're back in D.C. now. She landed at Dulles yesterday, but today we can't find either of them. They're nowhere."

Walter's ears perked up. "You lost them? At the same time? That's curious."

"I suppose."

"Does she have roommates?"

"She lives alone in a basement apartment."

"Well, someone knows where she is," Walter said, flipping through the paper. "She's a twenty-two-year-old girl. She has to have friends who gossip."

"One would think. We'll work on the other interns in his office."

"Fine. Get cracking. In the meantime, I'm going to see what I can find."

"Really? Who are you going to talk to?"

Thinking about a recent, steamy night in Palm Beach with Helen Sanders, Walter's reply was nonchalant. "Oh, a lady friend of mine. Let's just say she's got a read on the men in the Senate."

§§§§

On Saturday morning, Phillip dropped Anne off at the McEvoy cabin before he went over to Judge Clements's place to report her arrival. Anne poked her head inside the front door. "Hello?"

Laura York's voice came from inside the house. "Hello, Anne! Come inside. Don't worry. It's just us girls."

As Anne walked in, she noticed the difference in the rooms. Flowers were everywhere. The dining room was properly set for a romantic dinner for two. She looked out the French doors onto the patio, and another table with six places was set for what looked to be a post-wedding brunch. Inside the kitchen, she found Laura with an apron around her waist and her attention on the stove.

"Good morning," Laura greeted with her soft, southern lilt. "It's so nice to see you again and on such a happy occasion."

"Yes, it's good to see you, too, but Laura, this is too much. Thank you. Really, you're incredibly kind, but—"

"No buts. This is fun, and Lillian wouldn't forgive me if I left this day up to Stephen."

"But Laura . . ."

"Please. It's my pleasure. Stephen asked me to get some flowers for the place. I just happened to think of a few other things."

"Well, thank you again."

"You're welcome. Now all of your things are laid out in the first bedroom on the right. I steamed your dress. It's gorgeous, by the way—and perfect for a hot day like today. It will look lovely in your wedding announcement in the *New York Times.*"

"Thank you. I love it, too." Checking her watch, Anne calculated her time to primp. "I've got an hour, right?"

"I'm guessing you want to wear your hair up. I can get you a few flowers if you want . . . maybe something blue?"

Anne tried not to smirk as she thought of the racy blue panties she bought to wear beneath her dress. "Thank you. Flowers would be nice. Actually, I think I've got everything else—old earrings, new dress . . . um . . .

something blue. I'm just missing the borrowed part."

"I thought that might be the case." Reaching her hand into the pocket of her pink linen dress, Laura pulled out an embroidered handkerchief. "I've got a hankie for you."

"You're amazing. You've thought of everything."

"If I haven't, I will by the ceremony. Grayson wouldn't be a senator without me thinking ahead his entire career."

"That's usually the case, isn't it?" Anne chuckled.

"Yes, ma'am." Laura smiled. "Now go get changed. You don't want to be late to your own wedding."

When it came time for the nuptials, Anne waited for Laura to situate everyone on the lawn. Only a few steps across the patio separated the house from the lawn and its blooming wildflowers. Her nervousness vanished into a grin when she saw Stephen catch his breath and smile at the sight of her. She thought him dashing in his casual suit, sans tie, but with a matching red rose to her bouquet.

Judge Clements stood in the center with Buster at his heel; off to the side stood Grayson and Laura. They all beamed as Anne walked toward them. Performing his role as the behind-the-scenes man, Phillip stood in the background with a camera, though also with a smile on his face.

The actual ceremony was short, legal, and very sweet. The standard civil ceremony had few words, but Anne watched as the enormity of the event swept over Stephen, and she felt the same. Savoring every second, their eyes never left one another. The marriage didn't feel rushed or forced, rather the natural next step in their relationship. He couldn't have said his vows with more enthusiasm and determination, and Anne recited hers intently with misty eyes. When the time came to seal the marriage, Stephen pulled her close and she placed both hands on his face; they shared a loving kiss.

After a round of applause, Phillip took a series of photos depicting a respectable, romantic, and, above all, official wedding. The six then sat down to Laura's elaborate brunch.

"You know, Phillip," commented Judge Clements as he snuck a piece of ham for Buster. "I've never known an attorney to provide so many services to his client. You're a combination attorney, photographer, chauffeur, personal shopper, and spy. I'm sure I'm missing something."

"I have a varied practice." Phillip was known for his economy of speech. He cleared his throat. "I hate to break up the festivities, but we need to talk about an unlikely, but possible, situation. I want to make sure everyone here is on the same page if the press is tipped off before we choose to contact them."

"Well, I'd prefer it if no one commented until we tell our families," said Stephen as he looked around the table.

"That's very understandable. As a mother, I'd like the courtesy," said Laura with a nod, but her tone changed to one of warning. "But I also think if the press calls before you're ready, either Judge Clements or Grayson should make a statement."

"Hell, yeah," Judge Clements muttered. "I'm talking if asked—only if asked, mind you—but I'm talking. I always give my opinion."

"What will you say?" Anne asked with some trepidation.

"Oh, something like, 'Yesterday morning, I was proud to perform the marriage of a longtime friend. In the afternoon, I went fishin'.' "

Everyone laughed at the Judge's statement, and Grayson snickered. "Mine will be similar. 'I was happy to stand up for a Senate colleague and family friend. If you want to know about the dress or the flowers, ask Laura.' "

While they all chuckled, Anne turned to Laura and smiled. "And what will you say?"

"I'll bore them to death with every last detail of your dress, hair, flowers, and rings." She winked and leaned closer to Anne. "And if Phillip lets me, I might leak a photo."

Stephen twisted his mouth, hating to bring up something so depressing at a happy time. He looked at Anne apologetically. "And what if someone suggests it's a shotgun wedding?"

Anne shrugged. "Isn't that guaranteed?" She made light of it, though she dreaded the ordeal.

"Pshaw," said the Judge with a wave of his hand. "I'm a judge in West Virginia. I've been to plenty of shotgun weddings. I've officiated shotgun weddings. I know a shotgun wedding when I see one, and this wasn't a shotgun wedding. Don't you think that's right, Grayson?"

"Of course." Grayson laughed. "I'd comment and say 'despite the Second Amendment rights of the father of the bride, there was no need for firearms at the ceremony.' "

After brunch, Judge Clements left for his house with his Bible and dog, while Laura ordered Grayson to help her with the dishes. Anne and Stephen used the time to square away with Phillip the following day's announcement of their wedding to their families. When everything was taken care of, the newly married couple bid their guests farewell.

As soon as they were out of sight, Stephen lifted Anne off the ground and spun her around. "You're my wife, we're alone, and for the rest of our lives, we don't have to hide anymore!"

"I know!" She kissed him hard. The kiss and his gleeful expression made her gasp and she asked, "Why didn't we do this sooner?"

"Oh God. Don't you dare revise history here. I had this idea a long time ago."

"But I came up with it at a better time."

"My smartass." He put her down and kissed her joyfully. As his hands wandered up her bare back, he touched the tendrils of her hair, damp from the heat. "Maybe we should go for a swim. You haven't been to the swimming hole yet."

"Sure. Let me get my suit."

"I don't think that's necessary today," he countered, waggling his eyebrows.

"Are you sure?" She was still surprised by their newfound freedom.

"Definitely."

A partially dammed creek created a small pond with clear water, and a dock jutted out, providing both a patio and diving platform. When they arrived at the dock, Stephen unbuttoned his shirt while Anne found a place to lay her dress.

Just as she reached to undo her halter, Stephen rushed to her side. "No. Not a chance. That's my job." After he unfastened the dress, she turned around and smiled, holding the top to her chest. He lowered the dress so she could step out of it, and his grin grew. She was completely nude, save for lacy blue panties. "Oh, my naughty bride."

"I was supposed to wear something blue." She smirked, happy that her plan worked.

His hands ghosted over her breasts, hips, and finally the blue silk. "Rather than skinny-dipping, maybe we should get on with our marriage."

She laughed and took his hand. "I think that's a great idea."

Chapter 25

The following morning, Anne and Stephen were giddy as they sped across Interstate 66 through northern Virginia, nearing Washington, D.C. It wasn't simply the speed of sixty-five miles per hour which gave them a rush—it was also the experience of being out publicly as a couple, albeit in a car at a high speed.

A few times that morning, Stephen checked his messages. He smiled as he ignored Megan and Patty's annoyed pleas demanding his location. When his cell rang and he saw it was Helen, he grimaced.

"It's Helen. I think I should take it. Are you okay with me taking the call?" he asked Anne.

"It's fine," she grumbled and looked out the window.

"I'll keep it on speaker." He smiled and answered, "Good morning, Helen. How are you? I'm sorry I didn't get back to you yesterday."

"I'm good," she answered in a silky voice. "Although things always get better when I talk with you."

Anne sneered at the phone, and he shook his head apologetically. He warned Helen, "I've got you on speaker because I'm driving . . . with my family."

He winked at Anne's grin, while Helen's voice huffed, "Please pull over and take me off speaker. I need to talk with you about my border security amendment on the appropriations bill."

"Okay. Just a second." He muted the phone. "She actually does want to talk work. She's been trying to get me to vote for this stupid thing for a while now. The vote is on Wednesday, and I need to get her off my back. There's an exit coming up. I'll make the call quick."

Anne nodded, and he exited the highway. In a gas station parking lot, he answered again. "I'm sorry, but my position hasn't changed. I can't vote for that amendment."

"This is important to me. It was a campaign promise. I'm not sure when I can sneak it in again."

"But you're not up again for two years. You've got plenty of time."

"Stephen, I'm counting on you for this one. I need your vote." Her sharp plea sounded more like a demand.

"No." He'd lost his patience with her relentlessness. "There's no way I'm taking money away from airports, which actually have real national security threats, to fund crazy Idaho militias."

Anne suppressed a giggle and gave him a nod of approval.

Over the speaker, Helen snapped, "Those are patriotic Americans who want to keep this country safe from terrorists and illegal immigrants. They're some of my most devoted constituents. I won't have you talking about them like that. Take it back, now."

"No. It's the truth." He smiled at Anne, but he soon thought better of his harsh words to Helen. Needing to make some amends, his tone softened. "Come on, Helen. I accept it when you can't support my bills. Please do the same for me."

"This is different."

"No, it's not."

Helen didn't reply for a moment, and when she did, her voice was stern and cold. "I'm not used to being told no, and I'm tired of hearing it from you. Do I have to remind you that you are in no position to reject a request from me?"

"Do I have to remind you that you're in no position to *ever* threaten me?" His eyes opened wide in anger.

"Oh, really? Who has more to lose?"

Catching a glimpse of his wedding ring, he smiled at Anne. "At this point . . . I think you do."

"What does that mean?"

"Just speculating." He lowered his voice in warning. "You're playing a dangerous game here. Drop it."

"Huh. I'll think about it." Her line clicked as she ended the call.

"Is she going to be a problem?" Anne asked and winced.

"Not any more than usual . . . if she knows what's good for her." He squeezed her hand and rubbed his thumb over her wedding band, a constant reminder of his newfound comfort in the world. Without saying another word, he tapped on his phone a few times and rang his mother's line.

"Hi, Mom."

"Hello, Stephen. Are you home from your fishing trip with Grayson yet?"

"Almost. I need you to call a family meeting at the house in an hour, and please tell Megan to get Greg there, too. It's important."

"So are you going to make an announcement?"

Stephen heard the grin in his mother's voice in anticipation of an engagement. "Yes. Anne and I have something to tell everyone."

"I can't wait!" Her gleeful tone was one Stephen hadn't heard from his mother in years. "I'll go do it right now. Oh, and tell Anne good-bye."

Anne smiled at all-knowing Lillian. "Good-bye, Lillian."

§§§§

In less than an hour, Stephen and Anne entered the house hand in hand. High from anticipation, Anne smiled with nervous delight. Her smile vanished when she saw a stern Patty heading straight toward them, with Lillian following behind.

Before any morning greetings, Patty accosted him in the foyer. "Why haven't you returned my calls? Why is there a new woman's saddle in the garage? And above all, why did the two of you pull up together in the same car? What the *fuck* is going on?"

Lillian placed her hands on her hotheaded daughter's shoulders. "Now, Patty, calm down. Let's all sit in the living room before you interrogate your brother. I'm sure he'll answer all of our questions."

Stephen smirked at his sister. "That, I will." He whispered in Anne's ear. "Patty ruined the surprise, but the saddle is your wedding present."

"Really?" Anne exclaimed, her eyes big with disbelief.

He pressed his finger to her lips. "Shush for now. This isn't how we wanted to tell them we got married."

The entire family plus Greg assembled on the sofas and chairs. Before Stephen said a word, Megan spotted the diamond on Anne's hand. She gasped out loud and turned to look at Stephen's left hand. "Oh my God. You're married!"

The reactions around the room varied.

Greg appeared genuinely happy for Stephen and Anne. "Wow. This changes everything—and in a good way, I think."

Megan took her hand off her big, pregnant belly and placed it on Marco's leg. She looked him in the eye and rested her head on his shoulder. "I feel sick."

Marco clenched his wife's hand, and his smiled widened at his brother-in-law and new sister-in-law. "Well, hot damn. Congratulations." He kissed his wife's hair and said softly, "I think it's a good thing. They didn't have any good options. Why not take the one which makes them happiest?"

"Please, don't get me wrong," Megan said and smiled. "I *am* happy for you two—really, I am. It's just a surprise, and the press will be crazy."

Almost jumping out of her seat with glee, Lillian's hands fluttered around her face. "I'm so happy! I'm so proud of you two. It reminds me of Patrick's and my wedding. I want to hear all about it. Oh, I can't wait to see the pictures!" Her voice lowered in reproach. "You do have pictures, don't you?"

Stephen nodded. "Of course, Mom. Phillip took them." He turned to

Patty, who'd been uncharacteristically quiet.

"What the fuck?" She said with her eyes ablaze. "You went off and eloped? I swear to God, you're trying to lose this race."

"Now Patty, that is no way to speak to your brother and your new sister-in-law." Lillian shook her head. "I will not have it. Even your father would put aside politics at this moment."

Chastened, Patty hung her head down and mumbled, "Congratulations, but I have to think about this." She rubbed her temples in silence.

In the meantime, Marco went to the bar to grab a bottle of champagne. As he handed out the crystal flutes, the room erupted in hugs and cheers and questions asking how they had pulled it off. Everyone admired the rings, but they were far more impressed with the wedding story. While the impromptu party swirled around her, Patty continued to press her fingers into her forehead.

Marco was the one to confirm what no one yet had asked. "So you're going public, correct?"

Anne and Stephen smiled at one another. "Of course. As soon as possible."

"It's going to be one hell of a news day." Megan giggled. "And I'll love it."

After Anne and Stephen told all the details of their wedding tale, Patty piped up with a grin. "Okay. I've thought things through. I'm fine with it. This might even work. Congratulations."

"Don't knock yourself out there, sis." Stephen laughed.

"Don't worry. I won't. We've got to get on this. I don't know if a politician has ever tried to avert a sex scandal by eloping."

"I wouldn't refer to my marriage to Anne as my 'trying to avert a sex scandal.' "

A pang hit Anne in the gut. She gave him an uneasy look and shrugged. "I think that's what people will call it. Patty's right."

"Thanks, Anne." Patty smiled and turned to her brother. She was smug. "I've always liked your wife. She's smart."

Megan interrupted the squabble. "Can we talk about the announcement strategy?"

"Well, I'd like to tell my parents first, of course, and in person, if at all possible," said Anne.

Lillian smiled. "Lovely, then I'll place a call to them afterward. I'll tell them the truth—Patrick would have been proud to have you as a daughter-in-law."

"Good move on both parts," Patty commented. "We need your dad standing beside you and Stephen at the press conference."

Anne sucked in a sharp breath. "Um. My mom and brother *may* be there. But I have no idea how we'll get my dad there. He may think it's a campaign stunt."

"That's understandable." Stephen nodded. "I don't want to pressure your family to do something they're uncomfortable with."

She cringed as she thought of the awkward position she'd put her parents in, especially her father. She'd tried not to think about it over the last week, concentrating instead on her own happiness. Now she faced the political fallout of her marriage. Whether it was at a press conference or some later date, her father was guaranteed to be asked about his son-in-law. Would he buck his party and endorse Stephen over Langford? She was certain he wouldn't take sides, though she wondered how he'd convey his continued party loyalty, despite his daughter's choice of husbands. She had an idea which could make it easier for everyone.

"This is going to sound crazy," she said with some apprehension. "But maybe my father and I should tell Langford before we release anything."

"What?" Stephen asked, his brow furrowing. "I don't know what that gets anyone. Your dad will be uncomfortable, and then Langford and his campaign are prepared when we come out."

Anne shook her head. "We can get the timing right, and more importantly, it would allow my dad to be open and honest with Langford. I mean, let's get real. My dad's a Republican. He's friends with these guys. It would be nice for him to be able to do things on the up and up as much as possible."

"It's a brilliant idea," Patty announced and slapped her leg. "When Langford is asked to comment on your marriage, they'll have to disclose that you and your father spoke with them. They can't come out quite as hard if you actually give him a courtesy warning."

"Patty's on to something," Greg said from across the room. "It gives us another layer of respectability."

"It's a really good idea," agreed Megan.

Stephen looked around the room searching for support. There was none. Every member of his family nodded in agreement with Anne and Patty.

Lillian summed it up. "Tactically, it's very smart." She smiled at Anne. "It's also the decent thing to do."

Stephen sighed in defeat. "Okay. But only because your dad will be there. I'd hate for you to do that alone."

As the debate went on around her, Megan scribbled notes. "I think we should handle things this way. We all fly to Denver tonight, and Stephen and Anne continue on to the ranch. First thing tomorrow morning, they tell her family, and Mom does a follow-up call. Anne and her dad then tell Langford a few hours later. In the meantime, I'll have pitched *The Denver Post* an exclusive interview with you two, which will run the next day. That way the full story is out before we hold our press conference the next morning where you answer all questions."

"I like it." Patty nodded. "We break the whole story on our terms first, and then we're completely transparent at a press conference."

Marco snickered. "So in the sequence you've laid out, when does the shit hit the fan?"

Megan raised her eyebrows and took a deep breath. "The moment the reporter calls Langford's camp for a quote."

§§§§

Later that evening, Walter rolled off Helen as they panted from their second round. The smell of sex mixed with the lingering scent of disinfectant, common to every Courtyard Marriott. Walter asked to rendezvous outside Dulles Airport in Virginia so they wouldn't be noticed together. After a grueling day of twisting senators' arms for votes, Helen was happy for the distraction.

With his arms wrapped around her, Walter stroked her shoulder. "Helen, we're friends. I hope you don't mind me asking something of you."

"Not at all."

"Please don't be offended."

She laughed. "Why would I be offended?"

"Well, some women might find it insulting."

"How so?"

"Well, I'm guessing you haven't been faithful to your fiancé."

She laughed at the ridiculousness of his statement; at that very moment, she was naked in bed with another man. "What makes you say that?" She blinked in feigned innocence and shrugged. "I like the fact Smythe and I are engaged. I like that I've found someone to have kids with, but I'm not quite ready to settle down. Don't worry, though, if you're concerned about my reelection. I'm very discreet—as discreet as you, I might add."

"How do you know?" He raised his eyebrows.

"How do I know?" She laughed. "Isn't this the pot calling the kettle black? For starters, I know you've been screwing your receptionist for years. So if you add me and the secretary together, odds are there are others. You're just discreet."

"You're a smart woman." He sighed. "So if you're as discreet as me, I'm guessing you stick with men who have just as much to lose as you?"

"Yes."

"Like your Senate colleagues?"

"On occasion." She gave him a wicked smile.

"Have you ever crossed party lines?"

"Yes. That's not unheard of . . ."

"Pardon me if this is too forward." His voice changed from apologetic to interrogative. "But have you ever been with Stephen McEvoy?"

Still angry from their conversation that morning, she sneered hearing Stephen's name. "Well, yes, but who hasn't?"

"Funny you bring that up. Do you know any of his other . . . companions?" He looked at her dead on and spoke with determination. "I'm heavily invested in the Colorado race, and we have a lead he's had an affair with an intern. Do you know anything about it? I wouldn't ask if the race weren't on the line. We could take the Senate with that seat."

Helen was quiet for a moment as she evaluated his question. She never expected to be asked about Stephen by anyone—let alone Walter. In the end, Stephen's opposition to her amendment weighed little on her mind. Instead, party loyalty made her divulge the truth. Without hesitation, she declared, "I believe her name is Anne."

Chapter 26

Early the following morning, Anne led Stephen into the Norwood family home. "Hey! I'm here," she called out.

Still in his pajamas, Mark walked down the stairs and gave a sleepy greeting to his sister. "Hey." When he saw Stephen behind her, he raised one eyebrow and nodded. "You're here, too?"

"Morning, Mark," Stephen answered, as he walked up and offered his hand.

Shaking Stephen's hand, Mark looked between Stephen and Anne. "Huh." He scratched his head and headed to the kitchen. "This is gonna be interesting."

As they walked into the breakfast nook, Elton and Mary Beth looked up from their usual morning fare of hardboiled eggs, buttered toast, and *The Denver Post*. Neither seemed surprised at Stephen's presence. Instead, they glanced at one another as if to confirm their suspicions.

Elton spoke first. "Morning, Anne. Morning, Stephen. It's good to see you."

"Morning, Dad. Hi, Mom." Anne gave them hugs.

Stephen again extended his hand. "Good morning, sir. Good morning, Mrs. Norwood."

"Stephen, can I get you a cup of coffee?" asked Mary Beth with a hesitant smile.

"Thank you. That would be very nice."

"I'll get it, Mom. You don't have to get up," answered Anne.

"Pour me a cup, too," said Mark, as he rubbed his eyes.

Anne looked at her brother and could tell he was hung over. He spent most of his vacations reliving his college years of drinking and sleeping. Pouring a trio of coffees, she chuckled. "You're looking a little worse for wear."

"Thanks." He smirked. "We'll see if it gets worse."

Elton motioned to an empty chair. "Stephen, why don't you take a seat?"

"Thanks." He sat down, and as Anne distributed the coffee cups, he announced, "You're probably all wondering why we're here."

Anne's eyes darted about the room. Her call the night before saying she needed to talk had been short. Over the months since Christmas, they'd heard brief snippets of her life with Stephen. She made sure she always gave details of what was going on with his family, hoping they'd understand the relationship was serious. As time wore on, she got the feeling her mother was warming slightly to him. Anne hoped she'd help convince her father and brother.

Mark was the first to respond to Stephen's statement, but he directed his reply to Anne. "So *now* you're pregnant."

"Jeez. No." She rolled her eyes. "Will you give me some credit?"

Mary Beth looked at her husband, and everyone could see the relief in their eyes. Stephen gave Anne a nod and dropped the bombshell. "Mr. and Mrs. Norwood, Anne and I are married."

"What?" Mary Beth exclaimed.

"Oh my God." Mark shook his head and laughed.

Elton sat motionless and without expression.

After a reassuring glance at Anne, Stephen looked again at her parents. "I realize we haven't gone about this in the traditional route. I mean no disrespect; I did tell you at Christmas I wanted to marry her. So instead of asking you for her hand, I'm asking for your blessing. We eloped on Saturday."

"You did? How? Where?" her mother asked, her mouth agape.

"We were married at my family's cabin in West Virginia by a family friend who's a federal judge. Senator Grayson York and his wife, Laura, were our witnesses. It was a very respectable wedding. I love Anne more than anything in the world, more than my own life and certainly my career. Will you give us your blessing?"

Elton sat in silence, maintaining his expressionless stare. Mary Beth's eyes flicked down to the rings on their hands, and her eyebrows rose at the diamond Anne wore. She caught Elton's eye and gave the tiniest of nods toward the ring. Finally, Anne could decode their silent communication, for it was one she'd seen before. It was the look they gave one another when something serious had taken place that needed special attention.

Elton spoke calmly. "You told me you wanted to marry her. You said you wanted to earn my blessing. But you also told me you were going to wait until after the election. What made you change your mind?"

"I wanted to, Dad." Anne's voice was strong as she claimed her own ground as an adult. "There was no reason to wait."

Elton nodded at his wife, and Anne awaited her opinion. Her mother was a practical woman. Anne hoped that she'd see her daughter was happy with a man who loved her. And her new son-in-law was a United States Senator from a hallowed family with significant wherewithal. Mary Beth looked at the dazzling jewels on Anne's hand one more time. The ring said it all. Stephen McEvoy was a catch, and Anne had caught him—hook, line, and sinker.

She smiled. "Well, Anne, you certainly have made your life more complicated than it needed to be, but it *is* your choice. We still love you, and I see you're happy. Congratulations, sweetheart."

"Oh, Mom," she said as she reached to hug her mother. "I love you."

"I love you, too, dear. We just want you to be happy."

"Thank you, Mrs. Norwood." Stephen smiled.

Everyone looked at Elton, waiting his opinion on the matter. He cleared his voice and spoke directly to Stephen. "You have my blessing—not because I think this is a choice Anne should have made. Her mother and I both think she's too young to get married, and we'd say that regardless of who the man was. But you have my blessing because I love my daughter, despite her decisions, and you've acted about as honorably and honestly as you could, given your situation."

"Thank you, Mr. Norwood. I appreciate that."

"Thanks, Dad," Anne said as she walked around to give him a hug.

As they closed their arms around one another, he finally smiled. "I love you, Annie."

"I love you, Dad," she replied, holding back her tears.

Mark squeezed her arm as she walked to her seat. "I guess everybody's cool with it, so I am, too. Congratulations. Good going. Nothing I do in life will compare to this."

Anne punched him in the arm. "Yeah, right."

"I assume you're going to make a formal statement," Elton said.

"Yes, we will," Anne replied.

Stephen looked at his new in-laws with all seriousness. "Let me tell you how we've planned this." He described their plans to go public, but left out the meeting with Langford. Anne would raise that later.

"Mom, Dad, you don't have to be there if you don't want to," Anne said.

Elton looked at his wife, and she nodded. Without a wasting a moment, he replied, "We'll be there."

"We will?" asked Mark in complete confusion.

Elton shrugged. "They're married now. That changes everything. I don't want to be estranged from my daughter." He turned to Anne. "What statement does it make if we're not with you when you announce this? It makes it look like we've shunned you—maybe even for political reasons. It couldn't be further from the truth."

Mary Beth smiled. "We're still a family, Anne. We want this marriage to work."

"Damn," Mark said as he took a drink of coffee. "I guess it makes sense. I don't want you hanging out there alone."

Anne wiped away the tears that flooded her eyes. "Thank you," she whispered.

"I can't begin to express my appreciation to you all," Stephen said as he put his arm around Anne. "And I have to say my family is going to be very happy to meet you—my mother especially."

As they talked about the plans for the next day, Anne became anxious. It was time to bring up Langford. "Dad, I know you don't want to talk politics tomorrow, but I wondered if it would be best for you to give Langford a heads-up. Stephen and I think it would be a good idea."

Elton nodded. "I actually thought of it myself, but I didn't want to press it with you. It's your day tomorrow, not mine."

"Well, would you be up for it?"

"Sure, let me see if I can get some time with him today." He smiled. "We're going to Denver anyway."

§§§§

Stephen left Anne alone with her family to organize their meeting with Langford. They would all meet up in Denver later that day. As he drove, he listened to his messages; Megan's was tense.

"Call me now. I just talked with the reporter. He's received a tip about you and Anne."

Stephen yelled into the phone, "Fuck!"

The word was no sooner out of his mouth when the phone rang with Megan on the line. "I got tired of waiting for you. Did you get my message?"

"Just now. Tell me everything that happened."

"I pitched Dexter Olson the interview. After he listened to my whole spiel, he said something like 'Well, this is very interesting. I was planning to work on a story today about Senator McEvoy. I just got a tip he had an affair with an intern.'

"So I asked if it was from Langford's campaign, and he said no, it was from another source not affiliated with the campaign. When I said it must be Walter Smith, Dexter didn't deny it. Anyway, I told him you and Anne would answer all questions with an in-person interview this afternoon."

Alarmed, but still under control, Stephen blew out a steadying breath. "Langford's campaign has to know. Okay. Well, this is a wrench in our plans, but it's not the end of the world."

"Do you have any idea how someone figured this out? And who it was? Were they following you? Oh God. Did they go to the cabin?"

"They may have been following me, but I doubt they were at the cabin. Phillip was very careful in orchestrating how we got in and out of there."

"So where did things break down?"

"Helen Sanders," he replied without skipping a beat and with no second thoughts.

"Oh my God. Are you sure?"

"Just a guess . . ."

§§§§

As Anne and Elton were ushered into the ornate Colorado State Treasurer's office, Dan Langford rose from his stately desk.

"Welcome, Elton. Anne." He extended his hand.

"Good to see you, Dan," Elton said, shaking his hand. "Thank you for squeezing us in on such short notice."

"Hello, Mr. Langford," Anne said politely.

"Well, sit down. You said it was urgent. What can I do for you?"

After they took their seats, Anne looked at her father for moral support. He nodded, and she spoke with confidence. "We wanted to tell you something important before you heard it in the press."

"We wanted to do this as a courtesy to you and as a sign of the friendship between our families," said Elton.

"What's that?" Langford asked with deep suspicion.

The tone of his voice and his entire demeanor told Anne and Elton something important—Langford wasn't in the know. Someone had told *The Denver Post* about Stephen and Anne's relationship, but no one had told the candidate yet. They'd be springing the news.

Anne was confident and forthright. "Stephen McEvoy and I were married this weekend. We're announcing it tomorrow."

Blinking rapidly as he absorbed her words, a sneer slowly curled Langford's lip upward. "Stephen McEvoy. You married him? You're just a girl! And you work for him." He looked at Elton in disgust. "Why did you allow this?"

Elton shrugged. "Obviously, it wasn't my decision."

"It would be my decision in my house!" Dan stared at Anne. "Why would you do this?"

"We're in love. It's been a complicated relationship, and we wanted to get married. It's that simple." She was going to end it on that final note, but she remembered a crucial fact. "Oh, and of course, I no longer work in his office."

Langford's anger turned to Elton. "What are you going to say about this?"

"That I support my daughter."

"I don't understand how you could ever say that," Langford replied.

Elton shook his head. "Aw hell, Dan. I'm a prosecutor. I know a defendant is in a world of hurt if his family isn't with him in court. Mary Beth and I are standing by our daughter. She's married. We want the marriage to work. We're not talking politics here. This is a family matter."

The room was silent for a moment, until Langford stood up. Anne and Elton did the same, also without speaking. Langford extended his hand to Elton. "Thank you for telling me," he said flatly. To Anne, he was equally emotionless. "I wish you the best." He nodded to the door. "I need to get back to work now. Thank you for stopping by."

"Thank you, Dan," said Elton as he guided Anne to the door.

She forced a smile, but Langford ignored her and walked to his desk. "Thank you, Mr. Langford," she called out.

As Elton closed the door, Anne heard Langford's voice on the phone. "Get Trey . . . now."

§§§§

The day became increasingly surreal for Anne as she sat with Stephen, awaiting *The Denver Post* reporter. Stephen held her sweaty hand and stroked her hair, trying to ease her mind. "It's okay. Everything is going to be okay."

"How can you say that? This day just gets worse and worse."

Stephen shrugged. "I don't know. I talked to Mom. She's a little upset we're behind the eight ball with Walter, but she's hopeful. We'll learn what he's up to as we talk to the reporter. He'll give us information. We just need to tell him our story."

"I know, I know." She smiled. "It *is* a pretty good story."

He kissed her cheek and whispered in her ear, "Of course it is. It's a love story, after all."

Chapter 27

That afternoon, Langford arrived at his humming campaign office. Patriotic campaign signs, bedecked with sheriff stars and his name, covered the walls. When he walked in, he was greeted like a celebrity, only with more deference. While he appreciated the attention, he simply tipped his straw cowboy hat as he strode to his private office.

As he entered, he saw Trey sitting on the sofa while texting furiously. He shut the door and spewed, "You said you knew . . . When? Why didn't you tell me?"

"I didn't know for sure . . . I just had suspicions," Trey said with a shrug.

"When, though?" Langford sat down in his giant desk chair and placed his hat at its corner. "When did you first suspect something? What made you think of it? When we saw her in D.C.?"

"No. I thought I saw McEvoy with Anne at the Boulder commencement."

"McEvoy was at the graduation? *I* was there. Why didn't you tell me?" Langford pounded his fist on the desk, making the pens jump.

"With fifty thousand people, you can't be sure," said Trey, sounding defensive. "I called Walter. Then he—"

"You called Walter before *me*? I should have been told right there, on the spot."

Trey walked to the desk and leaned against it. "Boss, I'm sorry we kept you in the dark. We didn't want to distract you. It might've been nothing."

Langford grimaced and leaned back in his chair. "Humph." After a moment he sighed and resigned himself to the fact that if he wanted to win the election, he needed to be managed. "I suppose it was the right thing to do, though I feel like a fool. I would've had a lot more to say to Elton and Anne if I'd known." Trey's mouth twitched, and Langford caught on immediately. "*Okay.* I get it. It might not have been the best thing if I'd taken them to task."

"That was our thinking."

"So what have you learned?" asked Langford, getting down to business.

"Walter has discovered that they've been together for a while . . . since last fall. It's kind of crazy how they've been able to keep it secret."

"Since the fall? That can't be. McEvoy has been with . . . well, with everybody."

"Yeah . . . who knows what disease she's caught from him." Trey chuckled. "Not to mention, there's a chance she's pregnant. It's unlikely, but wouldn't it be great?"

"I thought of that myself," muttered Langford.

"Regardless, we don't have much time." Trey said with an eager pat on the desk. "We have to make a statement."

"So what are you thinking?"

"Well, we need to be as transparent as they are, or this could blow up in our faces. They've been pretty cunning by telling you first. I've talked with Walter, and he's adamant we need to disclose that. He suggests something like, 'Elton Norwood is a fine man who was decent enough to inform me of the news.' I think it sounds pretty good."

"Okay. This is what I want to say." Langford began scratching out his statement on a piece of monogrammed paper.

He handed it to Trey, who read it aloud. " 'The Norwoods are longtime friends. Elton Norwood was decent enough to inform me of the events. I wish Anne Norwood the best of luck in life, but I fear she is the victim in this situation. As for my opponent, I am very disturbed by his obvious lack of ethics and potential violation of the law. His actions should be thoroughly investigated. The people of Colorado deserve better in a senator.' " When he finished, Trey bobbed his head in agreement. "I like it."

"What's Walter doing?"

"Oh, he's got a few television spots in the works already." Trey smirked.

§§§§

As soon as *The Denver Post* website went live with its exclusive interview with Senator Stephen McEvoy and his former intern—now wife—Anne Norwood, the twenty-four-hour cable news cycle kicked in. Reporters around the nation and even the world scrambled for any bit of novel information they could find. Megan was glued to the television listening to predictions of her brother's uncertain future.

"Hey, Marco," she called out from the bedroom. "CNN has already tracked down the Pocahontas County clerk who issued their marriage license."

"Don't worry. I'm listening," Marco answered from the bathroom.

Unfortunately for the media, Judge Clements had picked the right clerk for Stephen and Anne. When CNN's Brian Nester met Shirley on her way into the county courthouse, she happily agreed to be interviewed.

His first questions were friendly, but pointed. "Can you tell me more about Senator McEvoy and Anne Norwood? What were they like as a couple?"

"Oh, they were real nice," she said in her deep West Virginia accent as she smiled for the camera.

"There must have been something that stood out—something different from the average couple coming in for a marriage license."

"No. They paid cash, just like everybody else," she said without missing a beat.

"Is there anything else you can tell us?"

"Pocahontas County is just about one of the prettiest places in God's creation. It's a lovely place to get married."

Marco guffawed with laughter and walked into the bedroom, wearing only a towel and holding a razor. "Well, she shut him up. I love that woman. She reminds of me of my Aunt Maria, who works in a library in Pueblo. You couldn't get her to tell you what books people checked out of that library if you threatened to skin her cat."

"And no one gives people like her enough credit. They're smart. They know what they're doing," Megan said as she pulled a blouse over her swollen belly. She sighed. "The press isn't that bad yet, but it's only the beginning."

§§§§

When Helen woke up that morning, she started her day as she always did and immediately picked up her phone. The number of messages surprised her, so she went to the first from her state director back in Idaho, Joe Riggs. Next to her chief of staff in D.C., Joe was her closest confidant. Since he lived a few time zones away, he often had news that came in after she'd gone to bed.

Catching her breath in shock, she placed her right hand on her chest as she read Joe's first text.

Unbelievable! McEvoy eloped w/ his intern on Sat. Announcing today. Rumor is she's pregnant. Another Dem bites the dust!

She scanned her remaining texts and e-mails; every one of them was about the scandal. She gasped aloud, "Oh my God. What did Stephen do?"

At once, she turned on the television, and Fox News appeared. The plastic morning news show personalities filled up airtime by picking apart Stephen and Anne's *Denver Post* interview, which posted online only hours earlier. As the female announcer read a quote from Stephen or Anne, her male counterpart batted it down.

"Let's be honest here. Senator McEvoy has been quite the high-profile ladies' man. He's been linked to everyone from Hollywood starlets to Members of Congress. Why would he pick an intern to marry unless there was something else going on? Is she pregnant? The interviewer never really asked.

Only a few months ago, actress Jennifer Hamilton called the senator her, and I quote, 'boyfriend.' Now, she's saying it was just to get some animal-rights bill through Congress. Was he seeing both of them?

The senator started seeing this girl while she worked in his office. You have to wonder if he's been with other staffers. Is this really a one-time incident? That's not usually the way these things turn out. The Senate Ethics Committee is going to have to investigate.

How will the voters in Colorado view a sex scandal? Is this the kind of behavior they want in a senator? Not many voters in the United States would put up with this. After all, this is America, not France."

With the chatter in the background, Helen raced through her other messages and listened to voice mails. As she learned more, she wondered if they'd gotten married because they'd been found out or if Anne was pregnant.

When her phone rang, it showed her fiancé's name. She let it go into voice mail. He probably wanted to gossip, but he wouldn't have any new information. Instead, she tapped away on her phone and pulled up the newspaper interview.

She shook her head as she read because Stephen came across as completely honest. When she finished, she was shocked. "I think he's in love with her."

Her lip curled in disgust. *Why would he want her when he could be with me? Everyone wants to be with me.* She wondered if Stephen married her in part because she'd disclosed Anne's name to Walter, but she felt no guilt.

"Serves him right," she said to the empty room.

§§§§

A few hours later, the briefing room inside the Denver Federal Building was packed with local, national, and international media holding cameras, microphones, and reporters' tablets. The small space was loud as they shared information with one another and awaited the start of the press conference.

In the anteroom, the McEvoy and Norwood families spoke in hushed tones, and Anne rubbed the sweat off her hands. Looking down, she squinted with anxiety and centered herself with a deep breath of determination.

Ever punctual at nine sharp, Stephen led Anne into the room, with Greg and the rest of the McEvoy and Norwood clans filing in behind them. Stephen looked his daily senatorial self in a dark blue suit, white shirt, and red tie. He stood at the podium with Anne at his side. She looked svelte in a pencil skirt, with a wide belt tightly cinched to counter any pregnancy comments. Stephen wasted no time in making his statement.

"Good morning, everyone. Thank you for coming for what we view as a very happy announcement. We'd like to make short statements and then open it up for questions." Letting the press corps nod in agreement, he said, "I'd like to introduce you to my wife, Anne Norwood McEvoy." Pausing for a moment and beaming with pride, he looked at her, and they shared a smile. "We married on Saturday at my family's cabin in West Virginia. A longtime family friend, Federal Judge Worthington Clements, performed the ceremony. Our witnesses were my father's best friend, former colleague, and my current colleague in the Senate, Senator Grayson York and his wife, Laura. It was important to me to have a reminder of my father at our wedding, as his presence has weighed heavily on my mind since I first met Anne. It's true Anne worked as an intern in my office. I was taken from the moment we first met, but I denied my feelings for her. I continually asked myself, 'What would my father do?' The answer was always the same. Patrick McEvoy would stay away from such a politically dangerous relationship.

"It was only when I found myself in too deep with Anne that I spoke with my mother, Lillian McEvoy, who eventually gave me the opposite answer. As she can tell you herself, above all, my father would want me to be happy. After spending time with Anne, she said if my happiness depended on pursuing a relationship with Anne, then I should do just that. Anne and I started off as friends, sharing a love of the outdoors, public service, books, and our families. I mention our families since we had a bit of an old-fashioned courtship, with my family almost always around us. With so much in common, our relationship soon turned romantic. In December, I sat down with her family and told them I had every intention of marrying Anne one day. That day came this past Saturday, and I've never been happier."

Smiling again at Anne, he moved aside and offered her microphone. She'd been coached for two hours that morning by Megan and Patty. While still anxious about the spectacle of it all, she was confident about her prepared remarks. They were short and written in her own voice, rather than public-relations speak, and they showed her to be a very normal, down-to-earth person.

She happily greeted the room. "Good morning. Please, first let me apologize if I stumble. I'm not accustomed to making headlines." The line was perfect, showing her as both humble and humorous.

"I'm also happy to be here today as we announce our marriage with our families at our side. I never expected my life would turn out as it has, but I feel very fortunate to have met my husband so early in life. I know many will say ours was a whirlwind romance, and it will never last. I look forward to proving them wrong." Laughter filled the room in response, and she waited for the chuckling to die down. "I went into this relationship with my eyes wide open to the risk I was taking, both to my personal reputation and future career. I quickly realized, though, that I'd make no greater mistake in my life if I didn't spend the rest of it with Stephen. Of course, I could say more, but I'm sure you have questions for all of us."

Anne stepped aside, and Stephen moved to the microphone to field the onslaught of questions, answering each one—no matter how personal.

"Could you tell us more about the timing of the relationship?"

"We started seeing each other in late October, early November."

"When did the relationship become inappropriate?"

"The relationship was never inappropriate. Internally, we followed all the rules and simple good judgment. My chief of staff talked with Anne to ensure it was a consensual relationship. While we kept the relationship private, our families were well aware, as were some friends."

"According to press accounts, you were seeing other women last fall. When did you stop?"

"As soon as I set my mind to be with Anne."

"Just a few months ago, actress Jennifer Hamilton said you two were still dating."

"Well, she was wrong."

"Why did you elope?" The local news station poked further. "What does it say that you didn't marry in Colorado?"

"Obviously, I couldn't get a marriage license in Colorado without it becoming public, and a public wedding would be a news event. We were lucky to have a private ceremony, even if it meant that our families weren't there."

"How do you respond to the comments that you only married to avoid a scandal?"

"Considering the hundreds of millions of people who will hear about our marriage, I'd say we haven't avoided public scrutiny."

"Are you worried about the Senate Ethics Committee investigating you?"

"Not at all. I have nothing to hide, and I've broken no law."

"Why did Anne continue to work for you after you started dating?"

"Quitting really wouldn't have solved anything. Suspicions would still be raised. The fact she'd worked for me would still hang over us."

"Are you concerned about the impact this scandal will have on your reelection?"

"No, because it's not a scandal."

"You said that your friendship changed to a romantic relationship. What does that mean?"

"What do you think it means? It went from a platonic relationship to a romantic relationship. I'm not going to elaborate more than that."

"The timing seems odd to many people. Is there any other reason why you married?"

"Other than we love each other? No." He looked at Megan with her hands clasped over her baby bump. Beside her, Lillian beamed at the room. "My mother is expecting only one grandchild." Stephen smiled. "I'm sure others want to speak for themselves. I'll let you ask questions of Anne and our families."

The local ABC affiliate pounced on Elton next, and Anne held her breath. Elton refused to be coached, saying he talked to the press all the time. The reporter asked a deadly question. "What did you think when Senator McEvoy first came to your house?"

"I thought it was peculiar."

"But what about when he announced his intentions with your young daughter? He's ten years her senior and her boss. You must have thought something of that."

"Like any father, I wanted to kill him." The room gasped, while Elton simply said matter-of-factly, "But in the end, my daughter is an adult. It's her choice who she spends her time with, and eventually, I saw him differently."

"Mr. Norwood, you're a Republican elected official, but you're now related to the McEvoy family by marriage. Who are you going to endorse in the senate race?"

"No one today," Elton quipped. "And that's all I'm saying on the matter. Don't even try to ask it again."

Anne smiled at her father in relief at his comments.

It was then Mary Beth's turn for a question. "Mrs. Norwood, how do you feel?"

"It's not how I would've planned things for Anne, but it's her life. She's happy, and we support her." She smiled for the cameras. "As for the elopement, I think it's terribly romantic, don't you?"

As the questions dwindled, an ITN reporter directed a question to Marco. "Mr. Zamora, you're a State Department Official. Does the Administration have a statement?"

"I'm here as a brother-in-law, not in my professional capacity, and I'm also a career diplomat, rather than a political appointee. And I will say, in my career of traveling overseas, I've consistently heard the question, 'Why do Americans care so much about a politician's sex life?' I've never found a good answer."

When he uttered the word "sex," Anne's eyes widened, and she glanced at Megan. Megan shot her husband a fierce look. As another reporter asked a softball question of Mary Beth, Marco shrugged and whispered, "I think it needed to be said."

When the press conference ended, the McEvoys met in Stephen's office conference room to review the remaining press strategy. As Megan laid out the additional interviews, Patty stared at the television, monitoring the current news. "Not bad, all things considered," she said. Her smile quickly disappeared, when a commercial came on the screen. "Well, shit. They wasted no time," she muttered. She adjusted the volume, turning everyone's attention to the commercial.

The room gasped when Anne's innocent-looking high school yearbook photo came on the screen. And everyone was instantly silenced as the commercial's narrator read the caption below Anne's photo. "Stephen

McEvoy. Sexual Predator."

Anne turned to Stephen. All her fears had come to fruition. "This is going to be bad."

His face was grim. "Yes, it is."

Chapter 28

The next day, Anne and Stephen arrived back in D.C. to face the music there. As they unpacked their bags in the house on Massachusetts Avenue, his phone rang. Anne continued to sort dirty laundry as he took the call.

"Hey, Patty." After a minute of silence, he said, "You're kidding me." He shook his head and looked at Anne. "You should talk to Patty. I'll put her on speaker."

Anne eyed him warily and sat on the bed. Over the last few days, Patty had warmed to Anne, but she still intimidated her. Anne took a breath and said, "Hi Patty. What's up?"

"Hey. I don't suppose you've seen *The Range* lately?"

"Er. No," Stephen said. "What's that?"

Anne shook her head. "That independent paper? No. Not for a while. Not since I lived in Boulder. Why? What's going on?"

"They've started something called 'Bump Watch' on their website. Every time there's a new photograph of Anne, they analyze her stomach to look for signs she's pregnant."

Throwing her hand over her eyes, Anne moaned. "God, that's embarrassing."

"That's horrible. She's a senator's wife, for Christ's sake. What the fuck?" Stephen's eyes narrowed in rage.

"Stephen, you two are in the middle of a sex scandal," Patty reminded him. "Normal rules of decorum no longer apply to you."

"So we should get used to being humiliated?" Anne said with a frown.

"In a word, yes," said Patty. "Walter Fucking Smith has ads running twenty-four-seven depicting Stephen as a perv who preys on little girls. You're already the butt of the late-night shows, and this stupid piece in *The Range* is going viral. There have to be a hundred photos of you on that site already, and Megan's getting calls about it."

Stephen grimaced. "Is there anything we can do about that paper?"

"No. I talked with Megan," Patty said. "She thinks we need to let the joke play itself out. If we do or say anything, it will only draw more attention to it. The story will end on its own as time shows she isn't pregnant."

"Wonderful. For the next three months, I'm going to be paranoid about looking fat," Anne grumbled.

"Yeah, might want to skip the carbs for a while," Patty said.

"Thanks," Anne said as she rolled her eyes.

"Sorry. That was a bad joke," Patty said. "Listen. I need you two to concentrate here. You've got four months until the election. That's four months to show to the world you're a perfectly normal, married couple."

"Which is what we are," said Stephen as he rubbed Anne's arm.

"Exactly. Go on a date tonight—somewhere popular. Show people how normal you really are."

"And in four months, rational people will then see the truth and vote for Stephen?" asked Anne with no hope, only sarcasm in her voice.

"That's the plan," said Patty. "But never underestimate the ability of the American electorate to behave irrationally."

§§§§

The following Sunday morning, Anne raised her head off the pillow to see the time. Disliking the number, she wrinkled her nose and whispered in Stephen's ear, "Wake up, sleepy husband. It's late."

Tightening his squeeze on her waist, he groaned. "One more hour? Can I have one more hour of irresponsibility?"

"Sweetheart, it's almost ten o'clock."

His eyes fluttered open. "Morning, sweet wife," he said, nuzzling into her hair.

"Last night was fun."

"It was." He smiled. "Our first date. Just like a normal couple."

"I know, and everyone was so nice to us—even the photographers were nice."

"They were. I'm sure Megan will monitor the press." He raised his eyebrows and poked her side suggestively. "After dinner was great, too. I'm surprised there haven't been calls."

She giggled. "We're pretty damn loud, aren't we?"

"We are," he answered, nuzzling into her hair. "And I love having our own place where it doesn't matter what we do."

"I know it's our own place, but it's a little upscale for most newlyweds, wouldn't you say?" she asked, curling up beside him.

"Yeah, though we do lack furniture and lamps." He chuckled as he tucked her into the crook of his arm. "Sorry. I'm just sick of living with my parents' stuff all around me."

"I don't want to be surrounded by all of your mom's antiques either. I'm glad we got rid of them, and this way, we get to start fresh."

"Some light would be nice, though." He gave her a kiss. "If we ever get out of bed, I might look for a stray lamp."

An hour later, they eventually left their marriage bed, and he began his search. In a few minutes, he called out from a closet in a guest bedroom, "I found some Christmas lights! Now we won't be in the dark."

"Great, but let's sit on the patio right now. It's nice outside," she said as she closed the front door with the morning papers in hand.

Walking to the patio, she scanned the front page, quickly digesting the stories the newspaper editors deemed important enough to be placed above the fold. *The New York Times* focused on the Middle East. She turned to *The Washington Post*, and gasped as she read the headline, *Senate Ethics Committee to Investigate Senator Stephen McEvoy.*

She didn't see Stephen standing in front of her with strings of Christmas lights. "What do you think? Should I put these on the mantle?" he asked.

She didn't reply. Instead, she held the paper so he could read the headline.

His expression soured, and he took a deep breath. "Even if you know something is coming, when you see it as a headline, it's still a shock."

"That's exactly how I felt."

He took the paper and examined the entire front page for a moment. "Oh good. There are three different stories dedicated to us. There's one about our time together, one about you, and one about my past." He flipped to the paper's interior. "There's also a timeline of our relationship inside. Can't wait to read that."

"I guess they were working on the stories all week to publish so many today." She shook her head. "Why didn't Megan or Patty call to warn you? They always tell you when something like this has happened."

"I bet Mom told them to let us be. We can't do much about it on a Sunday morning anyway." He kissed her forehead and patted her back. "Let's sit outside. I'll get the coffee. Fresh air will be nice as we read this shit."

The two devoured the papers as they sat on the porch with their coffee in hand. He dissected *The Washington Post* while Anne read *The New York Times*.

"I don't think the *Times* story is that bad," she announced. "In fact, it's kind of helpful. There's a chart of all the members of Congress who've had affairs with staffers and whether or not the member resigned. Many didn't."

"Were any of them with staffers ten years younger?" he muttered.

"Uh, Newt Gingrich, and he resigned. But of the others, a few of them got married and stayed in office." Then she remembered something and happily looked around the scattered papers. "Speaking of which, our wedding announcement should be in the paper today. Megan is a genius. This is perfect," she declared as she found their photo. "We look like your average couple, and the announcement doesn't make you look sleazy at all."

"Well, some of these stories definitely make me look like a sleazebag," he muttered as he looked up from his reading. "They also have Walter Smith written all over them. Langford's camp is still sticking to his original statement, saying he wishes you well, but there's a lot of conjecture in here about me taking advantage of you and hitting on all of my staff. That stuff has to come from Walter."

"How worried are you about the Ethics Committee?" she asked.

"A little." He shrugged, but she could tell he was downplaying his feelings.

She frowned and said, "Me, too."

He brushed his hand over her cheek. "I'm sorry, sweetheart. We just have to stay positive. We have a good, honest story, and we're living, daily proof of it."

"I know," she said softly.

He picked up his phone from the side table and started punching numbers.

"Are you calling Patty or Megan?" she asked.

"I'm calling Phillip."

"Why?"

"If I'm being investigated, I need a lawyer."

"So, Phillip will deal with this?"

"No," he said with a sigh. "I need a big gun."

§§§§

Later that week, Trey waited eagerly for Walter to pick up the line. When he answered, Trey didn't even say hello. "I'm calling with some good news for you," he said.

"What's that?" Walter chuckled.

"Our fundraising for this quarter has shot through the roof."

"Ah yes! I'd heard people had stepped up their giving to Langford."

"There's no way McEvoy can beat these numbers," Trey said proudly. "We'll blow him away this quarter."

"Good. You'll need it because I'm sure Lillian McEvoy will write as many checks as she has to in order to keep her boy in office."

"I know, but the Ethics Committee investigation is helpful. It'll keep up a slow drumbeat of negative news about McEvoy."

"Oh, yeah. That's good, though he's lawyered up by hiring Gene Nelson —he's formidable. He always gets his guys off."

"But . . . but," Trey sputtered. "McEvoy fucked an intern, for God's sake. At a minimum, there's a sexual harassment case here."

"I hope so, but it was consensual, and it was a brilliant move on their part to get married, especially with their families and all these solidly reputable folks lined up behind them. And by all appearances, they're a happy couple." Walter chuckled. "Not that I'd say it to the press."

"So everything's fine now because they're smiling all the time?" Trey grumbled.

"I wouldn't go that far, but we've got our work cut out for us. They're a good-looking couple. People are drawn to that," Walter explained. "And it's pretty obvious she's not pregnant, though I like keeping the rumor out there as long as we can. Anyway, let's proceed with what we've got. McEvoy is a sleazy, rich Democrat who will buy his way out of any mess."

"I like it." Trey smiled. "And we're working hard, as you can tell by our numbers."

"Good. Because I hate losing money and I hate losing elections. I better not lose either one here," Walter warned.

§§§§

After a long August day of campaigning in the southwestern corner of Colorado, the McEvoy family was quiet on the flight from Durango to Denver. Anne broke the silence as she read the comments on a political blog. "Oh, this is nice. I'm a gold digger and a shopaholic because I was seen walking down the street near Nordstrom. What the hell? I remember that day. I'd stopped to get a cup of coffee, and I was walking to my car."

"At least you're not pregnant anymore." Patty laughed.

"Yeah, right," Anne grumbled.

Patty looked at her sister-in-law with sympathy. "Really, Anne, you're doing great. They have to make up all this shit about you because you and Stephen are so squeaky clean and boring. And you're wonderful at campaign events. People eat you up. The Republicans can't stand it."

"Thanks, Patty. That's nice to hear," Anne said.

"Patty's right . . . and don't forget who writes all those comments," Stephen said with a yawn. He settled deeper in his seat. "They're Republican hacks or losers with no real lives."

"Well, that's true," Megan said as she looked up from her laptop. "But they influence the narrative in the media. They're part of what keeps the story alive."

"And it is alive," muttered Anne.

"The Ethics Committee keeps it out there, too," Patty said, placing *The Durango Herald* at her side. "Which is why our poll numbers suck, no matter how many people like Stephen and Anne together."

"Still that bad?" Stephen frowned. "I was hoping you'd seen some change in the last few weeks."

"Still that bad," Patty replied bitterly.

"It's not good to have that investigation hanging around your neck," Megan said, shaking her head.

"Why is the Ethics Committee so secretive and slow? I mean, they're slow even for Congress," said Anne.

"They don't like investigating one of their own." Stephen shrugged. "My lawyer says I'm going to be exonerated—before the election."

"But when? The day before?" Patty asked. "We need it sooner, not later.

Like right now would be good."

"I know," Megan said with a nod. "There has to be a change in the press, or I worry . . ."

"You worry about what?" asked Anne impatiently.

Megan raised her hands in helplessness. "I worry that even if the committee clears him, the cloud around Stephen's integrity will cause permanent damage."

"We won't just lose this election," snapped Patty. Her expression morphed into a frown full of sorrow. She gazed at Stephen. "I'm sorry to say it, but you could be unelectable."

"Forever?" Anne asked, leaning forward in fear.

"Yes. Forever." Patty nodded.

The cabin quieted at the hard truth. Stephen scowled and closed his eyes, and Megan went back to her computer. Staring at Stephen, Anne experienced simultaneous pangs of guilt and nausea. She heard Patty sigh. Unable to look at the pain on Stephen's face any longer, Anne turned away.

The four traveled in silence until they neared Denver. Anne looked up from her reading and saw Patty staring at her, a smile slowly spreading across her face.

"What?" asked Anne, wondering at the change in Patty's mood.

Patty grinned, her eyes afire. "We need a diversion."

"A diversion?"

"Yes." Patty nodded. "A diversion, and we have one."

"We do? What's that?" Stephen asked without opening his eyes.

"Never mind," Patty said, still with a smile. "I'll take care of it."

Chapter 29

Since Stephen's scandal broke, Helen had avoided him. She remained angry he never supported her amendment, and she didn't like thinking of him as married. To top it off, he was being investigated. She didn't want to be anywhere near him, lest anyone got any ideas.

Instead, she enjoyed his predicament. Stephen would lose his seat, the Republicans could then take control of the Senate, and she'd become the chair of an important committee. It was a wonderful turn of events for her.

When she took the call from her staffer, Joe, that day in August, she expected him to be as chipper as they'd both been since the McEvoy scandal.

Instead, he was curt. "Helen, I've got Chelsea on the line. We're having a three-way call. We're alone in our offices with closed doors. You should do the same before we speak."

Helen thought it odd that Chelsea, her chief of staff, was on the phone right next door. "All right. My door is already closed. What's this about?"

"This is a difficult call for me," Joe said in a determined voice. "I'm sorry I have to do it, but we must deal with this immediately."

"Well, get on with it."

"I'll be blunt. *The Idaho Statesman* has graphic video of you and Tony Anderson having sex. I'm not sure where, but it looks to be a storage room, maybe in a hotel or something. The images were taken by security cameras, but they're very close up."

Divine retribution caused Helen's hands to shake in fear. She swallowed hard at the news and breathed heavily as she remembered exactly what she and Senator Anderson did in that storage room. "How graphic?" she asked, her voice gruff with anxiety.

"It's . . . well, it's pornographic. There's no other way to describe it."

Everyone on the line was silent, and Helen envisioned the ugly demise of her political career.

After the strained silence, Chelsea said, "Helen . . . Joe and I talked. We have a plan. It requires full disclosure, though. We believe it's the only way for you to survive."

"Of course." Helen understood it was the only answer, but she needed more information. She cleared her throat. "I need to know who else has seen this footage. Who is their source?"

"Well naturally, they won't reveal their source, and I don't know who's seen it," Joe replied. "If you ask me, the timing is odd. You're not up for a few years. The Dems in Idaho don't have a real candidate to run against you. Who would do this? And why now? I don't see who—"

"Who and why don't matter right now." Chelsea's voice was firm and brooked no argument as she started laying out the plan. "Let's get back to what we need to do. Helen, you probably should take some time to think things through, but you don't have long. As a courtesy, the newspaper is holding the story until we decide on our response. I apologize for being presumptuous here, but you need to tell Matt. None of our plans will work without him."

Politicians only survived a horrible sex scandal when their wives stood with them at their confessional press conference. Matt, an elected official himself, would be put in the unenviable position of standing by a cheating woman. It would take a level of humility not found in most men— especially a politician. Helen took a deep breath. "Okay. I'll call you back."

She ended the call and closed her eyes, absorbing the horrible ramifications of the sex tape. She needed guidance. Her hands shook again as she found her phone and the name of the person she always turned to for advice. The line only rang once before he answered. "Walter here."

"Walter, it's Helen. I need your help."

"Yes. I've been waiting for you to call."

"What? What do you know?"

"I know everything, Helen—just like I always do."

"What? Who told you? Do others know?" Her heart stopped as she realized the disaster was already occurring.

"I have my sources, and I'd say that your secret is contained at the moment. You need to act soon, though, in order to deal with this on your own terms."

"I know I do, but I need you. First, I need advice on how to tell Matt," she begged.

"I have no advice other than to tell him everything and be contrite as hell —even if you don't mean it," he said with a chuckle. "I've seen the tapes, and they're definitely X-rated. You're at your fiancé's mercy here. And he must stand by you, or you're a goner. You've really gotten yourself into a pickle."

"You're not going to lift a finger to help me?"

"Um. No," he said with reproach.

"Because you could back me. Help me maintain some credibility with the public and the party."

"Why would I put myself in that position?"

His tone was as if she'd made the stupidest request in the world, nor was his advice what she would expect from someone she considered a trusted counselor. He was also her only friend who wasn't a staffer, paid to support her. His nonchalance at her political demise inflamed her, so she lashed out. "Well, there has to be a vendetta against me. There's no other way security videos would surface unless someone was tracking me closely. They might also know about us. You need to watch out yourself."

"Helen, Helen, Helen," he said in a patronizing voice. "You know the way things work in this world. Guys like me never get caught, and if we do, we always shake it off. That's just the way things are."

"Asshole! I'll remember this," Helen yelled and hung up.

§§§§

The following morning, Anne nuzzled into Stephen's neck as they lay in bed. The Colorado sun streamed through their windows as their alarm clock woke them with the morning news.

"The time is eight o'clock. This is NPR News. I'm Merritt Kronen. The newspaper, *The Idaho Statesman*, has obtained video footage depicting a sexual encounter between United States Senators Helen Sanders and Tony Anderson. The video was taken by a security camera in a storage room of the Willard Hotel during a recent Republican National Committee fundraiser. Senator Anderson represents the state of Nebraska and is divorced and single. Senator Sanders represents the state of Idaho and is engaged to Wyoming Congressman Matt Smythe. Congressman Smythe has issued a statement, saying, quote, 'To describe this as anything less than highly embarrassing is to mince words. I ask for your prayers as I work through this matter privately.' Sources say Congressman Smythe will not join Senator Sanders at her upcoming press conference later today where she is expected to resign from office. A spokesperson for the Republican National Committee issued the following statement, 'We are disturbed and saddened by this news. Obviously, this behavior does not reflect the high moral values of the Republican party.' In other news, China's artificially low currency rate continues to exacerbate America's trade deficit—"

Stephen switched off the news and stared at Anne, his eyes wide with shock. "Do you think Patty had something to do with this?"

"I don't know. Maybe," she answered through a yawn. "It couldn't happen to a nicer woman. Could it?" She smiled, rather enjoying Helen's demise.

"Wow. Helen's career is over."

"In a few years she could get a spot on CNN like all the other scandalized politicians do." Anne giggled. "Anyway, why do you care? You're pretty certain she backstabbed you."

"I know. Don't get me wrong. I'm happy she's gone. Plus, we look tame in comparison." He shrugged. "It's just hard for me to believe my mom signed off on this."

Later that morning, Stephen walked out to a secluded part of the garden and found his mother knitting a baby blanket for her soon-to-be-born grandchild.

She greeted him first. "Good morning. What do you think?" She held up her handiwork.

Stephen nodded. "It's nice."

"I think so. This giraffe is a little challenging, though. Lots of different colors. I think I should have gone with the zebra." She smiled. "Sit down and tell me about your date last night. *The Denver Post* had some nice photos of you and Anne. Did you enjoy yourselves?"

"It was great, but, Mom, I came out to talk about Helen." He sat on the lounger next to his mother.

"Yes," she said as she counted stitches.

"Let me preface this by saying I'm not defending her. I just don't think we agreed to destroy her life. In fact, I don't believe I even signed off on you hiring an investigator, which is probably how this video came to be."

"Oh, that," she scoffed and continued her knitting. "I agreed with Patty. Hiring someone was the prudent thing to do, and I didn't think you needed to worry about it." She looked up and smiled. "And I've been proven right. Helen now must deal with karma, and you and Anne are no longer the most interesting news out there. In fact, you two look rather boring."

"But, Mom, isn't this a little much?"

Lillian's warm, maternal side vanished for a moment as her political animal took over. "It was necessary," she declared. She nodded to a basket of yarn near Stephen's feet. "Can you please hand me the dark brown? I need it for the giraffe's horns."

"I can't believe Dad would've allowed this to happen."

"Hmm . . . oh, he might have balked at first, but he'd have seen the benefit, just as you will." She placed her hand on his. "This isn't only about you and keeping this Senate seat in the family. It's highly likely that the Democrats will lose the House. We must keep the Senate. Taking down Helen Sanders has many advantages—another seat is in play and the Republicans have to defend themselves. Don't worry. She's a cat. She'll land on her feet."

"Maybe it's not Helen that's bothering me here," he said as he ran his hand through his hair. "Maybe I just expect us—the McEvoy family—to be above this kind of thing."

"Well, we're not," she said, her voice icy.

"What if I lose? We've taken her down and have nothing to show for it."

"That's not true." The yarn flew through her fingers as she knitted. "We'll have lost, but we'll have given it our all."

Stephen nodded. He knew there was no reason to debate his mother when she was wedded to an idea. And the deed was done. As much as Stephen was uncomfortable with what had happened to Helen, he wouldn't lift a finger to change things. His mouth twitched as he accepted his complicity in the matter.

"Now you need to get on with your life," she said with a quick pat on his leg. "You and Anne need to go back to D.C. and finish this term. Hopefully, the ethics investigation will end soon. In the meantime, you two should be out—all the time. You need to proceed like there's nothing wrong."

"I know." He sighed.

"After all, there isn't anything wrong." She smiled and returned to knitting. "This may play out very well."

§§§§

Later that month, Trey sat at his desk on interminable hold as Walter finished another call. He tried not to take it personally, but he couldn't help it. He wondered if Walter was less interested in Langford's campaign. He shook it off, thinking it impossible.

"Good afternoon, Walter," said Trey in as chipper a voice as he could muster. "How are you?"

"Oh, I'm doing fine. Busy. I'm involved in a lot of races these days," he replied. "But I'm sure you're calling about my spending in Colorado."

"Well, I was curious as to what you were up to."

"I'm in for now. Two big factors are coming up though—the ruling by the Ethics Committee and the debate." Walter cleared his throat. "We need both to go our way, or I'm not running any more ads in Colorado."

"But we need those ads." Trey realized he sounded panicky and regretted it. "I assure you Langford can win," Trey said in a stronger voice.

"Well, I'll run ads until the debate in October. Depending on Langford's performance, I'll decide if I spend any more money there before the election."

"Oh, he'll do well." Trey knew Langford could debate, but the question of how he'd compare to McEvoy still remained.

"He needs to," Walter replied in a stern voice. "Sorry, Trey. I'm not in this to make anyone feel good. I'm in it to win. You should know that by now."

§§§§

Anne always laughed when Patty actually admitted to praying she'd win an election. Most people involved in politics, sports, or a war considered it poor taste—or even blasphemous—to pray for the other side's demise. In politics, the proper thing to do was to pray for a good race that benefited the people. Patty would have none of that. "I know I'm right," she declared with pride. "Why would I ever ask God for anything else?"

When they heard the news that the Senate Ethics Committee had cleared Stephen of any wrongdoing, Anne was overcome with relief, while Patty exclaimed, "Thank God!" She looked heavenward as she kissed the cross that hung from the platinum chain around her neck. "Thank you for answering my prayers."

"Thank God is right," agreed Stephen. Though he wasn't known to put much stock in the power of prayer, he appeared thankful, nonetheless.

"It's worked out exactly how I wanted—the committee ruled in September. We have almost two months to put it behind us before the election." Patty was smug. "Take that, Walter Smith, you little shit."

Over Stephen's shoulder, Anne looked at his laptop screen and read the one-paragraph letter dismissing the complaint against him. She wrinkled her nose. "It's awfully short. I mean, after three months of meetings, depositions, lawyers, and documents, all they have to say is, 'The Committee finds no direct violation—blah, blah, blah. The Committee dismisses the matter.' That's it?"

"That's all they *want* to say." Stephen chuckled. "Just in case it happens to one of them one day."

"It's true." Lillian smiled. "Even with all of today's partisanship, some things don't change. The U.S. Senate still is 'The Club.' They're loath to criticize their own." She wrapped her reassuring arms around the shoulders of Stephen and Anne. "But in this case, it was also the *right* outcome. I'm very happy for you two."

"Thanks, Lillian," Anne said, patting her mother-in-law's hand.

Stephen looked up at his mother, his eyes shining in a rare display of open emotion. "We couldn't have done this without you, Mom." He cleared his throat, though it didn't mask the waver in his voice.

Lillian's eyes misted as she beamed. "I've just always wanted my children to be happy."

"Things are looking up. I bet we'll see another bump in the polls." Megan smiled. "You've been cleared by the Ethics Committee, and you're no longer a joke on the late-night shows."

Anne laughed. "I suppose we can thank Helen for that. Her sex tape gave Jay Leno enough material for years."

"Or you could thank Mom and me," said Patty, straightening her jacket in pride of a job well done. Her voice sobered, though. "We're not out of the woods yet. There's a lot of time left in this campaign, including the debate."

"The debate. Yeah . . . ." Stephen muttered with a nod.

Patty frowned. "Right. The debate. Don't fuck it up."

§§§§

Few people actually watched a debate for a Senate seat, but the spin on who won and lost played in the media until Election Day. Davis Auditorium at the University of Denver hummed with murmurs and whispers as Langford and Stephen strode onto the stage. Before they headed to their podiums, they performed the customary handshake.

Stephen was pleasant. "Good evening, Dan. It's nice to see you again."

"Evening, Stephen. Nice to see you, too." He smirked and side-eyed the row of the McEvoy clan. "And your family also."

Stephen nodded, though he sensed there was meaning behind Langford's otherwise benign comment. He walked to his podium and put on his microphone. He looked at Anne, who sat between a proud Lillian and determined Patty. Anne gave him a reassuring nod and grin, and he was more at ease.

When the debate began, both men started off well. Stephen hoped Langford might stumble on more complex topics, but he handled them with his down-home common sense. While they weren't the more thorough and eloquent answers Stephen might give, they were effective. The debate appeared to be heading for a draw, and twinges of panic pinched at Stephen. He needed a decisive win, not a tepid tie. He glanced at Patty, whose expression was steadfast, though he knew she worried just like him. While Langford made the audience chuckle again at his corny jokes, Stephen straightened his tie as he tried to bolster his confidence. He knew what the next topic was going to be.

The moderator ventured into the issue everyone was waiting for. "This is a question for Senator McEvoy," the moderator announced. He was a crusty television reporter for the local ABC affiliate who spoke in a voice which made people want to stand straighter. "While the Senate Ethics Committee cleared you of any wrongdoing, questions about your morality linger. What is your response to those who think you're unfit for public office?"

Stephen kept his placid expression as he moved his pen aside on the podium. It was a practiced maneuver to signal a thoughtful statement on an issue. In this case, he was to deliver a message he'd done many times since his marriage to Anne—but this time the message would reach the widest audience. He wanted to make sure his statement was one which would define him. He looked ahead and spoke to the auditorium in a candid voice.

"I can understand why the public has an interest in a politician's private life. After all, we're people just like anyone, and it would be a lie by any politician who said they didn't use their personal story to influence voters." He gestured to Langford. "Both Dan and I have narratives about our lives which describe us and our values." He moved his hands to grip the podium. "If the events of the last year hadn't taken place, I'd still be standing before you with the same experiences I have today. I'd have a successful career as a district attorney and a strong record as a United States Senator, working in Washington, D.C. to better the lives of Coloradans. I'd also carry my family's dedication to fighting for the interests of the poor and working class. But my life has changed in the last year. Today I also have a wonderful wife who I happened to meet on the job. That's not such a different story than many Americans who find their partner at work." Turning his head to Anne and the rest of his family, he said, "Anne Norwood McEvoy is a part of my family. I love her dearly, and I'm a better man because she's in my life." He smiled at Anne, who returned the grin while Lillian patted her arm.

Silence took over the room for a moment, until a few members of the audience began clapping. As the clapping became louder, the moderator interrupted, "May we please have quiet in the auditorium?" He turned to Langford. "Treasurer Langford, do you have any comment on Senator McEvoy's answer?"

Langford looked down at his podium for a moment and frowned. For months, he'd barely commented on Stephen's scandal, leaving the vitriol to his surrogates. Everyone in the room waited for him to finally address the question with his opponent only a few feet away. His head rose and stared into the camera. "I'd say that's a nice sentiment, Stephen, but Coloradans care about family values."

"Really?" Stephen asked without waiting for the moderator. "Well, then I don't think there's an issue here since both Anne's and my family support us. But I disagree. I don't think people are most concerned about family values—however you define them. I think most people care about things which impact their everyday life—and my personal life certainly doesn't do that. What Coloradans really want are jobs that allow them to provide for their family. Good schools so their kids get better opportunities. Clean air and water so they can enjoy the outdoors. And a national defense to keep America safe and strong. Those are the issues I think this election is about." Stephen stared Langford down, daring him to respond.

"Treasurer Langford, what do you think this election is about?" The moderator raised his eyebrows.

"Sending the right man to Washington," he said with a nod as if to convince everyone around him he was the right guy.

Stephen gave a small smile and looked down; he knew he'd done well.

After the debate ended, the candidates' families rushed the stage. Langford headed over to his wife and grown children, while Stephen met Anne midway.

As he hugged her, she leaned into his ear. "You were great, sweetheart. It went really well."

Lillian said as she got the second hug, "Patrick would be so proud of you."

Megan and Marco simply congratulated him and smiled as they handed over the newest McEvoy for the traditional politician-with-a-baby photo-op. Lillian McEvoy Zamora, or Lil, as she was called, smiled for her Uncle Stephen and the cameras.

Afterward, Patty touched Stephen's arm. "I guess there's some benefit to everyone thinking you're political roadkill. People have low expectations of us now, so we're doing great."

"Thanks," Stephen grumbled.

"I'm joking. Nice job." She grinned, tugging at his suit coat. "I mean it. I couldn't have said it better myself."

"Thanks, Patty. I'm glad it's over," he said before heaving a great sigh.

Greg offered his hand. "She's right. It was awesome. Langford took the bait and imploded." He grinned and predicted the outcome of the election with his next words. "Congratulations, *Senator* McEvoy."

§§§§

The day of the election Helen sat on a Mexican beach, checking the political headlines on her phone. "Tsk, tsk," she said aloud. With a survey around the expansive beach, she saw no one was nearby. She smiled, saying to the palm tree, "I suppose the time has come." She picked up her phone and soon said, "Good afternoon, Michaela. This is Senator Helen Sanders. How are you?"

Normally, Helen didn't like drawing attention to herself or using her official title. She'd carry the title of Senator with her for life—whether or not she was in Congress—so she liked to throw it around when it was helpful. Speaking to a *Washington Post* reporter was just such an occasion.

"Hello, Senator Sanders. I'm fine. I hope you are, too," the reporter answered. She sounded eager to hear from the disgraced senator. "What can I help you with today?"

"I'm glad you're doing well," Helen said as she looked out onto the ocean. "I've always liked your reporting, and I wanted to give you a tip—confidentially, of course, and the information must be embargoed until tomorrow. I don't think it will be a problem because you'll need some time to write the story, and you won't want it buried in all the election coverage."

"All right. I can offer you confidentiality, but I can't promise an embargo. That, of course, depends on the nature of the story."

Helen checked the time. It was late afternoon on the West Coast—late enough so that even if the story broke it wouldn't hurt the Republican Party's chances that day. "Okay. We can talk."

"Go ahead and shoot. What do you have for me?"

"I've read a few of your stories lately on the FEC looking into campaign finance issues between Walter Smith and Dan Langford's senate campaign."

"That's right. Do you know something about it?" the reporter asked in a leading voice.

"Not really, but I thought you might like another angle on the issue."

"What's that?"

"Well, I happen to know Walter has been having extramarital affairs while he's spending millions to attack Stephen McEvoy's character. At least one has been with a public figure. I'm sure there are others."

"And how do you know that?"

"I was one of his affairs."

Michaela was silent for a second before asking in a firm voice, "Will you go on the record?"

"I'll answer a yes/no question, but that's all. You can do your own investigating of his other affairs. They won't be hard to dig up."

"Okay . . ." There was anticipation in Michaela's voice. "So did you have a sexual relationship with Walter Smith this year?"

"Yes." Helen smiled as she said it.

"Thank you," Michaela chuckled.

"You're welcome."

"You know, if you don't mind me asking—off the record—why are you doing this? Why do you want to take down one of the most influential Republicans? And why do you want to bring more attention to yourself? Don't you want some privacy right now?"

"Oh, I'm not worried about me. I've already been raked over the coals. Now I'm doing fine, and I'm on an extended vacation." She glanced at Mario, the cabana boy she'd shared a few nights with recently. He waved, and she raised her glass to him. "As for Walter, well you know this won't really take him down. He'll pay a fine to the FEC, and eventually, he'll repair his reputation and relationship with his wife."

"But he's still going to be hurt by this. His whole private life will be exposed in the media. You realize that, don't you?"

"Yes," Helen said with a giddy grin. "And I have to say—I like that idea."

§§§§

When the AP finally called the race for Stephen, he and his family were ensconced in a suite at a hotel, while his victory party went wild down in the ballroom.

As soon as Megan told him the news, he grabbed Anne ecstatically. "Come here."

When he took her to one of the bedrooms, no one thought it strange he might want to savor the moment alone with his wife. He'd soon be standing among thousands and speaking before millions when he gave his victory speech.

Just as he closed the door, Anne pounced on him with a giant hug. "You did it. You did it! I'm so happy for you."

"No, *we* did it. You and me." He crushed his mouth to hers with a warm, needy kiss. Their entwined limbs, coupled with the headiness of the moment, made him groan in exultant delight. When he felt her unbuckle his belt, he stilled for a brief moment. "We don't have time," he mumbled unconvincingly against her lips.

"No one will notice if you're a few minutes late." Unbuttoning his pants, she kissed him again, but stopped when his phone rang. "You should get that."

"Nah. Voice mail," he said as he leaned into her again.

"It might be someone important."

"Oh, all right," he grumbled as he gave his phone a perfunctory check. He was about to put it down again when his eyes widened. "That's a White House number."

If there were ever one call he'd take while his wife was unbuttoning his trousers, it would be a call from the leader of the free world.

"Stephen McEvoy speaking."

"Good evening, Senator McEvoy, this is White House operator Danielle Whitman. I have the President on the line for you."

As she listened to the conversation, Anne smiled giddily, and she squeezed Stephen's hand when she heard the President's voice boom through the phone.

"Congratulations, Stephen."

"Thank you, Mr. President," Stephen replied with a smile. He squeezed Anne's waist. "I'm very happy. It's a wonderful feeling."

"It is, isn't it? Especially these days. Thank you very much for giving the party some good news. We're short on it this November."

"Well, it was a long time coming. I'm sorry it was such a nail-biter."

"Oh, I always knew the McEvoys would pull it out. Please tell your mother congratulations for me."

"I will. She'll be honored," Stephen said while Anne rubbed his shoulders.

"I hope to congratulate you in person soon."

"That would be nice, thank you."

"Please tell your wife congratulations, also. Carol and I both want to meet Anne."

Anne's mouth dropped open in astonishment at the President saying her name. Clutching her hand, Stephen smiled. "Anne and I look forward to it, Mr. President."

3512083R00131

Made in the USA
San Bernardino, CA
06 August 2013